Morgans Run

Morgans Run

Carter Burke

To order additional copies of this book, contact:
Xlibris Corporation
1-888-795-4274
www.Xlibris.com
Orders@Xlibris.com
81153

BOOK ONE

The End

"Morgan, you just got a call from the agency"

Morgan was on her way out the door and to the party she had been desperately trying to make sure attended. All the people she hadn't seen in a long time were going to be there. Why in the hell would they call her now. She got out of her Corvette, which had been a present to her for graduating from college. Her father had told her if she took criminology and made it through with nothing less than an A average her would buy her dream car. And he did. A cocoa brown corvette, with white leather interior, and custom dash design. She loved the car and she loved her father. Her mother had passed away. She missed her, but her father turned out to be her hero.

"Morgan, they are waiting for you."

He screamed at her as if she couldn't hear him. She could hear him, she was debating on whether or not to act like she didn't hear him and to drive to this party or not. She turned the engine off and got out of the car.

"I'm coming daddy, I did hear you."

They lived off of a nice cul-de-sac in a quiet upper middle class neighborhood in Atlanta. The streets now dark with the evening light. People milling around their porches and patios, drinking sweet tea and or long island iced tea, whichever suited their fancy. The yards were very well maintained by the owners of these dwellings. Many a saturday morning, the sounds of lawn mowers intruded on Morgan's much needed sleep. But it wasn't a bad sound, pleasant childhood memories of Saturday mornings spent cutting grass and doing chores around the house when her mother was alive.

Morgan was an only child. Her mother was no nonsense and kept the young lady grounded, but her father was proud of his princess as he called her. Anything she did was fine with him. Morgan answered the phone.

"Yes, John, this is Morgan"

"What are you doing right now?"

"Well, I was actually planning to hit the party of the season at the Crows Nest, if you must know, but I guess you have other plans."

"Most assuredly, still a party though"

He explained to her the details of this particular assignment. Morgan worked as a freelance operative for a criminal investigation service in Atlanta.

"I need you to ingratiate yourself into the good favors of someone we have been surveying. He is reputed to be the link in the cocaine connection between Atlanta and Miami and New York and if we can nail him down, we can get the inside on when the next shipment is coming through and with whom it is being brought."

"Okay"

"The party is being held at Peachtree towers in the penthouse of a gentleman name Amir. He always invites the A list of Atlanta's finest and your character of Renee, the party girl is what we will need. She has been seen around at the A list parties before and she will be recognized and not draw any undue attention to you. He is a very tall, dark chocolate man, with tastes that run from the sublime to the totally outrageous and he has a taste for woman like your character Renee. People will probably tell him that they have seen you before and no doubt he will make the first contact. Keep on your toes, this guy is a brute when he wants to be. Feel like partying a little?"

"yes, but not this way, however I will see what I can find out about this man"

"Morgan, be really careful and remember to go with your gut instinct. Women have that instinct more than men. Don't take any unnecessary chances. If anything were to happen to you, I would hate to have to face your father."

Morgan knew what he was talking about and she promised to be careful.

It wasn't the type of party she had planned on going to,but it was a party and she hadn't been to one of them in awhile.

John gave her instructions on where to pick her brown mercedes that he had arranged for her. Brown was her color regardless of the car. He gave her the rest of her instructions and said good bye with his famous last words "go get 'em tiger". It had been a joke since she was young. When she played for the soccer team in her neighborhood, they always said that to her. John has known the family for years and use to send her father on different assignments around the country.

But if her father knew that he was using his daughter this way, he would have killed the man. But Morgan liked the excitement and the money was fantastic.

"Honey, was that the agency with another modeling assignment?"

"Yeah daddy, I have to be at a party tonight, the agency is hosting a take a look at our models party for some of the big advertisers in Atlanta and I have to be there."

"This late?"

"Its early in the real social circles daddy, we are just middle class folk who go to bed by 2 o'clock, these people are just starting." She smiled and kissed him on the cheek.

"I will probably be home late, so don't wait up. I'll stop by the waffle house and bring you some breakfast when I come home."

"Breakfast, huh, its going to be that type of night? Well, don't forget my hashbrowns, scattered, smothered and covered."

He always ate his hashbrowns from the waffle house that way. Has been for years. They use to drive to the waffle house off of washington road in East Point, before the neighborhood changed. There was a cook there who made the best hasbrowns, just across the bridge over 285. Its a different restaurant now, and the area has become a haven for crack heads and crack hoes. They don't go there anymore.

Moran slipped into her cocoa vet and started the engine. Vets make a purr all their own. She loved the sound of the engine.

She jumped on 85, headed north, the city alive with people going to parties or going somewhere. The skyline of the city in view. As she passed by the downtown exits, the city showered her with light. Her exit, Jimmy Carter Blvd was coming up. She maintained a studio apartment over their where she could change her clothes without being noticed by her father and kept her real identity a secret. L5P was a lively place with all kinds of people. The old pot heads, the Jerry Garcia fans, . . . , some hookers, lots of homeless and a parade of tattoo parlors and piercing. The bombay bicycle club with some of the greatest bikes she had ever seen. Crystal blue persuasion, a shop for crystals and tarots and other interesting gifts. Fellini's pizza was her favorite, and on warm nights you could sit and watch the traffic of cars and people parade by. Zestos was where she usually stopped for a great milk shake and then strolled the avenue to her place.

This time, no Zestos. She pulled in the parking lot of the apartment building. A mock brownstone, it had beautifully manicured lawns and was very quaint. She actually liked it here better than the place she lived in with her father. Her apartment was up on the 2nd floor, the top of the building. It had a little kitchen, bathroom, closet area, and very nice hardwood floors. It was furnished rather neatly. An orange sleep sofa, a huge stone table that was a present from some by gone lover that she didn't want to remember, a small stereo system, a few plants.

She went through her outfits and wigs and found the Renee look. Shoulder length brown wig, hazel contacts. Short black dress that fit every curve of her body. Stiletto heels and of course her knife that fit in a sheath on her thigh, in a little holster. The sheath fit inside her leg so it was not visible through the tightness of her dress. She pressed on some nails, not hoochie length, but fashionably long. In her real self, she kept her nails trimmed short for those occasional basketball games she had with her father.

She hadn't noticed the mercedes in the parking lot when she pulled up, but it was there now, on the street when she came out of her apartment. A few of the apartment dwellers were heading out to some late night revelry and they waved at her.

"Back in town for a layover?"

"Yeah, you know how it is"

They thought she was a stewardess. They thought she was eccentric because of the different looks she had, but she always went by the name Renee. It made Renee seem real. And in this business, occasionally people checked into you to see what you really did. Renee was her favorite character. When she had to go overseas, she was Armoire. She always told people it was a bedroom joke. They laughed at the irony of it. But it got her over.

She slipped into the chocolate mercedes and headed toward 85. She loved the lights of Atlanta. The skyline was beautiful in the dark. She drove through the barrage of traffic and exited on peachtree. The apartments were situated just north of the hotel district. The guard at the gate let her in.

"Somehow, I knew you would be here Renee. Its been awhile, how you be?"

Melvin was the security guard that most people hired for these clandestine functions. He was paid well and he kept his mouth shut. A retired Atlanta policeman, he knew many people in this town and knew who to let in and who not to. His information was what kept him securing the most elite parties and if he was here, it was going to be a good one.

"hey boo, you know I don't miss any social function in this little metropolis. Who is here that I need to know?"

"Everybody, little girl, every body. TLC just left a little while ago, they said they would be back though. That T-boz is sure a little cutie."

"Oh Melvin, you just a horny ol' man, but I love you."

Morgan parked the brown mercedes and headed for the festivities. It was a party, even if it wasn't the one she wanted to attend.

Riding the elevator to the pent house, she was crowded in with other party goers some she recognized and some she didn't. The ones she recognized smiled at her when she got onto the elevator, it was too close for any real conversation and she would get with them when she got off.

The elevator doors swung open and there was like a party in the hallway. Couples and groups of people were hanging around talking and drinking and creating a stir.

"Whats up baby girl?" The big man grabbed her and picked her up,slowly sliding her down his body.

"John, whats up?"

John was the local dealer to the stars. He also was well know by everyone and no one ever really tried to bust him because he kept his nose clean and didn't deal with the street knuckleheads, strictly star power. Renee had always liked John's easy way. He dressed nice, was very low profile and if he was fucking anyone, you never knew it. He didn't advertise, and he didn't have to. Dark brown skin, and a pleasant smile, 6'5" of pure man.

"I haven't seen you in awhile Babygirl, where you been?"

"You know I don't get lay overs in Atlanta as much as I like, I think they know I love it here. But I try to get in when I can. How you?"

"Cain't complain, just hangin'" She loved his soft southern drawl. He escorted her into the party.

"You don't have a woman hanging on your arm tonight?"

"I'm trying to get with your fine ass, but you won't let me."

"You know you just like a cousin to me"

"You never heard of kissin' cousins?" He smiled at her and disappeared into the crowd.

She stood in the background for a minute, but it didn't take her mark long to pick her out of a crowd. She was definitely his type. Once she realized he had a bead on her,she sauntered over to the little crowds of people, hugging the ones she knew and getting introduced to the ones she didn't.

The décor of the pent house was bachelor. She remembered this place. When she was here with Sharon Lee. She hoped no one would remember her. Dark colors and lots of african figurines. Photographs were everywhere from different locations that she could tell. Some Hawaiian photos, with flowers and hula girls. African animals. This man traveled a lot. These were very good photos. An amateur photographer. She made a note to keep that part of the conversation when he approached her and by all indications he was trying to make his way to her. She watched him watching her. As she flitted from one flower group to another, the social butterfly in her was reveling in the attention, but her peripheral vision was on her mark. There were silver trays with cocaine and gold trays with marijuana and she reached for a joint and strolled out to the balcony to smoke it. The balcony was large and there were smaller groups of people out here. Some she recognized but most she didn't. The ones she knew smiled at her but continued with their conversations. She picked the quiet spot on the balcony so that the mark had a chance to talk to her. She lit the little cigarette and the acrid smoke filled her lungs. It was the one part of the job she enjoyed. She had to fit in, and of course, being an avid smoker anyway, this was right up her alley. She never dealt with anything other than marijuana, no cocaine or heavy alcohol. A little white wine and champaigne once in a while, but the weed she kept as her personal vice. It also made it easier for her to smoke and maintain herself. Many operatives have tried to fit in and over indulged on drugs that they were not accustomed to and it almost cost them their lives. Trying to be deep cover. But you can't hang with a dope dealer if you don't do dope. Most dope dealers and smugglers always kept some weed around.

The view of Atlanta was beautiful from here and she watched the tops of limosines pulling into the Ritz Carlton, and the other upscale hotels in downtown Atlanta. Beautiful people being watched from above by other beautiful people.

She felt a presences behind her and knew it was her mark.

"I see you like my view"

"Yes, Atlanta is a beautiful city."

"My name is Amir"

She turned to face him because of until this point she had kept her attention focused on the skyline. When Morgan turned around, she looked into the eyes of the most gorgeous man she had seen in a long time. His skin was shining, his eyes were dark brown and piercing. She hoped in her heart he didn't remember her. She did remember him. Only, she didn't remember him looking this good.

"My name is ", but he interrupted.

"Renee. I know, I asked."

"Okay."

They stood quiet for a moment and he hit the joint she was holding. She really hadn't planned to share it.

They made small talk. His story was that he was retired military and did some work for the CIA which was why he could afford such a lavish lifestyle.

"The government pays well for certain positions"

"I guess they do. That's fascinating what you do. I am a professional party crasher by night and I freelance by day"

"Freelance at what?"

"Being a stewardess"

"Really, which airlines?"

"Like I said, I freelance, or more correctly I am floater. Different airlines. When a stewardess can't make her flight, they contact me and I do it for them. So I am on call a lot during the holiday seasons when stewardess want to extend their layovers in Atlanta and whatnot. Its an easy job and it pays well, plus I do a little writing."

"Anything that I may have read?"

"Just a few articles in the Atlanta Journal, but I am trying to get a book together."

"Like waiting to exhale?"

"No, not like that."

They were quiet again.

"I would like to take some time to talk to you, and this party is getting on my nerves. You wanna take a ride?"

"sure"

They left the party and he drove a Cherry red lexus. It had to be custom. Morgan hadn't seen anything like that. They drove out Peachtree, past the city into Buckhead, where the lights were just as bright and stopped in a little bistro just off Peachtree. He talked to one of the waiters for a moment then they left and headed to a quiet little table. He ordered pasta, and white wine for them both and they sat and talked.

"I've seen you at different parties, but never have seen you with a man. Are you a lesbian?"

"No, I just am particular about the company I keep."

"Me too. Women think I am an exciting man,but I have to be careful with whom I associate. You get the type of women who are gold diggers when you have money. And I have money."

"Really? I couldn't tell"

"And a sense of humor. Now, I don't buy the stewardess shit, but I do buy the writing. What are you really?"

Morgan had to admire the man, he was smarter than she thought.

"Actually, I have money because my mother died and left it to me. My dad disappeared many years ago, but my mom was attractive and she and my step dad managed to acquire a nice little sum of money, unfortunately their lives were cut short by the crash over Lockerbie and I have been on my own for awhile. I try to work, but writing is all I love."

"Poor little rich girl"

"I guess. My friends believe I am a stewardess and its easier than saying I have all this cash, women meet gold diggers as well as being them you know."

"I know"

"you seem lonely."

"me, lonely. Well, sometimes, but when I am, I go to Phipps and buy a nice outfit and hit a party or two and then I am fine again."

"and you go home to sleep by yourself."

"Most of the time"

"What about the other times?"

"You are getting very personal and I have just met you, Mr. Amir so I don't think I will tell you anymore right now. I thought CIA didn't tell anyone they were CIA?"

"You are right, but my friends don't know that. I am an art dealer by trade. I deal in articles that no one can get and I find them and make them available."

"Yeah, right, a black art dealer?"

"America is the only place who use skin as a prejudice, darling or haven't you been overseas? They attitude among thieves is one of monetary gain and it doesn't matter if the gain comes from a black man or whatever. If he has the goods, he gets the cash."

"Honor among thieves."

"Cash, is the only honor, darling. Cold hard cash."

They sat and made small talk for a while.

"Well, I guess I need to get back to my party to make sure everything is still okay."

"Yeah, some gold digger may be trying to get your booty."

"More accurate, I may be trying to get into some gold diggers booty tonight, unless you want to stay with me?"

"Well, not on the first date, darling, but maybe if we have a second one . . ."

"maybe?, you don't want to see me again? You are a different type of wench. My money doesn't impress money, huh?"

He kept looking at her. He had seen someone like her before, but it didn't connect.

"lets just say, it takes more than money. Money I have."

They drove back in silence. In the parking lot, he leaned over and kissed her deep and hard, his hands gripping her thighs. He felt the knife and slowly slid his hand back.

"Protection?"

"Every girls needs one. Especially when they run alone"

"are you coming in?"

"no, I think I will go home and sleep this one off. Its been a pleasure Amir, maybe we can meet again sometime"

"I guarantee we will."

Morgan departed the car. She wondered how he would set this up. But right now, contact was made. She would pursue at this present course because it was working. But, she made plans in her head to live in L5P for awhile.

II

Morgan home late last night and didn't want to wake her father. She put in a call to John to make the arrangements to have herself sent on a model tour of Milan. That way, she could live in L5P for as long as it takes to nail this guy. She told him that he made contact with her almost immediately.

"John, he said he worked for the CIA, it was hilarious. But he didn't buy the stewardess story so I told him I was a writer. I need some articles that are imprinted in different magazines to have around my table at L5P. Preferably out of print so that he can't buy it on the newsstand. I am going to need some show money, because I told him my parents died and left me a fortune in the Lockerbe air disaster."

"That's not very imaginative."

"Well, he won't check that out, but he may try to check my holdings. Get some postcards for Milan so I can send my father post cards and let him know I am okay Modeling in Italy. I left the Mercedes at L5P and drove my vet home. Pick me up around noon, I want to have breakfast with daddy before I get down to business."

"Do you think you can get him?"

"Yes, he is pretty taken with Renee and I guess she is his type. Financial secure, alone in the world. He hates notoriety. He's pretty sexual though, so make sure I have plenty of the sanitary implants available. I don't know who this guy has screwed and I don't want to catch anything. But I know sex is inevitable."

"Can you handle it?"

"Its just a job, John. I don't take this personally."

"I worry about you sometimes. The pay is sufficient for you I hope."

"You always pay me well. That's not the issue. If this guy is a major player in the cocaine connection, we need him. I can do the rest. Feelings won't get in the way."

"Everything will be ready. I will see you around noon."

"Okay John"

Morgan disconnected the call, put her robe on and headed for the smell of bacon and pancakes that was coming from the kitchen. The kitchen was designed by her and her father after her mother died. There was a stacked oven, copper pots hanging on the ceiling, with a wine rack in one corner. The window was broken out and a patio door added. A bar instead of a table, left lots of space for when they had their cooking experiments. The color scheme was dusty rose, which was accented with white and copper accessories. Her father, standing over the stove in his robe flipping pancakes eyed her.

"You had a late night, babydoll. Did you have fun?"

"Just a little. John has a modeling assignment for me in Milan and I wanted to have some Atlanta style fun before I hit the runway. It was the usual. Sorry about breakfast,but I knew it wasn't my type of party and I decided not to"

Morgan embraced her dad.

"You think you will like the assignment? Milan is very far away."

"I will send you postcards every day until its done. I have never been there and it should be a blast. Don't worry about your babydoll, she will be okay, I promise."

"I just wish you would find a man and settle down for a change. You seem to be going and going. I don't notice any men in your life except John. And he is just an ol' white man. You need to be around men your age."

"Men my age have issues and problems and I don't. I don't need someone else's drama cluttering up my life right now. I am enjoying myself and when the time comes and the right man comes along, I will do the right thing."

"Grandchildren would be nice, babydoll. Just one or two. One day you have to stop running."

"Sure they would. I promise after this I will take the time to find someone and settle down. You don't have anyone in mind do you? And, I am not running."

"Well, there is this detective that I play racket ball with and he has seen you here and there and wants to get to know you. I think he's a lot like me. And you are running. Running from relationships. I don't do relationships because I am me, you don't have to run from them. A lot of them are good."

"Oh, daddy, a detective can't be good!"

"When you get back from Milan, I will arrange a dinner or something so you can meet him. He is very good at what he does and he has no drama that I know of."

The doorbell rang at that moment and Morgan answered it. It was the detective, in his tennis clothes.

"Good morning, you must be Morgan. Hello, I am Steven St. John, I play racquetball with your father." He put out his hand and looked at her quizzically.

"I know you from somewhere. The hair is different, but I have seen you."

"No, I don't think so, but come in anyway."

Morgan felt a little chill come over her. She had seen him somewhere. But she couldn't quite place him. He kept staring and she turned away and headed for the kitchen. Mind was going fast trying to place this guy. She thought, he must have seen me as Renee, but he isn't sure. Lets hope he stays unsure.

They sat at the bar while her dad passed out the food.

"You met my daughter, but unfortunately too late. She is flying to Milan for some modeling work."

"Really, maybe that's where I saw you, in the magazine ads?"

"Its possible" Morgan spoke while concentrating on her food, she didn't want to look him directly in the eyes.

"Why are you modeling when I understand you have a degree in criminology? Don't you like police work?"

"Yes I do, but I am not ready to commit to it just yet. It takes a lot to be a cop."

"I know you would understand that because of your father. He is the greatest guy I know. I hope to learn all I can from him. Especially his racquetball skills."

They laughed and continued eating. The sun was shining brightly in the kitchen, illuminating the copper and dancing off the walls. Morgan thought that this was such a beautiful room. She loved it here, in the kitchen.

She excused herself from the table.

"I have a lot of packing to do. John will be here around noon, my flight leaves at one thirty. You know how hard it is to get around at Hartsfield."

"Go ahead, babydoll, I will straighten up here."

"Hope we get to meet again when you are not so busy."

She smiled at the men and went to her room.

She had moved her bedroom into the den after her mother died. Spacious and open, with a glass enclosed patio, she needed the space. She had wigs, clothes, shoes and other things everywhere. She grabbed her Renee clothes. Renee was a special character of hers. Free spirited and loose, She dressed in outfits that accented her best body features. She had several Renee wigs and made a note to get to the hairdresser to get the weave in so that the wigs would not have to be used. It wouldn't do for the wig to come off during a love session.

There were several contact lenses cases with Renee's eyes in them. Just in case she lost one. Going through the walk in closet she had built, there were shoes, shoes and more shoes. She had stiletto's for after 5, tennis shoes, sandals, sling backs, and others. Various colors. She loved shopping at College Park Shoes because they had the best variety and the best styles. She made a note to herself to get back there soon. Eve's at South Dekalb had the best selection of after five shoes. Although a little pricey, she enjoyed the fact that many of them were one of a kind. The idea of someone with smaller feet where her shoes and looking better in them made her feel bad. While she was arranging her attire, there came a knock at her door.

When she opened it, Steve was standing there.

"I never saw a model getting ready for a shoot before, can I watch."

"Sure"

He sat down on the wicker couch she had in the corner near her stereo. Weather Report, Heavy Weather was playing softly on it.

"You like jazz?"

"Yes, its sort of mood music."

"You have to get in the mood to model?"

"yeah, its not as easy as it seems. With all the make up and changes and fittings, its actually pretty tiring and you do have to have your mind set for it. The pictures look pretty and walking down the runway gives you a great feeling, but when you get behind the scenes its just an endless day of changing clothes, and changing makeup. Hair teasing and crap like that. But the money is good and the recognition is excellent."

"I would imagine."

He sat quietly for a moment.

"Who is John?"

"My, aren't we nosy!! John is my agent/friend. He oversees all the details of my trips and makes sure that I don't get into any trouble or anything like that. He is a 63 year old white man, not a boyfriend."

"White is not a problem is it?" And as soon as he said it he looked embarrassed.

"I wasn't trying to pry"

"Yes you were, but its cool. Color is only an issue if it is made to be one. My dad thinks very highly of you. He even hinted about me settling down with you. Isn't that funny?"

"No, I don't think so. We share a common interest."

"Modeling?"

"You know I mean law enforcement. You have a sense of humor. He didn't tell me that."

"what did he tell you?"

"we can discuss that when you get back if you want."

"Are you making a date with me?"

"Yes, if you don't mind. I would like to get to know you better. And what's so funny about us settling down?"

"I just never saw myself as the June Cleaver type, but you never know"

"Who is June Cleaver?"

"Oh, you don't watch TV Land, Beavers mom on Leave it to Beaver, you know, Ward, Wally, Beav and June. Oh don't tell me you didn't watch this stuff as a kid."

"Well, I didn't even see a t.v. Until I moved in with my aunt and uncle after my parents disappeared. By then, I was watching Speed Racer mostly."

"ah, the Mach 5"

"Yeah."

"Your parents disappeared?"

"One day, they just left me at my aunts house and never came back. After about a year, I stopped thinking about them."

"Oh, I am sorry. I didn't know"

"I don't know why I told you. I never even told your father that. I changed my name to St. John after about 3 years of waiting. My real name was Tobias. Stephen Anthony Tobias."

"I like Steve St. John."

"I hope you will."

He got up and headed for the door.

"Your dad wants to kick my butt at racquet ball so I guess I better go. Good luck and I hope to see you soon."

"You too. And don't let my father beat you. Once in awhile it does him good to win on his own."

He left, looking back at her quizzically again.

"I still think I met you before, but I guess it was the magazine layouts."

"I guess"

Morgan was glad he left the room. She had some sensitive things she needed in her move. Her service revolver, ammunition, knives and others instruments of protection. Her private cell phone that rang directly to John when there was trouble. Her sanitary shields. These were inserted into the vagina like a diaphragm, but made of a polymer that yielded under body heat and protected her from semen getting into her. The were usually good for a week or two, and then had to be removed and reapplied. A cool water and vinegar douche made them harden a little and she could remove them. This way, there would be no fluid introduced into the body. She would be safe as far as that goes. Kissing was another thing and they had not come up with anything to protect her from that. But, life was a gamble. For a female operative, sex was sometimes necessary in order to maintain the cover that she had. Renee was a sexual person. She could do the sex without getting involved personally. She would become Renee in those instances and when it was over she could be herself again. She wondered if that's what prostitutes did to have several johns every night. You have to have some sort of detachment she supposed. She often wondered if she could have a regular sex life after this. Would the detachment stay a part of her psyche forever? Sometimes it was hard to tell. A lot of her jobs did not involve sex, but the few that did were usually wild and furious.

She had learned a lot of techniques. A normal man would probably be threatened by her sexual knowledge and she made a note to always keep that part hidden once she decided to stop doing this type of work. But for the moment, it was a necessary evil.

She packed her numerous bags and made another note to get some groceries. She knew the place didn't have much. Some caviar and some champaign maybe. A few eggs. She tried to get through there once or twice a week to keep the dust from settling too much. And to keep appearance up that she lived there.

Morgan showered and put on her clothes. Just a pair of jeans and some sandals. A nice crisp cotton shirt. Earrings and a bracelet. She pulled her hair back into a pony tail and minimal make up. She was ready.

Taking her stuff to the front room, she went back into the kitchen to say her goodbyes to her father.

He was just about ready to leave. That was good. She didn't want him here when John came. He asked too many questions. She still had another 45 minutes before he would arrive. And her father was putting stuff in the car.

"You got your passport babydoll?"

"yes daddy."

"Is it updated? You have all your shots?"

"yes daddy."

They went through this everytime she had to leave. It was his way of reassuring himself and she didn't mind.

"Daddy, its going to be fine. Steve will watch after you while I am gone, won't you Steve. Don't let him eat too much and make sure he takes his vitamins."

"you too are more like husband and wife than daughter and father. I love this."

"you should have seen him the first time I left."

She kissed him good bye and Steve kissed her on the cheek.

"for luck" he said.

When they drove off, she stood and waved, then went to the car port where her vet was. She put the cover over it and locked it in place. The garage was so full of her fathers stuff that he kept meaning to clean out that she had to keep it in the carport. But she didn't mind. Their neighborhood was nice and nothing had happened to it thusfar. John drove up as she was finishing.

"locking up your baby, I see. Are you ready?"

"yes John, I am. Daddy had a detective over here who thought he recognized me. But I convinced him that it was the modeling stuff. I have seen him somewhere but I can't put my finger on it."

"If you feel any trouble, just remember the cell phone. I will make sure you get out."

He gave her another pack of sanitary shields, some extra contact lenses, bullets for her gun.

"from what we have gathered, there is a big shipment of cocaine coming in from the ivory coast in the next 2 or 3 weeks. If we can nail him with it, your job will be over quicker. And for my peace of mind, play as hard to get as you can with the sex thing. I understand he is pretty brutal with his lovers. A couple of call girls got treated pretty rough even by their standards. I understand he is hung like a horse."

"Don't worry, John. You sound like my father."

As they drove away, John put his hand on hers.

"Morgan, you are the best operative I have. This is the worst situation I could put you in. Don't take any unnecessary chances and stay in touch. After this, we will only use you on an as needed basis. We feel that we have been taking advantage of you. I, I feel very deeply for you, like you were my own daughter. Please be safe and don't get in over your head. If anything, and I mean anything goes wrong, you bail out and come home. I mean it. You will still get paid. I feel really apprehensive about this assignment. More than I have with the other ones."

He drove slowly down 85 toward Jimmy Carter. The taxi cab was a good cover. It looked like she was just returning from a trip somewhere. Morgan almost forgot.

"take me to Hair Happenings and let me get my transformation on. I have to get the weave done before I go home to L5P. Go and get some lunch and take my key and drop off my stuff. The maintenance man will hold it for me and I will call you when I am ready to go, okay?"

"you trust him?"

"yea, he is my friend. He knows that I have been out of town and it won't look strange if someone happens to be sitting around the place, you know. Besides its gonna take Sylvia a little while to get my hair right. I don't want you to wait, it wouldn't look normal."

"okay."

She leaned and kissed John.

"I will be all right, trust me."

John dropped her off in front of the beauty shop. It was off of Glenwood and Sylvia was the best at putting in weaves. She was waiting for her. For two hundred dollars, it was the best money can buy.

"hey girl, you got the style, I have the hair. Lets get started."

They made small talk for the next four hours while the transformation was complete. When John arrived in the taxi, Morgan looked almost not like Morgan. The only thing she needed was her contacts and she had them in her purse. She sat in the back of the cab, putting them in and then applying her makeup, the transformation was completed. She looked at the results. Perfect for Renee.

They arrived in L5P shortly after 5 in the afternoon. It was a Monday, so traffic was a little heavy, but the bars were not as crowded. She said goodbye to John, and walked to Larry's apartment. He was waiting for her. He was always excited when she came home. She sat and talked with him for a while and watched CNN smoking a joint. He ask her about her trip and told her that he had fumigated the place because the trashy people downstairs moved out and bugs were everywhere. He had fixed her air conditioner because it had to be cleaned from lack of use. He opened her windows and aired out the place. On his stove he was cooking ox tails and had some Bull in the refrigerator. He always cooked her favorite things and did it well. They sat and laughed for a long time. He kept trying to put the videos of Star Trek that he had. He was an avid star trek fan and so was she, but tonight she wasn't in the mood.

She walked up stairs to the back of her apartment. Her message light was blinking.

III

The voice on the machine was Amir.

"Hey beautiful woman, I called every Renee in the Atlanta white pages. Finally I got your voice. Call me at this number when you get in."

She was surprised. He really had to do that because she didn't tell him her last name. But she made sure she was in the book, it was part of the show.

She sat things down and begin putting things in place. She realized that she hadn't eaten since morning and weaving took a lot out of her. So she put on a pair of shorts and walked to Felini's pizza for a white slice and some beer. The white slice was her favorite because it was all white cheese. The michelob was good and cold and she drank two as she waited for her slices. The crew was glad to see her and she watched the local dead heads meandering around the square. Not much to do as of yet, this evening. The buzz from the joint she smoked with Larry gave her big time munchies. He had saved her a little pink packet for her return home. She was glad because she was out of her stash.

She took her pizza home, and waved at her neighbors who were coming in. They were always happy to see her. She was glad Larry aired the place out and she waited to turn the air on. There was a good breeze blowing in with a storm that was riding the waves into Atlanta. Good thing it happened after rush hour. This place had the worst drivers she had ever experienced. One drop of rain and pouf, thirty accidents. But summer rains were usually heavy and full of lightning in this city. She still hated storms, and always felt the need to hide from them when they occurred at night.

Getting her little home in order was the first business after she ate the pizza. The guys at Felini's put an extra slice in there for her and she put it in the refrigerator for later consumption. She shook the pink packet and cleaned the weed. She rolled a joint, turned on Michael Franks and began getting her house in order. She took down all the items that would not pertain to Renee. The picture of her and her father was replaced by her and a not so famous fashion designer that John had created for her. Her police magazines were replaced with fashion magazines with her pictures added for reality sake. Not Vogue or Cosmo, but lesser known and not easily obtainable magazine from Italy, France, England. The over seas magazines with her articles in them replaced newsweek. After the transformation was complete, she called Amir.

It was his cell phone.

"Hello Amir, I am returning your call."

"good afternoon Miss Renee, and how are you? Busy?"

"no, just writing a story."

"From your number I gather you live in the moreland avenue area. I am in that area now, can I stop by for a moment, I know its short notice."

"sure you can. I haven't been to the store yet, but you can come. I can't offer you anything."

"sure you can, but that can wait. I just want to see you."

Morgan gave him the address and told him to ring the bell and she would let him in. She told him to park on the street or in the alleyway because Larry would have his car towed away. Parking was limited around here. And the apartment didn't like people using their lot.

Five minutes later, the bell rang. He was really in the area. She got totally into character. There was no Morgan now, only Renee.

She went downstairs and let him in.

"You didn't say you lived in L5P. How bohemian. Just suited for you."

"yeah, I like it."

He could smell the weed in the air.

"enjoying a little evening libation. I brought wine and some munchies because I brought you a present."

It was another bag of weed. If it was the same that was at the party, it was very quality stuff.

"thanks, a girl can't have too much libation. Have a seat."

He sat on the sofa.

"There is no bedroom, where do you sleep, or do you just party all night?"

"I sleep where your ass is."

"oh, okay a sleep sofa."

"yes, its convenient. I like it here. The neighborhood is so different, and when you walk on the bike path over across the way, you can see the lights of downtown so nicely at night"

"You venture out at night? Isn't that dangerous?"

"not for me. Most people around here know me and know that I carry a weapon. Besides, the homeless population like me and they keep an eye and make sure that no one gets me. They are every where I want them to be. They even play my tag number in the pick three. I didn't even know my tag number. Its cool. This is a very secluded place. The outsiders always stay where the lights and the restaurants are."

"I would hate anything to happen to you."

"Don't worry about me, I am a big girl and can take care of myself."

Amir rolled a fat joint for her and she was reluctant to take it. She was as high as she wanted to be right now, but she hit it a little and put it out.

"don't feel like hangin'?"

"Its not that, I just had one and I have some writing to do. It wouldn't be good for me to be too high. I could mess up my livelihood and a girl has to make a living."

"smart girls have their livings made for them. Didn't you know that? Besides you don't need money, why do you bother. You should be the quintessential party girl, sleep till 2 party till daylight."

"fortunately, I realize that money doesn't last forever and I never liked that lifestyle. Its too hedonistic for me. I believe in working for a living. It a moral issue."

"You have morals, how refreshing. I meet so many women that the more money you offer them, the less important morals become."

"yeah, well that's not me. Dealt in any good art lately?"

"Actually, I am waiting on some which should be here in the next 2 or 3 weeks. Just some figurines and such. African art."

Morgan remembered what John had told her about the shipment.

"there is a friend of mine who is coordinating for me, and he will be in touch soon. You seem so relaxed here, not like at my party."

"parties are cool, but you never know who you will be meeting there. I have met more than my share of loonies at parties. So I try to keep a low profile. I enjoy the scene, but you never know what type of vipers hangout there."

"that's for sure. One party I had, after everyone was gone, I went to my room and there was this beautiful white woman laying in my bed. Of course, since she was in my bed, she must have wanted some. So I gave her what she wanted and then she refused to go home. She said that she was in love with me and that she would never leave me. I told her she was most certainly leaving here and had to call the cops to remove her. She tried to tell them I raped her. I wanted to put my hands around her neck and choke the life out of her. But the cops knew me and they knew her. They escorted her from my building and I had to have a restraining order put on her. She used to try to bribe Melvin to let her in. He didn't go for that. I pay him well, we all do in the building. He is priceless."

"yeah, I like Melvin. He is always good to me."

"I have a feeling everyone you meet is good to you."

Amir leaned over and kissed her deeply and began to rub on her. She backed him off a little.

"did you come over just to ravish me or what?"

"I am just very excited by you. I don't want to ravish you I want to eat you up. Like the chocolate candy that you are. But like I said, I can wait. I like to lick my chocolate before I eat it."

Morgan remembered that she had not put a shield on and she had to try to keep him from initiating sex until she could.

"I understand, and I know I am just a party girl, but I do have things I do and don't do. And fucking someone I just met is one of my don'ts."

"Don't worry, we will have sufficient time to get to know each other. I want to cook dinner for you this evening. Are you free?"

"Not entirely, but my fees are negotiable"

He laughed at that. But it wasn't a good laugh, there was something very sinister about it.

He stood up and stood her up also. Holding her closely, she could feel his hard on and the size of him. He definitely was hung like a horse. He just held her ass and rubbed himself on her.

"Come to dinner, I promise I'll be good."

"Only if you promise. Let me freshen up and I will meet you there."

"If you get there before I arrive, have Melvin let you in. I won't be far behind you."

"okay, but I don't feel comfortable being in your place alone."

"you are never alone in my place, big brother is always watching."

He kissed her again and left.

Morgan sat down on the sofa to collect her thoughts. Well, here goes nothing. She picked out an after five outfit and called John as she readied her bath.

"Are you going?"

"Well John, I have to."

"okay, careful is the key word, we want no more incidents like the chains."

"stop trying to scare me John, I can handle it."

Morgan hated the reference to the chains. She hadn't thought about that in a while. She dressed and put an overnight bag in her car, just in case. The brown Mercedes was ready and so was she.

Cruisin the streets of Atlanta on a Sunday night was cool. No traffic really. Everyone was readying for the work day. No one really had time to hang out on the weekdays although a few places offered happy hour prices to try to bring the crowd in on their slow nights.

Not too many takers, just the die hard party fans who decided not to let their work week get them down. But other than that, Sunday night was prime-time family night in Atlanta. The kids were out of school and up and down moreland, there were little pockets of kids playing under the lights or just milling around, trying to kill time until school started. Nothing else to do. You could only do six flags once in a while unless you were a die hard amusement park fan and in the heat of the summer she couldn't understand how anyone could be, white water, however was a different story. But these kids could never get to white water. In fact, she would bet that the majority hadn't been to six flags.

She arrived at the Peachtree, and Melvin was in his usual spot. He smiled as she drove in.

"I bet him 20 dollars that you wouldn't come and see him, that you were too busy for him. It took him a few days but here you are"

"I guess you lost your money"

"don't worry, I have plenty and its worth it to see you again."

"Here, let me park your car. I have a special spot for you, away from the riffraff."

He took the wheel and drove her to an entrance that she hadn't seen before

"this is the way to get in to avoid being seen. Its also a quick way out in case you need to. I know how Amir is sometimes and I want you to be able to get away if you have to."

"Okay"

"now to reach this from the apartments, you have to go out the front door, and back to the left. Follow the stairways, not the one to the laundry, the one that looks like it leads nowhere. Its dark down there but it will take you right here."

"thanks Melvin, but do you think I will need it?"

"you never know. I have seen some of the women leave his house looking rather abused. I would hate to have to kill that man over you, but make no mistake, Renee, I will. You are a good kid, even if you are confused. You need a husband."

"are you volunteering?"

"hell no, I can't handle my own wife. I am way to whorish for that. I fuck around way too much. But she accepts that and I treat her good. No, you need a good man."

He walked her around to the front entrance just as Amir was pulling up.

"you two having a rendezvous? Melvin, you know I get jealous about my women."

"no, man, she don't want no brokedown man like me. You are more her style."

Amir escorted Renee to the building.

"Renee, remember what I told you."

Amir didn't speak on that remark until they were up in the penthouse.

"what was that all about?"

"what?"

"that warning that Melvin gave you? What was that?"

"Oh, he was telling me I need to settle down and get married and stop partying so much, that's all. I remind him of his daughter."

"melvin doesn't have a daughter."

"well if he did, I would remind him of her, what's the big deal."

"I have never know melvin to get that involved with anyone who comes over here. Don't get involved with him, he's just an employee."

"are you warning me about that or what. I don't like warnings from anyone."

"Take it like you want, I am not trying to argue with you, lets not. I want to enjoy this evening. We will not talk about it anymore."

"okay. What's for dinner?"

"I made some beef tips and noodles, simple dinner, with the hopes that I could persuade you to come over. I am glad you did. I don't normally cook because cooking for one is such a hassle."

Morgan sat on the leather sofa. The place seemed different when it wasn't filled to capacity with party goers. She actually liked the décor. As she sat admiring it, his cell phone rang. Not the one he had in his pocket when he came to her house, a smaller one that was situated on a bookshelf. He answered it and walked toward the kitchen. Morgan tried to listen but he was whispering pretty good and she only caught bits of it when he became agitated.

"look muthafucka, I said my price and that's it. The cartel won't change their mind. Do your damn job, that's what we are paying for cop. Don't forget your place. No, not tonight I have company"

He disconnected the call and came into the living room placing the phone in its original place.

"one of my hired boys messed up a painting that I had worked so hard to secure for another client. He wanted to bring it by here tonight, but I am busy. I don't want anything to interrupt our getting to know each other."

They sat on the balcony and ate their dinner. The lights of Atlanta were shining brightly and there was not much traffic. Not like on the weekend. Sunday nights were so quiet in the city. Just a few limos and some shoppers were walking below. After all it was almost the height of the tourist season and with the Olympics scheduled in July, the city was enjoying its last bit of peace before the event.

Dinner was nice and they sat and enjoyed an after dinner smoke and some bubbling wine. The night air was fantastic and actually Morgan was feeling a little romantic. She tried to change that mood back to one of business, but the weed and the wine had her feeling a little more than romantic, almost randy. But she had to maintain herself. So she refocused her attention to other things.

"does it make you angry when people don't do what they are told? You seemed a little edgy with that guy on the phone. I couldn't hear anything until you got agitated."

"What did you hear?"

"nothing, except that you were agitated."

"you pay people to do what they are told and they always want to think. I do the thinking, not them. But you always get some smart ass who thinks he knows more than you and you have to put him in his place. I hate to talk to them like that."

"well, sometimes it has to be done. I understand, I just never really got use to people being agitated. It gives me a nervous stomach ache. I am fine now, but for a minute there I thought I would have to go home."

"Don't let harsh words do that to you Miss Renee. It just means that you are intimidated by harshness and people will sense that and use it against you. If you let people know your weakness, it will always be a weakness. The only way to overcome weakness is to work on the assumption that you don't have one."

"yeah, but you know what they say about assuming."

"well, in this instance, that rule doesn't apply. Remember there are always exceptions to rules. For instance, you are the exception to my rule on women. At this point, you should have been asking me about my money, my surroundings and yet none of this impresses you."

"actually it does, but I am much to polite to say so."

"Ah, then you were raised well. Most young women today are not raised, they are just put out in this world to be victims of whatever. Their mothers are so busy playing the victim that it carries over into the child and it is perpetual. If the mother was abused and not raised, so therefore the child won't either. You see a lot of that today. Young girls with no other direction other than to be pawns of many men. They crave it, and look for it because it is a normal situation to them and everyone looks for normalcy no matter how abnormal it is."

"So its not environmental?"

"On the contrary, environments are just where we live, our mind takes us to where we will be. The strong mind survives in this day and age, not just the strong. I have seen the strong become nothing more than crack heads and misfits. But strong minds cannot be bent like that. Its your mind willing you to survive, not your environment. That is why you have success from seemingly impossible beginnings. The boy who becomes a great scientist despite the fact that he grew up in the 'hood where schools were second rate and violence was everywhere. Where you see certain kids from Carver Homes and the other 'Homes' around Atlanta actually rise above it. Its not super human, its the mindset. It can happen and it does happen more often than it is talked about."

"How were you raised?"

"I wasn't. My mother was a heroin addict and my father was whoever. My mom's motivation was the next fix. I had to hustle for everything to stay alive. But I would go to downtown Atlanta, and see the people and know that there was something else. I stole art magazines and things that would remind me that i could be somebody. That's how I did it. I was lucky that I only had me to take care of. She only had one child and not countless like these girls today. And at the time she had me, she was straight. I wasn't born addicted to anything. The heroin came later in my life."

"oh"

"But I don't want to dwell on something that was past and best forgotten, you learn from, but you don't dwell on the past. I would rather concentrate on you."

He leaned over and kissed her, softly at first and then harder and deeper. He picked her up off the chair and carried her into his bedroom.

There, he lay her on the bed and begin to take her clothes off slowly and methodically.

"Are you sure you want to do this, we really don't know each other."

"I know that I am a man and you are a woman, that's all we need to know right now, my passion is very hot for you and I hope you will forgive me for not asking your permission, its how I am. Now, don't talk, just let me love you a little."

She lay there and let him take her clothes off. He stood over her and looking down at her, he began to take off his clothes.

She could see the big dick hardening as he looked at her and she wondered if she could handle this.

He began to kiss and bite her all over and when she tried to object and move away, he held her hands over her head and thrust very roughly into her. She let out a scream for although she was excited there was not enough wetness in her to lubricate this big thing. Again and again he thrusted and she tried to control her screams.

"No, don't hold them in, scream I want to hear it."

He bit her neck and held it as he thrusted again and again into her until he came. She could feel him cuming in her and she felt her own body responding in kind. The hot wetness only fueled his fire and he turned her over to enter her from the back. Under his weight, she couldn't move and he did not try to anally penetrate her, he just rode her from the back, which lessened the severity of the thrusts and he came again.

He never took himself out of her and maintained a semi hard condition while he lay on her and talked in her ears.

"I am being very gentle with you this first time Renee, but let me assure you that I am a firm believer that without pain there can be no pleasure. I won't inflict myself on you as yet, because I want to keep you as my woman. But the things I have planned for you will heighten your sexual experience and no other man will be able to satisfy you as I can. I want you to be in love with me. I don't want you to fuck me and leave me. I am tired of that. I can give you so much more than money. I can give you what no one ever wanted from me, myself."

He began slow, rhythmic soft thrusting until he came again. He then rolled, holding her and she was now laying on top of him, while he was still inside, her back to his front. He began to manipulate her clit and as she responded he began thrusting again and they came together this time. It was very intense. He squeezed her so tightly as he emptied the last of himself into her and bit her on the shoulder as he did so. The pain was horrible, but with the clitoral stimulation and the cum she was experiencing it was altogether an experience she didn't forget.

She knew her shoulder was bleeding. She could feel when he punctured the skin.

When he released her, she got up from the bed and grabbed her shoulder.

"Why in the fuck did you bite me like that?"

She stormed off into his bathroom and slammed and locked the door. She turned to see the damage. Perfect red teethmarks in her shoulder. She looked into the drawers and cabinets for some antiseptic to put on it. It was bleeding profusely right now. Damn the bastard. She thought of Sharon Lee, the party and the night she first saw Amir. She would be glad when this assignment was over, this guy was a nut. Did Sharon Lee go through this? Suddenly, she felt sorry for her.

He knocked softly on the door.

"Renee, open the door, I will fix your wound. I didn't mean it, but I got so carried away."

"fuck you Amir."

He knocked with a little more force.

"Renee, you are not a child, open my damn door."

She held fast.

"go to hell Amir, when I fix this shit I am going home."

She didn't hear anything for a minute and the next thing she knew the door was coming loose with a force that knocked her to the other side of the bathroom almost into the sunken tub. He was standing there, the look on his face was something she had never seen before. He reached for her, took her back to bed and fucked her again harder and harder. She was screaming for real now because she felt like she was dying. He kept screaming at her.

"Don't ever defy me, girl, don't do it. I am the man, me, you feel this dick in you, its a man's dick, not a boy."

He bit and tore at her skin and it was all she could do to keep from passing out. But she redirected her mind and let him vent his rage. She took herself, back to when she was playing in the yard. This current abuse had disappeared and she was not there. When she came back to reality, she was being sponged off with a cool rag and he was talking very gently to her. It took her a minute to realize where she was and that she was on assignment. She reached her hand up and slapped his face as hard as she could.

"You bastard, you take me home, you sadistic fucker. Have you lost your mind. Look at me. Look at this shit."

Large bite marks and bruises it seemed were everywhere.

Morgan tried to remember that she was Renee and kept acting accordingly. She took the rag from his hand and pushed her off away from her and tried to stand. However, her legs were not in the walking mood and she fell down beside the bed in a lump.

He picked her up and put her back on the bed.

"Renee, I am sorry, I don't mean to be such a rough lover, at least not yet. But I couldn't help it. I am not use to women defying me. And besides, the more I cum, the more I want to cum and the more intense it is. Please understand and don't leave me right now, stay the night. I can prove to you that I can be a gentle lover too. The desire for you was just so much that I didn't control myself like I promised I would. Just relax and let me make you feel better."

She looked at him. She couldn't really walk out of here right now anyway. As bad as she wanted to. Her muscles just were not cooperating and she lay there in the bed, trying not to cry. She didn't want her contacts to come out. It would mess up everything. Stay focussed Morgan, she kept telling herself, just stay focussed it won't be long just a couple of weeks. The doorbell rang and he shut the door and went to answer it.

There was man there and the voice was one she recognized but she couldn't place it. She had definitely heard it before, but where? Her mind was so jammed with what just happened that she couldn't concentrate on it.

"Man, I told you not to bring yourself here."

"what you got one of those little freaks in there, I want some too, man, you always share."

"Some other time man, just tell me what you have to tell me and get the fuck out my house."

"I tried to call, but no one answered the phone."

"I was busy."

"yeah I bet, I have seen what happens when you are busy."

"You want a drink?"

"yeah."

"Have a quick one finish your business and get out."

Morgan could hear the glasses moving around and wanted a drink really bad, instead she reached for the joint that she had put out and began to smoke.

She listened to the conversation.

"Everything is all set, the stuff will be here in 2 weeks exactly, with your fuckin' figurines. But the cut has gone up, I need 2 more grand to make it an even mil. No more, and definitely not less."

"why the increase?"

"because there is word out that someone is trying to get you. I don't need this bullshit, and I think since the degree of danger has just gone up, so should the price. I could take less, but then I would be more inclined to help you get caught if the other side was paying more. Right now, all I know is that someone has been planted from the outside into your party circle. You need to choose your friends carefully."

"Yea, and you aren't the one?"

"no, way man. I need that mil. I found a young lady that I want to settle down with and this is my last big score. After that, its the happy married life for me."

"yea right, who is she."

"Just a friend of a friend."

Suddenly, Morgan realized who that was. It was Steve St. John. What the fuck. Would he recognize her. She didn't think so, but she wouldn't take any chances with him. So he was the connection to the police force. She and John figured it had to be law enforcement involved because of the way no one got caught. You had to have some type of back up in the police department to move that type of merchandise. Damn.

She could hear the voices fading some, and she relaxed. Getting up finally, she turned on the shower and got into the cooling water. Each bite screamed when the water touched it and she could imagine cutting this guy in 15 different ways. The sadistic fucker.

It would be good bustin' him and she had to get in touch with John to tell him about Steve, but then he was a friend of her father. That complicated things somewhat.

IV

Steve St. John drove through the quiet streets of Atlanta. There was nothing much happening tonight. The weekend is usually when the fun began. Just minor skirmishes on Ashby street and in the general area, but nothing earth shattering. He was prowling, looking someone to play with. He hated when that fuckin' Amir talked to him like a common person. He was Atlanta's finest. Not one of those piss ass drug dealers. He drove the Ashby area, looking for a plaything.

He circled a few more times and his desires were about to be fulfilled. There, standing under a burnout street light, near a darkened store, was a prostitute. Thin and tall, she was definitely a crack whore, but it didn't matter. She was all alone and as he surveyed the area, there was no one around. She jumped into his car.

"Man, I hate Sundays. Ain't never shit happened out here. I just need a ride to my friends house okay."

"sure."

She smiled at him showing that she had no front teeth. The better to give head with.

"You don't mind. Why you out here like this? What you lookin' for?"

"I found what I was lookin' for honey."

"I know you a cop, I can smell cops, but cops need love too. Don't they?"

"yes we do. Can I get a freebee?"

"not tonight cop man, I got to make a little something."

Steve took twenty dollars out his wallet.

"You gonna bust me as soon as I take this ain't you. Phuck, I don't wanna go to jail tonight."

"you aren't going to jail, I promise honey."

He drove her, past the projects down 20, past Adamsville, past Fulton Industrial and past six flags.

"How far out we goin' man?"

"I know a quiet spot so that we can have some fun and not get caught. You know the cops have nothing to do tonight but patrol."

He gave her another twenty and she smiled and shut up.

He came to a secluded area with just enough low grass to drive into. He use to fish here when he first got into town. The dried up lake was just beyond those trees.

There, he took her out the car and let her suck his dick. The toothless bitch felt good, those gums rubbing his hard dick. He pushed her head lower and harder until she tried to fight him off.

But she could feel him getting ready to cum and she had forty dollars so she stopped fighting and tried to fight back the gag reflex. Ad he began to cum, he let her pull her mouth off of his dick and he came, he felt his knife going into her soft, skinny flesh. Deeper and deeper as the cum came. When he finished cumming, she was dead. A knife all the way into her. He took her clothes off, wiped the dripping semen off his dick and put them in a garbage bag, wiping the knife off too. He took his forty dollars and stuck them back in his wallet. He stood there looking at her for moment. He thought to himself, now, you don't have to work anymore.

He backed out with his lights off, no one could see his backing lights, he had disabled them in this vehicle. He drove off down the deserted highway. Back to the city.

Stephen Anthony Tobias drove home. He liked the area around Lindbergh Station. Buckhead without the price. The Gold Club loomed in the distance and he could see the limos pulling in and out. He went to his one bedroom apartment and took a shower. He placed the garbage bag with his regular garbage to be placed in the dumpster. Dumping a lot of food from the refrigerator that he saved up for these special moments, the garbage was complete. He would dump his garbage in the apartment dumpster and the one with the food and the clothes in one somewhere else. Moreland avenue was as good a place as any. Down near 285.

He lay in his bed to sleep. He was dreaming of Morgan. Sweet, sexy Morgan. He was seeing her father tomorrow. He really did like the man. But the ideas he had about his daughter would have turned the man's stomach. Nothing like the poor hooker that he killed. No one missed black hookers, they just disappeared. And lately they have disappeared pretty regular. But no one cared. He checked the papers regularly and no one even reported them missing.

They were the throw away women. Society didn't hold much for crack prostitutes. And no one missed them when they were gone. That was the 10th one in the 10 month period. Once a month was usually enough to satisfy him. He didn't want to do more. He needed a woman of his own that he could fuck. But she had to special, like Morgan. Clean, from a good home. Until then, he did what he had to do. The heat of the Georgia nights would take care of the remains quickly. And in the areas where they were dumped, there was never any one there. Deserted patches of overgrowth that development had overlooked for the time being. By the time they did, all they would find would be bones. No DNA evidence, no fibers, nothing but bone.

He lay there, thinking about pretty little Morgan and his dick got hard again. He masturbated saying her name softly as he came.

The phone woke him shrilly. He was still holding his penis.

"hello?"

"hello old man, you ready for some golf today?"

Morgan's father.

"sure old man. What time is it?"

"Its about ten o'clock, but I figured if we had brunch, we could tee off around noon."

"you cookin?"

"You know it. Hey, I got a postcard from Morgan. She arrived safely and everything is fine. She told me to tell you hello."

"Did she?"

"Yea, I told you she would like you. She is just a little hard to get. She doesn't like just anyone."

Morgan was clean and special. Steve St. John smiled to himself. She doesn't know just how special.

"Okay old man, I will be there. Give me time to shower and get ready"

"pancakes good for you?"

"Yours always are."

Steven got into the shower and washed himself. He was still stimulated from last night and his erection just kept coming back. He may have to do something against his feelings and get another hoe. But hopefully he won't kill her this time. He would select a little better and hopefully can get his knutt without murder. Let someone live.

He dressed in his golf attire and headed to Morgans house. Her father was in the kitchen in his golf attire. Eating some pancakes and drinking his orange juice. On the counter was his vitamins. Morgan had said make sure he takes them.

He did.

"My babydoll would kill me if she thought I didn't take my vitamins. But you know, she needs to have a husband to fuss over and not her old man. I can take care of myself."

"it will work out, just believe it. Don't press so hard or you will have the opposite effect. Just let it happen. I can charm her. I promise."

They ate in silence. The pancakes were good and Steve St. John was enjoying the prospect of being a part of this family. And, with the money he gets off this last score, he can bring something to the table besides himself. Most families with money are looking for others with money. He didn't feel this way about this family though. They didn't care, they just liked him. He just wanted to make sure that he could offer her a little something. So their kids can have their own money. Not like him. Money was not always there. His father made good money, just decided to take it somewhere else. Even detectives who made a little better salary were always searching for easier ways to get money. They did extra duty and other things on the side. Some of them became involved with the small time dope dealers in the city and got kickbacks from them. But with the Olympics coming to town, maybe the gravy train won't be so far away. There are plenty of jobs for cops who want to make it.

Everyone in Atlanta pinned their hopes on the Olympics. It was like pennies from heaven. Steve thought about the cops in Atlanta.

They were no worse than cops in any other metropolitan area. They had families, low pay and stress. They had to deal with dredges of society and people who hated them simply because they were cops. They had to deal with groupies who liked them just because they were in uniform. It was not just an eight hour day, because if you believed in what you did, you tried to make a difference in everything you did. Being a police officer was a source of pride to a real cop. But your pride was tested every day. You had good cops and bad cops and Atlanta didn't have an over abundance of either. They just had cops. Dealing with the the tremendous growth in the city and the problems that go with it. Atlanta was the mecca for every black person in the fifty states, which included the thugs, druggies, and other people who came here hoping that Atlanta, the chocolate city would fulfill their dreams and make them feel better about themselves. Most were disappointed, because if you brought nothing to Atlanta, you got nothing from her. She wasn't the one to give out favors. Those who didn't bring nothing and stayed, managed to ingratiate themselves with the other deluded people and form the backbone of crisis in the societal frame. Others, having the balls to get what they wanted, rose above the mainstream to be that entrepreneur that they dreamed of and ride with the success of Atlanta. And black success was here. Here, it wasn't necessarily who you knew but what you knew. Others, the drug dealers, come here thinking that they can take advantage of the laid back southern hospitality and what they perceived as weakness and end up with a bullet whole in their heads in back of some country road. Or a knife in the belly. Kindness or southern charm can be just as treacherous as city charm, only here, you don't always see it coming.

Steve and Morgans father drove out to the golf course off near the airport. Camp Creek parkway. It was a city run golf course and it played as good as all the others. There were quite a few people out there. Enjoying golf. Tiger Woods has sure blackened the game. But most black executives had to know the sport also, many a promotion was decided on the 18th hole.

They practiced their shots and didn't keep score. They ribbed each other on their form and tried to not keep focussed on Morgan. Both men were thinking of her, but for reasons as different as the north and the south.

V

Amir had made a breakfast of eggs benedict and lightly toasted english muffins for Renee. She was sore all over and really hated to look in the mirror at herself. She was afraid that she looked as bad as she felt. But her reflection told nothing of the brutality of last night. Her bruises had already started to fade and the scar on her shoulder was covered in cocoa butter. It felt soothed.

Amir made her lay down and he fed her. Every time he reached for her she jumped and it made him sad.

"Renee, please don't jump from me. I'm not a brute. I am just into sexual extremity. I won't ever hurt you again now that I know you can't handle it. I can be gentle. But, some women say no to that type of stuff and they actually like it. I should have known that you weren't that type of girl. I want you to be my woman. I'll save my brutality for the hookers that come to me. I promise. I can't tell you honestly that I can forget it completely because it really turned me on, but I won't hurt you again."

"Why do you like that? Pleasure Pain Pleasure?"

"Its a fact of life, baby. Violent storms are always followed by clear pretty days. How can you truly experience pleasure if you have nothing to compare it to in contrast. There is heaven, hell, good, evil, right, wrong, pleasure, pain. The whole world is based on it. My mother use to spank me for being bad, not spank but kick my ass. Then, she would hold me and rock me in her arms. I could smell her womaness and feel her breasts on me and she would kiss me and tell me she was sorry. It was so beautiful. I realized that if I did bad, she would kick my ass, then hold me and let me feel her breasts against me and kiss me. I think it was something she learned. When my father left, all she had was me to hold."

"that's kind of weird"

He looked at her and she was suddenly sorry she said it.

"no, Amir that's not what I meant, please, please don' hurt me."

Morgan heard herself begging him and she wanted to slit his throat.

"Baby, don't be afraid to talk to me. I won't hurt you for having opinions. Its not that type of show. I am not a dominator, I just love pleasure and pain in the sexual context. You always speak your mind with me."

He took the breakfast tray from her and lay her down on the bed. This time, he was gentle with her. He kissed her passionately and moved slowly inside her already tender body. He made soft, gentle love to her. She came numerous times. Each time, he pulled out slowly and sucked her clit and licked her juices. He would get back into her and take her there again and again. Finally, he held her tightly and thrusted as hard as he could and as he did, he climaxed in her calling her name . . . Renee, Ooh Renee.

It was something again, she never felt before. She had not cum so much in her life. She kissed him with hot passionate breath and wanted more. He made love to her until early in the evening.

"Baby, we gotta get out of this bed. We have a dinner guest tonight."

"really, who?"

"no one you know, but that ass hole that interrupted us yesterday. If I don't keep him happy, he will do sloppy work, so I am inviting him here for a little positive reinforcement. Sometimes you have to kiss some ass to get some head."

Damn. Steve St. John. This was the test of her cover. She wondered how hard he looked at her at her house. The changes were subtle and maybe she will only remind him of someone that he knew. That was the positive side. If he recognized her would he say so. She counted on the fact that he was a cop and inside he would be a cop. She hoped he was in this for the same reason she was.

When Amir left to get the dinner things, she stayed behind. She went to her car and called John.

"What the hell happened to you. I was ready to call everything off and come get you."

"relax John, its okay. There is a cop involved in this situation a Steve St. John, who knows my father. I hope my disguise would be enough to fool him. If not, I will call you. I don't know what his involvement is in this yet, but I hope he's on our side. His real name is Stephen Anthony Tobias. If you have anything on him, let me know."

"try to call me when you can. Are you okay, you sound a little strange."

"Well, I survived the trial by fire, this man is a sadist in every since of the word and apparently it started from childhood, but I survived it, just barely. Supposedly he will save the brutal stuff for the hookers and save the best for me."

She could almost see Johns face when he spoke to her. The sadness.

"I am so sorry. I would never want you to experience anything like that. Please please forgive me for what we are having you do. I want you to leave now. We will send another operative. Someone I don't care so much about."

"John, I am a big girl and will complete my job. I love you for caring and I promise that I will bail out if it gets any rougher okay."

"okay Morgan."

She disconnected the call and got her evening clothes out of the car. Melvin was there and he just waved. He looked around and mouthed the words—don't forget how to get out of there.

She smiled her acknowledgment and went back in. Amir must have told him plenty because he has never been afraid to talk to anyone before. She would ask him but she was afraid that it would get him trouble she made a note that when they busted this asshole, Melvin would get a cushy job somewhere. She would make sure John did that for her. He did owe her.

She arrived back in the penthouse and showered for the party. She didn't dress right away. Taking a vinegar and water douche out her bag she cleaned herself and removed the shield to replace it. There was blood on the inside. She flushed it, finished cleaning herself and inserted another. She powdered herself and fixed her hair. Applying her make up just right. Maybe a little heavy on it because of who was going to be there. She had to make sure that none of Morgan remained. It was important to her. It was important for the case.

The dress she chose was seductively tight and black. It showed her figure, something that Mr. St. John/Tobias had not had a chance to see. Maybe it would be enough of a distraction to take him off the track. For once in her life she was apprehensive. Most of these jobs went off without a hitch, but this was getting more complicated as it wore on. She needed that shipment to come fast. She didn't know how long this could last. She promised herself that after this, she would take her father's advice, find a husband and settle down. This would be her last case. Her nerves were getting jumpy so she smoked a joint to calm them. The joint took away the nerves and she felt she could face the music. Her body, still a little sore from the over stimulation and physical abuse, was feeling better. It was a good thing she was in shape. The past few nights would have killed her. She so wanted to go home not to L5P but to her home. Morgan's home. Back to her room. She wished she was in Milan. Doing the model stroll down the runway.

She sat in his room. Looking at the furnishing. It was actually a very tranquil setting. It had nothing to do with the atrocities that probably went on in here. The ways were a robins egg blue, the floor, beautifully finished teak. The rugs were soft white, and the comforter was a mix of blue and white. The artwork was different African men and women in love positions. Beautifully colored in rich blacks and browns, textures and gloss. Bright reds, subdued oranges and blues. Gracefully done. The music that constantly played was soft and bluesy. Nothing harsh. In fact the only thing harsh about the room was the owner of the room himself. She thought about his mother and thought about how freaky it all seemed to her. But its like he said normalcy is a perception. She finished the joint and poured a glass of wine in a crystal glass. She clinked it with her fingernail to here the clarity. Perfect. She lay on the couch and dozed into a deep sleep.

Steve St. John was finished with his golf game and had headed home, making sure Morgan's father was fine. He was a sweet old man, and he wished he was his father.

He showered in anticipation of dinner at his majesties abode. He wondered if the little honey was still there and if Mr. Amir was feeling generous enough to share. He had on numerous occasions and it kept the killing instinct at bay. He was able to do anything he wanted to the girls including penetration because they were a different class of hooker than that trash he disposed of. Still nothing in the paper about any of the disappearances. He made sure he kept his eye on that. Nothing floating around the squad room except for the occasional joke about the possibility of one of the hookers finding Jesus and going straight. They found Jesus alright. And he sent them straight to hell. He dressed in his black outfit because it showed his physical attributes and he was comfortable in it.

He took one of his dinner wines with him as a gratuity. Must show manners to the big dumb ass. He was the money man. He only had to be dirty for just another week or so. Then, he could be free of this ass wipe. He got into his car and started the drive into the city. He always liked Atlanta. He would leave as soon as this was over. Take Morgan and her dad to a nice place in California where they could lie on the beach and salt water fish.

Amir had been home for a while when Morgan awoke.

"My sweet Renee. The guest will be here soon. Get pretty for me."

He kissed her and held her hand and she got up from the sofa.

Going into the room to redo her makeup and refix her hair. Hit another joint and put on the black dress, stiletto heels and seamed stockings. She stood in the doorway for effect and she actually felt herself wanting Amirs approval.

He looked at her and smiled brightly.

"I could eat you alive."

"I think we have had that little scenario."

"I'm sorry, I didn't mean it like that baby. You look great. This dumb ass won't know what to do with beauty like yours. He is use to me sharing my friends with him and he will be very disappointed to learn that you are not a gift to him. I couldn't stand the fact that another man would touch you. He wouldn't live if I found out he tried anything. Watch him because he is a cop and cops are basically treacherous sons of bitches. Dirty cops are even more so."

The table was set for three. The man was a great host. He had the right glasses and silver ware and everything. There was fresh garden salad in a bowl on the table and the dinner was shrimp scampi with a pasta of his own creation. It smelled wonderful. Amir took her hand and led her to the balcony where they smoked a joint together and he hugged her close. The lighting was pleasantly muted. Hopefully enough to shield her from prying eyes. She picked the chair that was the most in the shadow.

"I think I love you baby Renee, make no mistake about that. Of all the treasures I have, you are my favorite and most cherished. When I was growing up, I dreamed of having a woman like you. Clean, nice and wonderful. It was hard for me to do the things I did to you and that never happened to me before. I never felt remorse about anything I did to women. My pleasure/pain theory doesn't work with you. For you I just want pleasure. No more pain. Never any more pain."

He held her close and she could feel his tears on her neck. This guy was cracked.

The doorbell rang and he took her hand and let her with him to answer it.

There was Steve St. John and he looked at Renee with hot eyes.

"Steve, this is Renee, Renee, my friend Steve."

"The pleasure is mine Renee."

"Don't be so sure man, you gets no pleasure here."

Morgan ignored that barb.

"Its nice to meet you Steve."

He took her hand and looked into her eyes. She felt herself crumbling but he showed no sign of recognition. He just leered at her.

They both escorted her to the table and they took their seats. Conversation was quiet and normal for awhile.

"where are you from Renee?"

"here in Atlanta. I grew up in Buckhead"

"really, what high school?"

"North Atlanta."

"Fine school. School for arts or magnet school or something isn't it."

"yes, but I didn't participate, it was just the school in my area. But I enjoyed going there."

Steve felt a hardening in his groin. He wanted this girl. Not to kill, but to fuck, and to fuck all night long. Long legs slender frame, small succulent tits. Ohhh she was almost as luscious as Morgan. Morgan, he thought for a moment, looked at her really hard. But Morgan is in Milan. But she definitely has a twin. No not a twin a double. He felt that twinge again in his groin, the same twinge when Morgan answered the door. He wasn't wrong, he was never wrong. This was Morgan, but what the hell was going on. Why the story about Milan. He tossed it around over and over in his head. Then, he cleared it out of his mind. Morgan is in Milan. But if he fucked this girl, he could easily imagine it was Morgan.

"You're unusually quiet, man, what's up with you?"

"Renee has taken away my thoughts. I just feel dumbfounded right now. That's all."

"yea, she is a beauty. I found her in L5P. Hiding from the world. She's a writer you know."

"Really, Renee, what do you write."

"Just articles right now, different overseas magazines, stuff like that. I haven't caught on in America yet, but maybe."

"She lost her parents in the plane crash over Lockerbe Scotland, remember that? She is all alone in the world except for me, her protector, and maybe she will let me be her husband."

He held her hand.

Steve almost choked on his wine. You won't get that one, you sick bastard. Then he thought, damn, has she experienced his sexual deviant behavior. The thought sent cold chills down his insides and the urge to kill was welling up inside of him. He had to find a hooker tonight, and he had to be extremely brutal. He must.

They got up from the table and Morgan walked to the balcony and sat in the night air. There was something up with Steve and she felt that he recognized her. Something about the way he looked at her. She would call John tomorrow and call it off. Her intuition was good and this time she didn't give a fuck about the case, she had to get out of this one. She felt afraid for the first time. Her luck was running out.

Steve joined her on the balcony.

"You don't have anybody? How lonely that is for you. Who do you talk to when you get lonely. Amir?"

"Not really, I haven't known Amir very long."

"I know where I saw you before, at one of his parties, right?"

She sighed inside.

"yes, I like his parties."

"So do I, such people. All kinds."

He had moved so close to her, she could smell him. The sweat was forming all over her, a cold sweat.

She repositioned herself to put a little distance between the two of them. As he smelled her fragrance in the heat, he felt new urges. He wanted her, and he was going to have her. She made him tingle inside and he kept trying to get closer to her but she kept moving away. He sat down.

"I know what loneliness is. I was abandoned as a child. My parents just went away. I had no brothers and sister. Raised by my aunt and uncle. I didn't have anyone to talk to either Renee. Maybe we can talk sometime."

She sat down away from him.

"Well, I don't really socialize too much. I am a private person."

"I don't mean here, maybe at your place. When you can get out of here, I mean. I don't want to cause no trouble between you and Amir, maybe we can be friends."

Maybe he didn't know. Her thoughts were clouding her intuition. Maybe she was just paranoid.

"Maybe"

"I hope so Renee. I am so lonely sometimes. I have a good friend that I hang around with but he is more like a father to me than a friend. I really love him."

Morgan knew he was talking about her father. But she ignored that.

"Its nice to have someone like that. I have never been able to find anyone like that."

"maybe you have now."

Amir joined them on the balcony. Brandy and coke for her, straight brandy for the men.

"Renee, baby, could you excuse yourself we have some business to discuss. I left you a present in the bedroom and later I will take you home okay?"

"sure Amir, it was nice meeting you Steve."

"my pleasure, Renee."

She left the balcony, holding back the need to run. She walked to the room and shut the door.

Morgan sat at the desk and smoked the joint that Amir left for her. She needed to go home. Breathe a little and talk to John about what to do. This was a confusing turn of events. She tried to listen to the conversation through the balcony entrance in the bedroom, but it was muffled with that damn music playing. But she heard that the shipment would be one night during the Olympics. Security would be high then and no one would be really paying any attention to the other world. But to make sure, Steve had a diversion set up for that night. But she couldn't make out what it was. It was just days. 10 days of strangers overrunning Atlanta.

VI

Amir talked with her before she left.

"Renee, will you come see me again. I am having a party this weekend and I want you to be by my side."

"Yes Amir I'll be there, you know I love your parties."

"I remember when I first saw you there. You walked in and put everyone else to shame. You set me on fire. Now you are mine. You are mine, aren't you?"

"yes."

"Did Steve make a pass at you. I left him out there purposely to see if he would."

"Not really a pass, I think he was smelling me or something, he is definitely weird."

"Not weird baby, just a different parody of normal."

"No Amir, that guy is weird."

"Maybe you are right this time, cops are definitely weird."

She kissed Amir good bye and began the drive to her apartment. The sun setting over L5P was beautiful. She went upstairs and for some reason making sure all the doors and windows were locked. She even turned on the air instead of leaving the windows open. It was just a feeling.

Outside, in the alleyway, Steve watched Renee arrive. He got out of his car and walked up to the apartment building. Her door was locked downstairs but the door in the building across from her apartment was open and he crept up the darkened stairway and had a good view of her window. She was on the phone and taking off her clothes. Her blinds were closed but the light cast a shadow of her on the windows like a macabre dance. He was fascinated and felt his dick getting hard. He left his hide out, and went walking through L5P, looking for a victim. There were plenty of crack hoes over here, all he had to do was go to the cut. All the cops knew about the cut and once in awhile they raided it when the tourist started complaining. Lots of drugs and sordid sex over here. He found his victim, a skinny crackhead that the homeless called Laura. She was dirty and foul. Perfect for him.

Amir had things on his mind and decided to drive. Getting in his cherrymobile as he called it, he slowly cruised the streets of Atlanta, thinking about Renee. He actually liked this girl, no loved this girl. His pain fetish was slipping from him and he didn't think it would be possible to change like that. But she had. When he saw what he did to her, it made him sick instead of excited. He hoped that he hadn't ruined his friendship with her. She was the perfect hostess for his lifestyle and after this last shipment of coke was on its way to New York, he would take her to the island and show her just what type of man he could really be.

The streets were strangely deserted. He rolled past all the detours that were going up for the Olympics. They had transformed Atlanta into a travel nightmare. It was bad enough during regular summer tourist and visitors, but this Olympic shit had taken control. He was ready for it to end. It didn't benefit him in the least. The only thing he liked was track and field and the tickets were few and far between for the people who actually lived here. They Olympics weren't for the Atlantan people, it was purely a money making venture and only those chose few would benefit from it. He remembered all the street vendors that came to town. Hoping to cash in. He almost got a vendors license. The crush was maddening.

He hoped it would be over soon. He drove back to his penthouse, made a few phone calls, and went to sleep.

Morgan was talking in Ernest to John as she disrobed. She still felt uneasy about this whole set up.

"John, I don't think he recognized me, I think I was paranoid. I smoked a lot of weed earlier and I think my nerves were on edge because I knew him."

"What did you gut say?"

"My gut said to come back here, pack the place up and go home, but later in the evening, it went away. I feel in control now."

"I think you should pack it in."

"John, you just feel bad because of what happened. It happens in our line of work John. I am fully recovered."

"I don't know, but if you want my advice, if your confidence is up and you feel you can nail this guy. Do it. But no more sex with him if you can help it please."

"I will try, I don't know Steve's involvement in this. Amir paints him as a dirty cop, but maybe he is in deep cover. It happens you know. And my dad would never fall for a dirty cop. He could smell them a mile away. Steve spoke in reflection about the relationship between he and my dad and I think that's what calmed my nerves. If he had know who I was, he would have looked at me when he mentioned my dad, to see if I reacted. But he didn't. He looked inside himself. Apparently, the shipment is to come in the night of the big party. At Olympic park. Steve mentioned something about a diversion, but I couldn't hear anymore. They figure the cops will be to distracted to watch everybody. And with all the international attention, Olympic Park will take precedence over some drug deal.

The stuff is coming in figurines or artwork or something like that. I did hear that. But I will find out exactly. Amir is giving a party this weekend and I am going to be there. I will give you more details later, John, I am very tired and just want to sleep."

Morgan lay on her couch, too tired to open it into a bed and fell asleep.

VII

The day was beautiful when Morgan got up. She felt relaxed and renewed. It was nice. She stretched a little and put on her jogging clothes. She didn't want to jog today, just walk through the bike path and see Atlanta from a distance. She pulled on her sleeveless red pullover and some short red shorts. Little red socks and white tennis shoes. Her hair, pulled up in a pony tail, the cap covering all but the back of the pony tail which she pulled through the back of the cap. The new turner field cap. The Ted. She had never seen a baseball game and when she got free tickets, she usually gave them to Larry, who would enjoy it a lot more than she would. Her dad was a braves fan for many years. No matter how bad they were, he always had season tickets. Morgan walked out of the building and started toward the bike bath. The Jimmy Carter library sat in the distance and she made a note to go check on it.

She saw Larry, getting ready to begin his day.

"Hey."

"Hey you."

"You going jogging."

"yep."

"Be careful, they found dirty Laura in a dumpster off of Moreland avenue this morning, right across from my friends house just up the street."

"really, what happened to her?"

"somebody stabbed her"

"did she have family."

"if you sleep out here, this is your family. Not that I know of, I fed her from time to time, let her come in and wash her ass once in awhile. She was the cut queen, fucked every body and any body. Sometimes they pick the wrong john. Wasn't no one in the cut that night. The church up the street had fed them that day and they stayed in that area waiting for tomorrow."

"Damn."

"come see me later."

"okay."

Morgan walked a little more slowly. She didn't know Dirty Laura, but she had seen her around. They all came through here once in awhile. Larry let them do odd jobs and her favorite, a big quiet talking man named JB, was here a lot. He is the one that kept all the other homeless away from her. JB was quiet and well spoken. She couldn't understand why he was homeless. Larry said he drank a bit and was on the rock. So, when he got out of jail, he would come back to L5P. This was his home. He was the one that always played her license number and always hit.

She wondered how he took the news. He must have been around her for years. She made a note to look for him and find out.

The path was quiet this morning, most of the people heading to work instead of enjoying a jog or walk. She looked at the beautiful cars going through the neighborhood heading into town. She made a note to wash her car. Seems like she was always making note.

Morgan thought how she missed her father. She wishes he was home now. Having pancakes with him and talking to him. Almost time to go but not quite. She wasn't finished with her work yet.

Most of the traffic was being rerouted through downtown and for a few businesses they changed their work hours to accommodate all the Olympic hoopla. It was an inconvenience but the powers that be figured it was worth it. It was giving Atlanta international attention. Dirty Laura didn't get international attention. She probably won't even get a line in the AJC. She probably won't have an obituary. That was a sad thought. No one to care enough about you to make sure you get a proper burial. She wondered how it felt to be that alone in the world. Then she thought about Steve. He wasn't particularly alone in the world. He was a cop and cops had their family ties together. A single cop was always includes in some other cops family. Steve was a part of theirs for right now. She hoped he wasn't dirty.

She walked slowly, listening to the birds chirping and thinking about what she would have for breakfast. For some reason, she had a ravenous appetite. She thought about the sex that she and Amir had. Why did people have to inflict pain on other people. Wasn't love suppose to be nice and gentle and beautiful. She knew that Amir loved her in his mind, but she could never love anyone with that much rage inside of him. And it had to be a type of rage that makes someone do that to people.

The more Morgan walked, the more she felt strong in herself. She had confidence in her self again. She was going to get her man and then go home. She turned around and headed back home, her hunger had overcome her need to exercise and she walked a little faster home. She headed for her door. Larry had already headed to begin his work day. She was sure of that. He always wanted to talk to her. He actually talked to everybody. He was an integral part of this neighborhood. Everyone knew him and if you needed anything, if he didn't have it in his apartment, he knew how to get his hands on it.

There was a beautiful blond artist that lived in his particular part of the building. She painted pretty mermaids and mermen on the walls. Morgan thought she was very beautiful to have no man in her life. She probably thought so too. But strong willed women never had a real man and she was way too confident about her knowledge to make a man comfortable. Its a pity that strong women frightened men. They could probably accomplish a lot together.

Larry had been cleaning out the yard area. There must be a party planned. She liked the neighborhood parties. Well not the neighborhood just this apartment building. Everyone got together and made special dishes and ate and got to know who was living where. It was something that Morgan had missed during her times at home with her dad.

She saw a police car slowing down coming toward her. It was not the regular Atlanta car, it was white and unadorned, what people mistakenly call a narc car. But you could definitely tell it was a cop. She noticed it was Steve St. John. Damn. She didn't want him to know where she lived. But, here it goes.

He stopped in front of the building.

"hey beautiful, this where you live"

"Oh, hi, Steve was your name wasn't it?"

"Did you forget me already?"

"No, not really, not the face, but the name."

"Been jogging?"

"No actually walking."

"really"

"You must be around here investigating the death of Dirty Laura."

"who?"

"Dirty Laura, one of the homeless hookers that hang out here. They found her in a dumpster up the street."

"Oh, yeah, I am. How did you hear about it?"

"Most of the homeless know me and they tell things. I had seen her around."

"Well, it happens when you are that type of person. I wouldn't worry if I were you."

"I don't worry, but she was a human and no one will probably even have a funeral for her"

"What you doing later on?"

"Nothing."

"Can I come visit you for awhile. I would like to talk to you a little. I don't bite"

Morgan didn't think that reference was funny. The smart ass bastard. She didn't want to, but she couldn't think up a way to beg out on the spot.

"Okay, maybe about 7 okay."

"Okay. Should I bring anything, some wine maybe"

"that's fine"

"see you later, Renee"

He drove off slowly, looking at her through the rear view mirror. He gave her the creeps since she saw him at Amirs. It wasn't bad at her home, but its like this is a different side of him. She can't tell if he was toying with her or really didn't know who she was.

Well, she was in for it now, but at least she was on her turf. But just in case, she would let Larry know and smoke a joint with him. He would watch out for her. He always did.

She walked down to the corner market, past Euclid, across from the Zestos. She needed a paper and coffee. There she ran into JB, and the other homeless talking about Dirty Laura.

"Hey Miss Renee. How you doin'"

She loved his slow southern drawl.

"Did you hear about Laura, man that was a shame. I was s'pose to meet her in the park that night, but I got tied up with somethin' else'"

"Really JB, I am sorry."

"We gonna get some flowers and put them in the park for her. There ain't even nuthin in the paper 'bout it. I know she had a cousin but I cain't think of her name right now."

They all seemed a little sad. Morgan decided that someone did care afterall and she gave the a couple of dollars to help with the flowers or the wine, whichever.

She walked home.

Once she got there, she climbed up the back stairway, feeling that someone was watching her. She looked around and she couldn't see anyone. Her phone was ringing and she hurried up the stairs to see who it was.

It was Amir.

"Hello baby, how are you? Rested"

"Yes Amir I am rested."

"Good. What's going on this evening? Are you up for some company?"

"Well, I sorta have plans."

"What plans"

She debated briefly not to tell him then, thought about it. Maybe it was good to cause a little dissension among the ranks.

"I ran into Steve in his cruiser when I came back from my morning walk. Apparently someone stabbed a hooker last night. He sort of invited himself up here."

There was quiet on the line. Then,

"He did, well maybe I will make a surprise visit, what do you think?"

"I think that would be a good idea. I don't feel too comfortable with him and I couldn't think fast enough to get out of it. Would you come by. I will leave the downstairs door unlocked. Just get here when you can."

"What time is he coming"

"He said around seven, so I guess then."

"the fuckin' rat bastard. I told you you couldn't trust the cops. I'll be there baby, you watch yourself okay."

"Don't worry just get here."

Morgan thought about what she had just done. To her it was the lessor of two evils. At least this way, she could stay in Amir's good graces until the case was solved and she wouldn't have to be alone with Steve for more than she had to.

Although Amir was a freak, she trusted him more than Steve right now. And Amir was the one she needed to keep an eye on not some rogue cop.

She begin to prepare for the evening. She made sure everything was put up and put on some decent music. Not too sexy, just quiet. She looked around for traces of Morgan. There were none that she could see. She never remembered that he had seen her packing her bags at home. All those bags were on the top of her closet space, for all to see.

Right around seven o'clock the bell rang in her apartment. She had on a pair of jeans and a big shirt and her hair was down. Contacts in. Renee was ready.

Morgan descended the steps and there was Steve, smiling a big smile. He had wine and flowers. She let him in and did the lock, then as she pointed him the way up to her place, she turned the lock again, unlocking the door.

He looked around her place.

"What a cute place. I didn't know that these looked like this. Hardwood floor, how nice."

"Yes and not too expensive"

"I would have never knew these were here if I wasn't looking for suspects."

"suspects?"

"In the murder."

"Oh are you investigating that. That's right you told me that. The homeless friends of mine are so upset. Apparently someone loved her."

"Not enough to keep her off the street."

He sat the wine and the flowers on the table. He looked around the place again.

He looked at her again.

"You look different in casual clothes. That dress you had on the other night was kickin' I liked that."

He walked a little too close to her and she motioned him to the couch.

"Have a seat."

She sat on the floor in front of him.

"I live over by Lindbergh. Its a nice area. Lots of Mexicans but I kind of like their mariachi music playing through the night on the weekends. During the week, they seem to work as hard as me."

He kept staring at her.

Then the next thing Morgan knew, he was on the floor beside her.

"Renee, I have been wanting to kiss you since I met you. I know this is sudden and I apologize, but may I please, just a kiss."

"I don't know, Steve, I . . ."

And before she could finish, he was kissing her deep and passionate and hard. Morgan's mind was taken back, he had lain on top of her on the floor and was holding her and kissing her and calling her Morgan in her ear.

"Steve, please get up, the floor is hard on my back."

"Morgan, oh Morgan"

His hard dick was pressing into her on the floor and she was hurting. He was grinding into her, and she could feel his heat rising. He continued until she could feel a wetness in his pants. That seemed to bring him out of it.

"Oh Renee, I am so sorry, I got so carried away—"

He was stammering and staring at her. His dick was still hard and the wetness in his pants was large enough where he couldn't hide it.

"Renee, forgive me. I love this girl, Morgan, she doesn't know and you remind me so much of her."

He reached for he again and she backed toward the closet space. As he held her and pushed her into the wall, his eyes looked up and saw the bags. He did recognize them. He hesitated for a moment, then turned her face to his and kissed her deeply and softly, he grinded into her again, and she could feel his dick hardening again, the wetness spreading to her clothes as well. He grabbed her hands and let her to the couch. As he held her hands he was fumbling with his zipper which was sticky and he couldn't get with one hand.

Morgan kept thinking of all times, where the hell was Amir, he promised to be here. He pulled his service revolver and held it on her while he fumbled more with his pants.

"Pull down your panties, now Morgan. I don't know why you are being Renee but I think it has something to do with Amir, but that's your business, my business is now, right now with you."

Morgan stood and pulled her panties down. He put the revolver down and watched her. She wasn't close enough to the door to run, but she glanced at it and he read her mind.

"Don't think about it Morgan, I'll shoot you before you get to the door. Then I will kill myself, but it won't matter because you will be dead."

He got his pants undone and pulled out his dick. It was swollen with hardness and although not as big as Amir's it was still a pretty good size. He threw her down on the couch and inserted himself in her, no foreplay just in. He thrusted for just a few short moments and he came again, all inside her. As he came, he grabbed her throat and held on tightly. Morgan gasped and tried to fight him scratching him in the face with her fingernails. She finally grabbed his eyes and scratched and he released her neck. She slid to the floor, grasping for breath and he grabbed his eyes.

"Morgan, you better play nice with me. I know your little charade and if I tell Amir, he will kill you. Slowly, sexually and brutally. You know that."

"You tried to kill me."

"No, its just a part of sex, like Amir likes to bite. I like to feel your pulse in your neck when you cum. You didn't cum."

"You better go."

"For now, Morgan, just for now. But I will be back and you better play nice or I will blow the whistle on your little scheme. I won't kill you, I promise. That's what that throw away trash is out there for. I think I could love you for a long time. Your father thinks so."

He kissed her face and she turned away.

"Don't be stupid Morgan. Your daddy will miss you when you are gone. And then he won't have anyone but me to be with, someone to make sure he takes his vitamins. You understand"

The thought of him being with her father made her sick.

"You bastard. Amir said dirty cops were the worst."

He laughed.

"Dirty, not me, I have been trying to nail that guy for a long time and he likes me, thinks I am his friend. Then here you come dressed like a harlot and he gives you all his trust. Well, I am going to nail him, but not before I finish fucking your brains out."

"You are a sick fuck, you know that."

"Yes, but my fantasies will be fulfilled and all by you Miss Morgan/Renee. Don't worry, your secret is safe with me as long as you play with me."

He left by the back stairs.

Morgan lay there on the floor. Then she remembered that Amir was supposed to be coming. She got up and as she did she caught sight of the closet. Her bags, all her bags were up there in plain sight. He had come into her room that day she was packing, saw the bags. Detectives have an eye for details. She reasoned that he may have thought so, but he didn't know for sure until he pushed her against the wall and saw the bags. Fuck. She went into the bathroom to straighten up. She washed her face and straightened her hair and changed her clothes. When she thought about calling John there was a knock at the door.

It was Amir.

VIII

"Did that creep show up?"

"Yeah, but he was a perfect gentleman. Left me some wine. He didn't stay long, just wanted to say hello."

"The rat bastard."

Amir hugged her and told her to get her purse, they were going out to eat.

She was glad for the diversion.

Steve drove through the streets of Atlanta, Ashby street was where he was headed. He had a good rush abusing Morgan. Trying to be undercover. As he drove through the streets and thought about it, how much did she really know? Had she bought the story of him getting ready to bust Amir? Damn, she complicated matters. He would have rather met Morgan, on his own terms, living the suburban dream at her fathers house. He would have taken care of her and married her, treated her like she should be treated. There would have been plenty of prostitutes in Atlanta to take care of his craving and he would have never let her know that side of him. They would have had kids.

He pulled to a darkened lot. The skyline of Atlanta shining in the night. For this area to be so run down, it had a beautiful view of the city. Where people like Amir lived in pent houses and fucked people like Morgan. Or Renee. Where tourists stayed in posh hotels, never even seeing that there was a little boy standing under the streetlight, looking to see if his momma was going to come home and cook for him. All his friends, in their rundown housing, but at least fed, and probably sitting in their room, playing a video game that came into their home from a crack deal, or from an uncle who boosted it from McCrory's. The kids grew fat off of the salt from the many days of Ramen Noodles and grilled processed cheese sandwiches and white bread. Starting their young lives with health problems looming in the future from all the processed cheaper foods at the corner market. He had shopped in those markets on the way home from work sometimes. Processed cheese food that when you mixed with hot grits, it should have melted but it clumped and never quite melted. Bologna sanwiches. The boy standing under the street light unsettled him and he circled the block and asked him why he was there.

"'cus"

"'cus why?"

"you da poleece?"

"Why"

"Nuthin'"

"Go home and go to bed."

"I'm waitin' for my momma"

At that moment a Marta bus pulled up across the street and a young lady got off. She had on the clothes of a fast food worker and she had her purse in her hand. She smiled at the boy then looked at the man in the car.

"Tobias, don't you be standin' out here talkin' to strangers. Why you ain't at home?"

"I was scared momma, I heard a noise."

He ran across the street, not bothering to look for traffic and to his momma.

She eyed Steve suspiciously.

"Don't worry ma'am, I am cop in this area and I was asking him why he was out here by himself."

"He got a home, he don't have to be here, his sister is watching him"

"C'mon, let me drive ya'll home"

She was reluctant and he showed her his badge. He drove her to a dilapidated house where she had rented two rooms upstairs. The boy got out the car and waved at the man and he called the girl back to the car.

Taking the 40 dollars out that he had given a hooker once, he gave it to her.

"What's this fo'?"

"Buy him some Krystals or something. He's a good kid worrying about his momma. Take care of him."

"I will."

She looked at him really strange, but she took the money and went upstairs. Looking back at him.

Steve drove off.

He hated to see women who were trying to make it have to make these types of choices. It was always harder to work and take care of your family. You worked at a place that paid minimum wage. Their kids always suffered. She wasn't like those crack hoes, just a working woman with too many kids. He admired women like that. Someone who didn't take the easy way out. Someone who didn't decide to make a living on her back. He would go home tonight. He made a note to check on the little boy once in a while. The Olympics meant nothing to them. He smiled a weak smile, the boy reminded him of himself.

The city lights smiled through the darkness.

Morgan rode with Amir through the streets of Atlanta. The pretty lights always made her feel better. It was a beautiful city. With all the lights and the Olympic building and planning. The city was in an uproar and she was glad to be here for it.

She wondered about the experience she had with Steve. What makes people take a pleasurable act and turn it into a perverse power trip to hurt and kill? What makes sadism take root in a person and grow?

"You are very quiet"

"Yes, I am just in a pensive mood I guess"

"why, did Steve mess with you?"

"no."

"Look, Steve won't be around much longer. He will get his money and thats the last we will see of him for awhile, I'll make sure of it."

Morgan thought about the prospect. Is there really honor among thieves? Obviously not. She watched as they approached the penthouse.

"Can we just ride for awhile?"

He changed his direction and continued down Peachtree, down past Five points, and onto Lee Street. They drove past Garnett, West End, and slowing near the Lakewood Station, turned and continued.

Coming to Washington Road, they drove and she could see the lights in the apartments. Families, people having dinner or watching t.v. There were a few people at the bus stop when he turned onto Janice Drive. There were some beautiful houses. She thought about what her father may be doing.

Morgan sat back and wondered why her life wasn't normal. Why things turned out they way they did. Was it because of the job she had. One day she would find the answer.

She sighed as they made the left back onto 85 and headed back downtown.

It was a short trip through normal land, but it felt good.

"I want to take you to dinner, and then take you home, to my house. I want to hold you. Not make love, just hold you Renee. When I first saw you, I felt a sexual desire, but watching your face as we drove through the hood, you want that type of life. I have never had a normal life, but I think I could have one with you. I have some issues, and up until this point, I was willing to accept that this is who I am, but with you, I want to be different, I want to better. I want to be good for you. I realize that if I want to keep you, I have to change. You couldn't change me, don't forget that because you can't change people. But I want to change, and I can change me. A person can change themselves.

No one minded my abuse because it wasn't me they wanted anyway. They wanted what I had. You didn't want what I had, so I decided it had to be me you wanted. Really me. So, you deserve to have the best of me. Where would you like to eat tonight?"

She could only think of one place right now.

"The Varsity."

They went to the varsity and had the best greasy meal of their lives.

"I would have never thought to take you to the Varsity. Why the Varsity?"

"My dad use to take me here after the Braves games."

Morgan wanted to go home. To her dad. But she couldn't. There was unfinished business.

IX

Steve sat at home, alone in his apartment. He had driven past the Gold Club with all its lights and limos and felt jealous about that.

Why was it that people can enjoy some of the finer things in life, and a lowly peace officer, the persons who keep this town from turning into a jungle, can't even get a good woman.

He thought about Morgan, her perfect little life. She had a good father and although her mother was gone, her father loved her. He had wished that his mother had loved him

What makes a mother not love her own flesh and blood. Do you hate the father so much that it transverses to your offspring. Or was she the type bitch that didn't give a damn. He thought about the little boy, standing in the shadows, waiting for his hard working mother. He was really worried about his mother and he didn't care about the mean streets. He just cared about his mother. If his mother had been nice he would have been like that little boy. Braving anything to make sure his mother was alright. Taking care of her and helping her. The thought of that little boy did something to Steve. He would get that boy something. Something nice.

He lay in his bed, fingering the knife he used when he killed his victims. They weren't his victims, he rationalized. They were society victims. They could be on Marta, coming home to their little boy standing in the dim streetlight. It was easier to lay down and open your legs. Ignore your little boy and lock him in the room. Let the men come in and out and forget your little boy. Your lonely little boy who listens and looks while you spread your legs. Listens while you tell these men you love them, but say nothing like that to your little boy. Your own little boy. Your child.

He thought about the homeless feeling bad about losing that smelly woman. Morgan said they actually were going to put flowers out at the cut where he got her. He wondered how long she had been homeless and what she was before she got that way. Was she a little girl whose parents left her and disappeared. Black people always had a aunt or uncle or cousin who would take them in when no one else wanted them. He always knew that. But some chose not to be there in the family and they take to the streets because they want to. He wondered if he had been in a black family would someone really had taken care of him. He never lived with an aunt or uncle, he was a homeless boy except for an old black woman who use to feed him. Some black people have compassion that sees past color. They truly believe in what the bible says. His black mother did. But he wouldn't have been there to watch out for her. If he hadn't sent her to God she would have been at the mercy of anyone. He had to do it.

He lay there playing with his knife, thinking of Morgan. He really didn't feel good about the abuse he inflicted on her. It was something different about her despite what she was appearing to be, but he had to find out and if she was playing in the big league, she had to accept that type of treatment. He realized that her father really did think she was in Milan and he would keep that secret. He really didn't want to hurt the old man. But if Morgan was playing big city games, she had to play by big city rules and he had to find out what was really going on. Did she know how deep he was in this?

The Olympic mark was on Atlanta big time. The downtown area was transformed and you could not recognize it. It was a blur of activity and people talked among themselves on the Marta trains about how they would reap the benefits from this event. People in the black neighborhoods planned on renting their homes out to Olympic people, but it was not meant to be. The Olympics was planned in a tight circle and most neighborhoods that didn't fall into the circle. The Olympic Circle.

Morgan and Amir had lain together all night, no sex, just holding each other. Amir told Morgan all his hopes and dreams and Morgan was very interested. Had she met him under different circumstances, she could have fell for him. She realized that she needed to contact John, but not now. She could hear Amir in the kitchen, cooking breakfast for her and she briefly wondered where Steve was. She imagined him having breakfast with her father, getting ready to play racquet ball.

She made herself believe that he would never hurt her father, despite what he told her. She felt that he actually liked her father, and that he would not harm the man. She prayed silently, and hoped openly.

Amir's private phone rang, and she strained to listen to the conversation.

"What do you mean the shipment is delayed. I have people waiting for that and the plans are in the works. I can't stop the ball now. I don't give a fuck if the army is marching through Atlanta for the second coming, get my shit and get it here on time!"

She heard him slam the phone down and then call someone.

"Those motherfuckers are screwing this shit up. My ass is on the line and I'm not taking the fall for nobody. Fuck that, lets just say if I go, you are going first. Look, you rat bastard, I knew involving your ass was a mistake. Take your connections and fuck yourself with them. I want my shit on time and you better break your ass to get it done Steve. Don't give me no fucking speech, just get my shit. Pick a cemetery cop boy, you're a dead ass."

Morgan got out of bed to see why it was suddenly so quiet.

Amir was sitting on the balcony, the breakfast halted before it was finished. He was holding the remains of a battered phone. She went back into the kitchen, pouring two cups of coffee and went back. She handed him a cup and she sat down in the chair opposite him with her cup. Morgan wished it was dark so that the lights of city would shine. Right now, it was just a fine haze as the city was waking up. It was going to be a hot day in Atlanta.

Steve was planning to go to Morgan's father's house for a little breakfast and a game, but he called and canceled. He had a little boy on his mind this morning.

He drove to the house where he had dropped off the woman and her son. There was a girl sitting on the porch outside, and he realized he forgotten the little boys name. As pulled to park, the little boy came running out the door with a sandwich in his hand. Steve got out of the car.

"Hey man, what up?"

The little boy looked for a minute then responded.

"oh, hi. You da' cop ain't you—Mom, the cop is here"

The lady came outside. She looked at him a little less suspicious, but still not trusting him.

"I have tickets for the Braves game, can I take your son to the game with me?"

The boy's eyes lit up.

"I won't keep him long, and I promise to bring him right home when we get finished. Okay? If you don't trust me, you can call the precinct and they will tell you who I am."

She still looked at him.

"Why you wanna take my boy to the game? You don't know him."

"Because I think he is a nice boy to wait for his momma to come home in the dark."

She let him go, but not before she made him run upstairs and change his shirt. She told him that she had to be at work for him to come straight home and stay in the house until she got home.

Steve asked her where she worked so that he could take her there. Turns out she works at the Picadilly's at Ansley mall. No wonder it took her so long to get home. She had to ride this bus to five points, take the train, and then get another bus. She stated that she wasn't ready to go to work just yet, but he could go ahead and take her son.

The little boy jumped in the car and waved to his momma. She and the girl sitting on the porch watching them drive off.

She shook her head and walked into the house.

"I really don't like no white poleece"

Steve and the young man stopped at Kentucky Fried chicken near the ball park.

"Do you want to eat here or you want to wait til we get to the game?"

"I want some chicken."

They sat and ate chicken and drank coca cola.

Steve as thinking about the little boy, and then his thoughts went to Morgan or Renee or whoever she was this time of day. He wondered if she had spent the night with Amir and what they were doing. He thought about how he treated her and he didn't really feel bad about it, but he didn't feel satisfied either. He had to see her again.

X

Morgan decided that if she was going to get this guy she needed to find out more about what's happening. She had really been thrown for a little while since finding out that Steve St. John was involved, but now she felt she was back on track. She needed more information about the shipment and when it was coming, the type of diversion that Steve was planning. She needed to know all these things and time was running out.

She showered and dressed and Amir's mood was bit lighter.

"So what are we going to do today?"

She playfully kissed Amir on the neck and slipped into his lap. He put his arms around her and kissed he face.

"What do you want to do?"

"I don't know baby, you seem so upset after the phone call that I think we need to go shopping or something. It cheers me up. Is every thing alright? Can you tell me about it?"

He thought for a moment. Then he looked at her.

"Renee, this is the biggest deal of my life. A major accomplishment. If I pull this off, I will have everything that I have ever thought about wanting. I will have the means to collect my art and sit back in comfort and not have to work at anything if I don't want to. In five days, all will right with world. People say that money doesn't buy happiness but I can tell you that it does. I have been hustling all my life, trying to get in where I wanted to fit in, every since I was a little boy, and now, its over."

"What's going on Amir?"

She moved from his lap and sat down at his feet, her head resting on his lap, looking up at him.

"What are you into Amir?"

He took her by the hands and stood her up.

"You don't have to ever sit at anyone's feet, baby, you are too beautiful for that. I don't really want to tell you what I do, because then I will have to kill you."

He smiled and kissed her face.

"C'mon lets go to Phipps"

Steve and the little boy were enjoying the game. The Braves had a double header against Cincinnati, it was the bottom of the 9th of the first game. Cincinnati was leading.

The little boy talked and talked. Steve laughed, the more he ate the more he talked. His name was Tobias, but he liked to be called Little T. That was his street name, he said. He was 9 years old and he goes to school sometimes. He doesn't like school because the teacher are just stupid. He likes to draw, but his momma makes him go outside and play so that he won't be stuck in the house all day. His sister was 13 and she had a boy friend who came over when his mother was at work. He didn't like his momma coming home in the dark because people get killed in 'lanta everyday. He saw a girl into the car with someone and he ain't seen her again. He knew her because when he used to wait with him for his momma sometimes, she would talk to him. She was ugly, but she was nice. Sometimes people look ugly but be nice inside. She would walk away when the bus came so that his mother didn't see her, 'cause she said that his momma wouldn't like him talking to her. She had a little boy but the white people took him away from her. Tobias said he liked her and he had not seen her in a long time. He thinks she dead.

Steve thought about it for a moment, then let the conversation continue.

His daddy came over once. And he brought him a pair of air jordans. But momma said he didn't need no shoes that s'pensive and she took them to the store and got him a regular pair of shoes and a toy. She brings him food from work sometimes. She works at the Picadilly and sometimes she takes him wid her. Her day off is on Tuesday. She likes beer, but she don't like no white people. Tobias stated that he knew some good white people and some bad white people like the ones that took the ugly girl's little boy. Sometimes people need their little boys and that the girl seemed lonely without him. Tobias said that he didn't really like no poleece 'cause they beat up black peoples. He said he thought Steve was lonely like the ugly girl.

Halfway through the second game, Tobias had fallen asleep on Steve's lap. He decided to take him where his momma worked and they would give her a ride home.

Amir and Morgan walked through the beautiful Phipps Plaza. She really didn't want to shop here, just like the ambiance of the place. She liked walking in the money. Phipps was full of people who were actually shopping and more than that, people like her who enjoyed walking though Phipps but didn't even think of paying those prices for things they could get at Lennox for much less. However, Amir went to an art store and looking and appraising its contents, bought a huge vase that he said was a ming vase. Morgan thought about that and he couldn't possibly be talking about the Ming Dynasty could he? For the price he paid for it, it could have actually. The gentleman wrapped it and placed it lovingly in a box of with lots of peanuts in it, and smiled suggestively at Amir as he pulled out his platinum card and some cash.

They would deliver it later.

"Let's go to Lennox and have some food at Mick's"

"Great Idea. This noveau riche is getting on my nerves"

"Really dahling, I hadn't noticed."

They laughed and walked hand in hand to the car and drove to Lennox to Micks.

There they ate a really good hamburger and drank red beer and watched the people going by. Morgan much preferred the atmosphere at Lennox to Phipps anytime, although,once in while you got to hit Phipps to remind yourself that people actually do have money in this town. And lots of it.

Steve waited outside Picadilly's while Tobias ran inside to get his momma. She looked surprised but she was glad for the ride home. They sat in the car in silence. She didn't feel comfortable with this cop showing her this attention and she wanted to tell him so. A cop had killed her father and although her son was enjoying the man, she was going to put a stop to it here and now.

When they got in front of her house, she sent Tobias out the car.

"Listen, I know you want to be nice and I appreciate it, but you are not welcome to my house or my boy. You white cops just kill people, like my daddy and I can't try and pretend I like any of you. My friends think I am fuckin you and I don't fuck white boys. Don't let me see you 'round here no more or I am going to call the police and tell them you are harassing me and my family. You understand?"

She got out of the car and threw his forty dollars back on the seat.

"I work everyday. I don't need no cop money."

And she walked way. Head held high. Tobias stood in the yard and waved, but his momma called him in the house and he went. But he looked back very disappointed.

Steve drove off. Slowly at first, then he was suddenly very angry. How in the fuck can she say that shit to him? He didn't kill her father and he was just watching out for the boy. He looked at the forty dollars on the seat. He wasn't giving her no hand outs he wanted to make sure the boy was alright. He forgot about the attitudes that some southern blacks had toward white people in general. The treatment at the hands of southern whites was legendary. He knew that and he forgot being a northern boy. He didn't treat blacks that way, and he never really knew anyone who did. Sure they didn't socialize with them, but that was the way times were. He didn't mean any harm and it hurt him to think that she felt that way. He wasn't trying to get into her pants, but he figured there were probably some that were. In a different set of circumstances, she would probably be a beautiful woman. But she worked too hard for her little money and it showed. He just felt for the boy and he made a promise that he would still ride by from time to time. He thought about what the boy said about the lady who use to talk to him. Had he seen him? He knew the girl was dead. He knew someone killed her after they picked her up. He didn't know that the someone was Steve. He drove in intense silence, heading for Metropolitan Parkway. To him, and other people, even out of towers, it was always Stewart avenue.

XI

Steve decided that it was time to pay Morgan/Renee another visit. He was pretty brutal the last time and he needed to know just how much she had found out and how its going to effect him. He had a hand in this and wasn't going to let this girl mess up his gravy train. Not this time. He liked her and loved her ol' man, but this was the chance of a lifetime, a chance to not be just a cop anymore.

He called Morgan first.

"Morgan?"

"No Morgan lives here, you have the wrong number."

The bitch hung up. Damn.

He called back.

"Renee"

"Yes."

"This is Steve, don't hang up Renee, I just need to talk to you. To apologize for what I did to you. I just lost my head. Please let me talk to you. We can sit in the courtyard in public or wherever but I need to talk to you, okay?"

Morgan hesitated, at least in the courtyard, he couldn't hurt her. Larry would make sure of that.

"Okay you asshole, c'mon and you can't stay long"

"Amir coming to see you?"

"None of your damn business Steve."

They sat in the courtyard that was between the two buildings. It was nice and airy. Morgan didn't have enough information on the shipment because for as nice as Amir was,he was tight about his business regardless of how much he cared for her. Now, Steve was another mess. Steve could be tricked, she thought, because of his tendency to over react. She would play the Steve card to find out what was really going on. Steve was under the impression that she was really into Amir and that Amir was really taken with her.

So, here we go. Morgan took a deep breath because after what Steve did to her she didn't really want to see him anymore, but this is why she was being paid the big bucks.

"I talked to Amir, I guess its getting ready to go down."

"I know, I was there when you called."

"Are you always over there."

"Pretty much."

"So what else did he say. I know he hates me"

"He doesn't hate you so much Steve, he just feels you are just a little overreactive and that you might ruin things."

"What??? did he say that?"

"I am not going to tell you what we discuss in the privacy of our bed, Steve, not out here in public."

"C'mon upstairs for a minute"

Morgan was really apprehensive as he pulled her long.

"I don't have time to fuck with you Renee, this is not pleasure, its business. I need to know what's up. I gotta make sure my cover isn't blown."

Morgan couldn't tell if he was pretending to be on the case instead of part of the case.

They sat on her couch.

"Basically, Steve, I don't think he knows your cover, I think he just doesn't like you or the way you handle things. He thinks you are sloppy and will get everyone busted."

"Fuck him, what???"

Morgan sat back alittle, Steve was losing it really fast.

"he said the plan for the diversion was unclear and that he couldn't really trust you. You are too hair trigger."

Steve paced the floor, he had taken the bait.

"That wannabe African or some shit mothafucka. I got the whole deal set up for him. My guy at Hartsfield is going to make sure that there is no security around to check the artifacts, they are going straight through. He couldn't have arranged that shit. The diversion is so sweet. With all the activities going on around Atlanta anyway, it will look just like another terrorist attack or something. They will be so busy watching for it, they won't see it coming. We will be able to get the art through, get it to the limo and on its way to New York in a matter of 45 minutes. When it hits 75 and heads north, not through the regular 95 route, but through 75 to Ohio,where one of my Columbus boys takes up the run and traveling across Pennsylvania, into Newark, then to New York. Its the long way, but it has to be done that way and that stupid art collecting Mothafucka couldn't have thought of a plan like that."

"I think he wants to cut you out completely."

Steve froze.

"Are you serious Morgan"

He looked around quickly and lowered his voice.

"I'm sorry Renee, do you think so? Is he on to me? What's up what did he say. C'mon Renee we are on the same side, you sleep with him and I don't see no bruises so he must like you. I owe you, I know, but you gotta tell me."

"He just said that you weren't to be trusted and that the pot looked much bigger without so many people involved. He said something about Honor among thieves or the lack there of when money is involved. What did you do to him?"

"I don't know, did he know I came to see you?"

"I didn't tell him."

"Look Renee, I didn't mean that. I was just being an asshole, I can be one you know. But you need to watch my back for me. I would never hurt your father or anything like that. I just wanted to see how much you knew. We are in this together girl. We can get so much."

"In order for me to keep you posted, I need to know what's really going down, this bullshit about diversions and crap ain't tellin' me nothin'. You tell me what the diversion is. I need to make sure that we are on the same page."

Somehow, she knew Steve would fall for that. He was too emotional and worried at this point and just the fact that he believed she was on his side was enough. He was really a strange man, but he was easy to read. He had so much riding on this.

"Cool, this is how we set it up. There is a huge vase, African I think that is coming through hartsfield to be shipped to a store in Phipps. Amir goes to Phipps, purchases the item and tells them to wrap it and ship it to his home. He pays cash. Once it arrives to his home, the merchandise is redistributed, cut a little and packaged for distribution. Amir moves it as far as Cincinnati with the guise that a buyer is interested in his artifacts. The cops know who he is and this has to go to the letter because all they need is a reason. But they also know he is a prominent citizen and art collector and Atlanta takes care of its prominent citizens. That's why they are here. John picks it up from Cincinnati, on his way to visit relatives in Columbus. He's made that trip before so many times. The cops don't even watch him anymore. They know when they see him where he is headed and have already investigated the family. Church going folks thats all. From Columbus, one of Amir's people picks it up and takes 70 toward Pennsylvania. Staying off the turnpike in Ohio, and heading for Newark NJ. The guy driving from Columbus, is seeing the cousin of John. So they are having one big family reunion and exchanging all at the same time. Perfect. From Newark, it hits the big apple. Hopefully untouched."

"In the meantime, since the cops know that at least it is coming through Atlanta, I still have to create a big enough diversion to take the attention off of us temporarily. And with the Olympics in town and the big party downtown that night, all eyes on Atlanta, none on anything else. Its going to be a blowout!!"

Morgan had to call John at some point tonight and let him know. She wasn't sure. But she was sure she needed to get Steve out of here now.

"That sounds like a plan. Does Amir know about that?"

"That stupid fuck. He thinks he's dealing with an idiot, but I know the score. I know he wants to cut me out. But he may be taken care of and soon."

He started for the door.

"I am sorry Renee that I did what I did to you. It was a mistake. I am glad you forgive me. Sometimes I get the ass and I took that out on you."

He left but she could see he was thinking about what she had said.

She called John.

"Where the hell have you been? I have been worried. I sent another post card to your father and pulled out some of your glossy's to send to him. Whats going on?"

"Well, from what Steve told me, the stuff is coming in through a big vase that is supposedly going to Phipps to an art dealer there. So I think its going down a lot quicker than I thought."

She explained how Steve said they were going to move the stuff.

"Can you find out if Amir is taking a trip?"

"Sure, but in the mean time, you need to station people at the locations for the exchanges and get those involved in case he slips us here."

"Right. They are taking the round about way aren't they? That will take the trip a lot longer than taking 95."

"But they know 95 is the route that is expected. If we don't catch it before it hits Newark, its a done deal. I'll go and see if I can hook up with Amir this evening or in the morning early, see what his plans are."

Her phone rang while she was on her cell with John.

She checked the i.d. Private caller, that was Amir. She held the cell phone so John could hear.

"Hello"

"Hello Renee."

"What's up?"

"I want you to make a run with me. Pack a bag."

"Where are we going?"

"Just out of here for a while. You game? I have to see a man about some art in Cincinnati."

"In Cincinnati? Are we flying?"

"No baby this is a road trip. I don't like flying too tough. I do it when I have to but this is a short hop. We can do this and get a chance to see some sights on the way. Just get out of town while this Olympic shit is happening."

"Okay baby, I'll be ready. You want me to come over there?"

"No, no, baby, I have some business here tonight. I will pick you up bright and early in the morning."

"In the morning okay, Amir. I'll be ready."

She hung up one phone and put the cell to here ear.

"Did you hear?"

"Yes, do you think its going down now?"

"I don't know unless it was already at Phipps. Which means Steve is definitely cut out the loop. I don't know for sure. I guess I am not playing this right, am I?"

"You are doing fine, you are in and that's more than any of our other operatives have been able to accomplish. You know the stuff is coming and how its going to be moved, the time frame is what's missing. But don't doubt yourself now, you are great. Just keep me posted."

"Okay, John, gotta pack. Talk to you tomorrow. I will check with you on the way, so if you don't hear from me, come get me, find me okay?"

"Why, what's wrong."

"Nothing, I just like to be sure. Steve made it sound so cool, that I don't trust it. But if I don't go, if I am set up, it will look like I know and we won't get anything."

Morgan hung up the cell phone. She had to find a way to keep it available. Something didn't feel right about this trip. The set up was too easy.

XII

Steve drove home. He didn't stop by the hoe strolls that he normally visited. There would be no killing tonight. He was going to save that for tomorrow. He had set that bitch up good. If she thought she was going to ruin his plans by catching Amir before he had a chance to get his money, she had another thing coming. Money was money and bullshit ain't nothing.

What Amir didn't know was what he picked up at Phipps was just a vase, nothing else. The connection had been made hours before he got there by Steve. Steve knew that Amir would try to cut him out, especially since he was thinking about marrying Morgan. The right woman makes a man do stupid things and this was not going to happen to Steve. He would lose his career, his credibility and his money. Not for any bitch, not even Morgan. The stuff was already on its way up 95, should be getting to its destination about the time he will get there. He pulled into his parking lot and sat smiling in his car.

Inside his home, he pulled out the knives he had used so many times before. He was going to fuck her before he killed her. It would be so bittersweet. He already had a plane ticket reserved at the Cincinnati airport to go to New York. He had one more meeting with Amir, playing it like everything was cool. Dumb ass Amir, trying to cut him out. Well, the cut was already made.

He had put his belonging in storage the other day and had his bags packed. He was going to leave this town and start over in New York city. He could be anything there with the money he was going to get. He decided he would open or buy a little newsstand in Manhattan and watch the people come by and get papers and have conversation with him.

And there were boroughs of hookers just waiting for lover boy and his little friend. With a city that large, he could kill for years and no one would notice. He was going to feel bad when he offered Morgan up as the sacrifice, but he had to protect his interest and she was going to fuck it up. Besides, she would have made sure he went down. He had bruised her ego and he could tell by the way she talked to him that she didn't like him. Funny, she could take that damn abuse from Amir, but not from him. He knew that what the real reason was. She probably liked it. Freaks come from all social-economic backgrounds.

Morgan had gotten ready for the trip. She still felt apprehensive and couldn't shake the feeling. Something just didn't feel right. She called her father on her cell phone. She felt the need to talk to him before her trip.

"Hi daddy"

"Hey my babydoll, how's Milan?"

"great daddy, I will be coming home soon."

"I know, I got your postcard. What's wrong babydoll, you sound strange. Has anything gone wrong with the shoot?"

"No, I'm just tired I guess. Missing you a lot. How's Steve?"

"I haven't seen him in a couple of days. I guess he's too busy to hang out with an old man. But, I enjoy the peace and quiet. He was grating on my nerves anyway. Too much of a good thing I guess."

"Oh. Well, I'll call you back when I get to Hartsfield okay?"

"Sure honey, I'll make sure I'm there."

"No, daddy it might be late. I can get a cab."

"No, I don't want those camel jockeys driving my baby home, not to mention they charge too damn much money. Come to this country and you think they picked the cotton around here. See you when you get here babydoll."

"I love you Daddy."

Morgan hung up the phone.

Morgan's father looked at the receiver for a long time. Something just didn't sound right about his little girl and he hoped that those people in Milan were treating her right. He knew how the modeling business was. People think its just show and glamour, but its hard work, long hours and very little appreciation. He never wanted her to do that in the first place, but she was very pretty. May as well get paid for it for a little while before she started having kids and getting that roundness that women who have kids have. He never thought it was a bad thing. Women running around trying to cut off the extra little meat that came with motherhood. He liked his women with a little meat on them. Those sculptured bodies looked good, but give him a real woman anytime. A woman who was shaped by the passage of time, gracefully, beautifully.

He steadied his thoughts. Maybe he should think about dating that nice lady in church. She was always making eyes at him anyway, and she had the pleasing face and smile and build of a mature woman. Sometimes he thought about her, naked in his bed. But he laughed. Maybe back a few years ago. He was too old for that foolishness now.

Amir showed up the next day, on time in a rental car. It was a beautiful black Lincoln, but Morgan kept thinking hearse or mob car. She smiled at him as he put her bags in the back of the car. He laughed at the amount of luggage and she laughed with him about being a woman and needed things for a road trip. Men never understood those things. A shave and a toothbrush was their arsenal for the road. She needed other things.

She had packed carefully for the trip. Including a note addressed to her father, because she figured if something happened to her, he would dispose of the bags without going through the contents. Never expecting them to be found. So she wrote a note telling her father about everything and how sorry she was that it ended this way. She hoped that he would never get to read what she put in that envelope. But, if it did go down like she suspected, and John didn't get to her in time, she would be covered.

They headed to 75 north. Out of Atlanta, past Dave and Busters, driving. There was a lot of traffic in this area, but there always was in Marietta. Lots of suburban whites lived in the north and the suburban blacks tended to migrate south. Sometimes, you would find the new rising stars in Roswell, and Buckhead, but the older stars, Millie Jackson, and people from the old school, tended to stay in the south end. College Park, Forest Park. They were quiet for most of the journey. Amir playing cd's and humming to himself. He asked her if she were hungry and she said not yet. She was good. He had packed a cooler with some wine coolers, bottled water and coca colas. Atlantans and their coca colas. She actually preferred Pepsi, but people automatically assume coca cola. Or co'cola as she has heard to called time and time again.

The music was nice and riding in the Lincoln was an experience. It was like floating on air. Morgan moved the cd case from in between she and Amir and sat closer to him, putting her hand in his lap. He smiled, and took her hand and kissed it. He held it as they drove, still not really saying anything. He just smiled a strange little smile.

Into Tennessee, she decided she needed to check in and take a break. Amir was cool with that, he said he needed something in his stomach. He offered to buy her a sandwich and she wanted fish. Nothing heavy. Road trips always messed with her stomach.

When they stopped, she grabbed her purse and headed for the ladies room. In the ladies room, she tried to call John. The reception was awful, but she was afraid to let Amir see her on the little phone. She did hear a little of what he said before the bathroom door came open.

"Morgan, its a setup—static—stuff going up 95—picked up—static—try to get"—then it broke completely. She was in the stall when she heard the door come open loudly, hitting the wall.

"Lets go Morgan."

It was Amir.

"My name isn't Morgan, its Renee."

"Get out that stall now, Morgan."

She heard the ominous click of the 9mm. She came out the stall. Phone still in her hand. Amir took the phone and threw it up against the wall. It shattered into pieces on the floor. He grabbed her arm and escorted her to the car. It was fruitless to scream. They were in a town where travelers came and went, but they didn't seem like they were interested in helping a pimp and his hooker and was just glad to see him take her and go. They didn't want any trouble here. She could tell by the way the old folks traveling in their winnebagos looked at her and Amir. The women with disgust in their eyes, the men with what was left of their lust in theirs.

In the car, he began to play Frankie Beverly and Maze, southern girl. She was quiet and he just looked at her, glancing in between the road and her.

"Steve must have been really pissed that you didn't give him any pussy. He told me all about you. He said he had seen you at the main police station many times. I told you about dirty cops Morgan. So you were going to bust me?"

"Not just you, Steve too."

"really?"

"So, you're going to kill me, huh."

"No Morgan, for what's its worth, I liked Renee. I probably would have liked Morgan better, but I met Renee. But inside I knew I had seen you before. It was nagging at me. You were at a party once, with Sharon Lee. It didn't dawn on me until after I talked to Steve. I knew it was too perfect. But I had grown to like Renee.

I don't dirty my hands with killing, that's what I pay ass wipes like Steve to do. He's a cop and he enjoys killing anyway. I'm just going to give you to him and continue my journey. I know you didn't get in touch with you contact, because the bathrooms are not very conducive to cell phone use, I know, I tried mine."

"Dirty cops are all around. The shipment you have is not real Amir, Steve set everything up around you. The shipment is already on 95 heading to the east coast."

Amir squeezed her hand.

"How do you know?"

"That's all I could pick up on my phone. The package was stopped on 95. I couldn't hear anything else."

"Fuckin' dirty cops. I will have to take care of Steve, but only after he takes care of you."

"What's the point. My people are on their way to get me, if they aren't staked out already. You have no product, you have no money coming, he double crossed both of us."

He sat quiet. Gripping the wheel tightly, straining his knuckles against the wheel.

"Both of you fucked up a good plan. I wasn't hurting anyone. People who do drugs will do them whether I give it to them or not. Drugs legal and illegal are everywhere. Half the people on the rode are under the influence of something, whether it be prescription drugs or illicit. They can't stop that. Its a drug oriented society, always has been, always will be. All I wanted was to get a little bank and pursue my art. Now I'm going to have two murders on my hands and this was just not necessary. It shouldn't have gone down this way. Why did you have to come into my life?"

"I am on the side of the law, Amir, its my way of life, my family."

"How much they paying you?"

"Actually Amir, its not the money. When I see the crack hoes standing there, when I see kids without their mommas, when I see good neighborhoods go bad, I know its because of people like you. Besides, no one gets paid enough to die."

"No body expects to die, Morgan, its one of those little pieces of toilet paper that sticks to your shoe when you are trying to look your best. Fucks up the whole scene. And you are so young and pretty."

"You think Steve doesn't know that we talked about this. Don't you think he's going to be ready for you?"

"Not necessarily. I told him that I would let him spill the beans, he thinks I want to watch him sexually abuse you. He thinks I am into that shit. But, that part of me has changed. I'll just suggest he shoot you and get it over with. That way, I can kill him and not have your blood on my hands. Everything works out. He's a bad cop, no one will miss him. No one will give a damn."

They sat in quiet. Heading up 75. Morgan was frantic in her mind, but her face was cool and calm. She won't die. She wasn't meant to leave her father alone. These situations happen. John knows they are somewhere on 75. Unless they detour. But that didn't look likely. Amir was unsure of his route and he wanted to stay with what he knew. She was aware of that. He didn't like taking stops at places he wasn't familiar with. He needed familiarity. Not a true road warrior.

Steve drove 75 as far as Chattanooga. Then he detoured to 127 and took that road to Monticello Kentucky and then followed the back roads toward London. That's where the rendezvous point was. He looked at the bag in the seat next to him. The shiny knives waiting to feel the soft flesh of Morgans skin as he penetrated her both with the steel blade and the blade of his own. He got hard thinking about it. The roads were deserted except for small farms and little trailers dotting the landscape. The drive was calming. He knew that Amir would be surprised when he shot his ass. He would die first. All he could think as he drove the small winding roads that people mistakenly called freeways, more like backroads to hell, was his new life in New York. The city of dreams. That's what the song said. The irony is that the ones down by law will get fooled, not him. He would be so respectable. In his newsstand, selling the wall street journal, magazines, coffee and hard rolls. Smiling at the street vendors with their hot dogs and sausages and pretzels. Having conversations with the business men, running their New York lives at the frantic pace. While he relaxed, and hunted the streets of times square for the sordid women who hung there.

He never forgot his first visit to time square. The taxi's and the XXX theaters, the hookers. The bums and the drug dealers all mixed together in a whirlwind of trash and human deviants. All waiting for the knifeman. And he wouldn't let them down.

He briefly thought about the diversion he had created for the big Olympic party. He forgot to cancel that, but the man was paid already so it was too late. They could never trace it to him, he was long gone. He made a note to get the paper after all this is over. He could just see the headlines from coast to coast. The thought of the innocent casualties didn't phase him in the least. They should have stayed their asses at home like good citizens. He thought about the pissed off vendors who came to town, hoping to cash in on some Olympic action. They were placed outside the loop. No one would profit from this monumental event but those who planned it. Didn't people see that. The Olympics weren't for the normal hardworking Atlantan. It was for the people who didn't need the money in the first place. It was a chance to spotlight the city on behalf of the richer half, dispel those myths of a chocolate city. All the black colleges in town and their own black college celebrations was shoved under the red carpet like a dead bug. Lots of dead roaches. Freaknik was systematically shut down. Chocolate city be damned. All those rich college kids, looking for a place to be black and have fun. Where else but Atlanta? Not.

He remembered fondly his first freaknik parade through downtown. He was off duty and joined the fun. Pretty half naked college girls riding on top of beautiful cars. It was a sight. He got out of the parade and decided it was more fun to watch from the sidelines. Old men drinking wine out of bags, leering at the young girls. Old women wearing freaknik t-shirts, titties hanging down to their navels. Their college days way behind them, if they even had any. The downtown workers annoyed and afraid of the frenzie. Good decent tourist scared of the influx of black sexuality on their streets. Beautiful raw sexuality displayed for the world to see. He had killed three prostitutes that weekend. And no one noticed, trying so hard to keep these ruffians from destroying their fair city. Those few paranoid idiots that shut their shops missed out on a motherload of money. The only ones arrested were the poor larcenist Atlantans who had more of a till to rob. And they were the opportunists who took any event as a money making event. It looked bad for the college students who just wanted to unwind and have fun like the white kids in Cancun and Dayton. White kids partying and drinking and having random sex was a chance to let off steam. For black kids, it was a riot that warranted a city shutdown. How absurd reality is. Which is why Steve took his leave of reality a long time ago.

He hated these country roads. He couldn't believe that he had actually lived like this once. Stuck in the country away from the real world, creating a pseudo reality. Thinking that this was the way it should be. People who never even saw another city. Just read about them in newspapers. He made sure his gas tank was full and had a reserve. Stopping around here would immediately call attention to him. They would never forget that he was a from somewhere else. From the city. They didn't have that many here. So he made sure he would not have to stop. People, what few he saw just assumed he was lost. This was too close to home. He never imagined himself having to come back to this place. It made him think of bad things. It made him think of the little boy whose parents drove away and never came back. He kept his map close at hand and pulled it up to look at it overtime he passed a pickup truck or a what use to be one.

Morgan was thinking of a way out of this. She was hoping the Calvary would rescue her, but she wasn't sure. You never knew about the Calvary.

"Morgan?"

"Yes, Amir?"

"Did you ever really like me, or was it all a game."

Morgan thought about this.

"Well, I guess I can be truthful since I am not going to live long. I didn't like you at all at first. Especially when we slept together the first time. You were a brutal, mean man and it was my pleasure to bust your ass. But, after you tried to change, I almost lost sight of what I was really there for and actually considered you to be a man worth spending my life with. I guess had situations been a little different, I could actually love you. But reality has a way of coming back and slapping you in the face. I had a job to do Amir, that was it."

He said nothing at first, then he spoke, quietly.

"all my life I have wanted a nice woman. But first, I was hustling and everyone is about the hustle. Women want men who have the hustle, but if you lose it, they move on to the next. So I would sit at home and look through my momma's art magazines. She had lots of them. She would look at them and decided which ones she would buy if she had the money. I didn't like school. It was boring and it didn't teach you things you needed in life. Not in our neighborhood. We learned a lot about black pride. Pride in being poor and left behind. Go to church and be a good person and you will get your gold and reward in heaven. The prayer of the damned. I wanted my gold now. It started out innocent enough. I was just a runner, going here and there, exchanging this for that. But I met this white man who was up in the business. He had stopped me on one of my runs and took me to his place to help him host a party. He said it looked good to upstanding people to have a black serving. Made them feel superior. So he dressed me in one of those monkey suits and I served at his party. I didn't know how to mix drinks or how to serve. He taught me that. He said that a man should know social graces, no matter how poor, because it was a good sideline. People paid good money to have someone who knew how wait on them. It would be useful if I ever wanted to go straight. So he taught me how to do that. He had a great art collection and he caught me staring at his art on the wall and the vases. They looked like the things in my mother's magazines. He taught me about those too. How to spot whites original and what's fabricated, what's tasteful and what's not. Where to hang certain prints and how to display vases and things properly. I enjoyed it.

I did bartending and catering on the side at every opportunity, but the drug trade was too lucrative. I was earning a thousand dollars a week before I was 20. I would talk to my mentor about how to keep it. I saw so many getting money like that and then buying flashy cars and having all these girls. But I remember when they went to jail and getting out had nothing, no cars, no money and no girls. That type of investment was too short lived. So, I bought art, and learned to appraise it. I invested in good cars, cars that befitted a man in the art world, not a drug dealer. He got me the penthouse as a present. He said to live here, you have to know how to act. And I did. My parties were for show and to keep the drug underlings happy. They wanted to live large like me, but I knew they wouldn't achieve it like that. But, once in awhile, I let them hang there. Bring me women who would do anything I wanted because I was the big man. So I took advantage of it and took out all my frustrations and fantasies on them because it was expected. That was the price they paid to hang out in the fast lane and they didn't mind. And if they didn't mind, neither did I. You were the only one who complained.

Even Sharon Lee, who I really liked, never complained. She just went with the flow. Detached from really enjoying her experience. I should have know something was up with you then. You renewed my faith in woman, only to cut it back down. I won't trust again. Well, maybe not ever again, but it will be along time. You don't meet people like you every day, and one day, if I don't go to jail or die, I will meet a Renee again, and she will be mine. And it will be for real."

The rest of the journey was in silence. Morgan was glad to see they weren't deviating from the course. She wanted to make sure she was found. But her gladness was short lived. They made a detour heading toward a town in Kentucky called London.

As they were approaching a town called London, Amir turned into the State Park that was situated there. Morgans heart sank. This was really going to happen. She couldn't tell John where she was. Her people would be scouring up and down 75 and they would be in the big woods, where no one could find her. She hoped that at least if she did get killed, they would find her before her remains were too bad and her father couldn't identify her. It was hard to have a funeral with a body that you identified through dental records.

XIII

They wound their way around the park, getting deeper and deeper into the woods. At the end, of a long narrow road, they parked the car and Amir motioned her to get out of the car. She thought about running, but Amir had his gun out, so she decided that if she could prolong death, she could maybe find a way out.

They walked to a break in the trees and there was Steve standing there. He had an Uzi and he motioned to Amir to drop his pistol.

"Mr. Amir. I thought about letting you stay and watch the festivities, but you already had Morgan, several times, this won't be a thrill for you. Besides, I don't like to share."

"Hey Steve, man, I thought we—"

But he never finished his sentence. Steve shot him and watched him fall down. He smiled at Morgan.

"See, no sweat. The trash is disposed of."

He went to the body and was moving it. Hiding it under some leaves. As he did that, Morgan broke and ran.

"Morgan!!!"

She ran, but she had no idea where she was running to.

Steve went to his car and got his knife.

"My little Morgan, why do you think I chose this place? I grew up here. I know all about these woods. There are so many people and things buried up here that no one ever found. They will never find you either, not after I am through."

And walked in Morgan's direction. There was no hurry. The paths is what she will take and they all lead to one place. So, he headed for the little ranger cabin out in the middle of the park. The paths were set up that way so that no one would really get lost. He headed for the ranger cabin, service revolver in his pocket and knife in his pants.

Morgan ran down the path. Paths always lead back out of the park, she hoped. She had never been a woods person, in fact, she was scared of them. Piedmont Park was the most woods she could deal with. She made a note that if she got out of this, she would learn the woods and how to survive in them. If she did survive.

Steve walked and whistled through the woods. He loved this place. He could be as perverted as he wanted. No one really came to the woods during the week. Just the die hard campers during vacation and this was off season for that. They usually enjoyed it in the fall when the leaves were turning colors. Camping is cool in the fall. He stopped by the spot where he put his first victim. A ratty boy who bugged him, wanting to hang out with him. A misfit just like him, but Steve was too arrogant to believe he was a misfit. Everyone thought that bad boy ran away. They were glad to be rid of him. The boy's family was just like his own. Didn't give a shit about him. Was glad he was gone. It took them a week to file a missing person report and they actually told the cops that they think he ran away and not to try real hard to find him. He'll turn up, they said. But with no more mouths to feed or kids to worry about getting to school and doing things for, the mother and father packed up and went away. They left the key under the mat, with a note in the house. Steve knew because he went into the house and lived for awhile. At least this kids parents tried to give him a home. For a while. There wasn't food in there, just old liquor bottles and beer cans. But the boys room was clean. It had matching sheets and curtains, and a Bowling Green pennant.

Steve stayed there for about a month until the neighbors started coming around thinking he was the boy. It was his first sexual experience. He remembers the boy screaming as he stuck his dick into him. It didn't feel that good to Steve either and he ended up just stabbing the boy and jacking off. He didn't know how fags did that ass shit. It hurt. There were hitchhikers that came through here from time to time. Trying to get to Columbus, or Cleveland, or Athens. Country girls from Mississippi and Alabama, looking for their boys who went away to college or who moved up north. Hitching was fun in those days, or was it.

The towns people never paid him any attention. He did odd jobs for the shop owners. Saying that his parents were working the mines, and that he didn't want to. He worked a little, didn't steal from them because then, they would have been suspicious of him. As long as he pretended to be normal, no one cared where he came from or where he lived. He worked a little for food and beer. And slept at that boy's house. It wasn't bad. When the electric was finally turned off, he bought candles. They had a well out back for his water and an outhouse.

When those southern girls came up here lookin for some place to sleep, he let them. He always had to kill one in the house, to isolate the other. They always traveled in twos. Safety in numbers they would say. He would put them to sleep in separate parts of the house, each girl anticipating that he would come to them because he was a nice looking boy. The nicer of the two he would visit first and quietly stab her while she slept. The other, he would lure to the woods, under the guise of looking for the other. It always worked. He said he took his knife for bears but he could never remember seeing a bear, but again it worked. They would walk and he would hold her because she was scared. A country girl scared of the woods. Maybe because they were northern woods. Like the south didn't have woods. They were all backwoods girls.

He would talk them into sitting and resting under a tree, the kiss her to try to calm her down. They always wanted that. Then he would lay them down, get on top of them, some would fight, which he enjoyed, others wanted to give it to him and he hated that and tried to be more brutal with those hoes. But in the end, he came and they went. And he would bury them and wait for the next. There was always someone else.

Steve arrived at the ranger cabin. Like he knew, there were no rangers here. But there was a ranger suit in the closet. He put it on. It didn't quite fit, but it would serve its purpose. There would be one here in the fall. They tried to stay staffed then when the tree watchers were out. Folks that knew nothing about the woods always wanted to be in them. He put on the uniform, and sat and waited.

Morgan sat behind the tree breathing deeply. She wanted to find the road back to the freeway, but all this tree shit looked alike. She figured the best bet was to stay on the path. Paths always led somewhere, didn't they? She wanted to cry, but she was a professional. She thought about Amir laying there by the car. Someone would have to see him. Eventually. A dead black man in this neck of the woods should arouse some suspicion. She laughed at that, this neck of the woods. She looked up through the trees. Not much daylight left and it would be darker in here than out there on the road. She had better continue. She was sorry her bags were in the car. Everything she needed was in there. She looked at her shoes. The path wasn't very hard, crushed rock to a fine dust. She took her socks off and put her shoes back on. She left the socks by the tree. Just in case she thought. Wished she had some breadcrumbs. At least Hansel and Gretel had breadcrumbs. But she had some skittles. Who the fuck could see skittles in the dark. But she dropped them one by one until they ran out. Laughing at her stupidness. Skittles, hansel and gretel. Is this what the end was like?

She didn't hear anyone behind her. Where was Steve. He was probably looking for her and as lost as she was. He was after all an Atlantan cop not a nature boy. She began running again. She thought about her dad, something to divert her attention from this physical exersion. She would really go to the gym if she made it through this. A joint would have been better.

She thought about what her dad and she would be doing tonight. Sitting in front of the t.v., watching the track and field events. She loved to see the women run. They were graceful as gazelles and strong. She noticed their muscles and their build. Small breasted just like she was. Less wind resistance. She smiled. Her father would have made some popcorn and cheered his favorite runners to victory. She wondered why he never married again. There was a sweet lady at church that had the hots for him. She could tell. She was always making her cookies and taking her to dinner. She could have been partying at the Crows Nest. Dancing til dawn with the fine brothers in Atlanta. There was a whole city of fine brothers in Atlanta, but some of them were crazy as all get out. She knew that. Usually you didn't find that out until you invited them over and by then, it was almost too late. You had to almost fight them to get them to leave. Not her though, she just pulled her gun. She had been called a crazy bitch more than once by one of those fine crazy brothers. But they were great to look at.

She wondered how her life took such a turn. Fuck. She just wanted to do her part for society. To get some of the drugs off the street and get the people who profit from them the most. Not the street dealers, they had to get them from somewhere. They didn't have charter planes and limos to pick this stuff up with. They were the low men on the totem pole. Just getting the stuff to the people who want it. And they do want it. Drugs don't start with the street dealers. It stops there. It starts with the people who have the means and the money to get the stuff, to cut it, to package it and to get it to the street dealers. The people with the private planes or the money to get one. The people with the passports and the visas. The connected people. The people who party in their penthouses or suburban homes, untouched by the street unless they want to be touched. But the cops bust the street dealers, and the flow is not stopped. Its just diverted. Until they get the people who have the connections, drugs will continue to trickle down to the streets. Where the people wait with open arms. And noses. People think that the folks that do drugs are just the dredges of society. Morgan remembers how many times she went in crack houses and saw suited businessmen, getting their high on, spending their paychecks with their white skin. She remembers lonely housewife from suburbia, slummin in the crack house with the hoes. Sitting by herself like it would isolate her from the stench. Cocaine became popular with the rich and famous before the hood could get it. Alcohol was always apart of the social scene, but it was the neighborhood bums who were looked down on. At least they had the courage to be who they were in front of everybody. The crack hoe was looked upon as dirty, but the businessman sitting beside her sharing that rock, just needed a little rehab. Society sure has ways of coloring the truth to fit whatever. Black will always be worse doing the same thing that whites have always done. She thought about the young black man, just 20, who went to jail for murder. His mother wanted him to live in a better neighborhood for better educational opportunities and the chance to meet and be a better class of people. She wanted him to be accepted. They accepted him and his mother was glad. He was accepted by the right people. They introduced him to hanging out, cruising in their nice cars, crystal meth, diet pills, ecstasy and ritalin. They introduced him Quaaludes,acid, prescription valium and their parents stash of weed and alcohol, pain killers, sleeping pills, lithium, stelazine. When he went to jail, he was just another black dredge on society. The white kids were in rehab, again, with scholarships bought and paid for to Ivy League schools. This is society, on the real side. Urban kids don't go to school and shoot everyone. They may go after a particular person. But the better neighborhoods do it one better, of course. They kill their parents, kill their teachers, kill students and kill themselves. Which society is scarier, black or white? The media will always let you know that is still more dangerous to be in a black neighborhood. She thought about the rapist in the Buckhead area, where the news was broadcasting it daily, with composites and everything. But in an apartment complex in not so affluent East Point, where women caught the bus often alone at 5:30 in the morning, at the corner of Washington Road and Janice Drive, where it was dark, that there was also a rapist, but, it wasn't news worthy. Not really. The women in the area had to make a noise to get any coverage. Our citizens were alerted. But, most of the women that needed to see it, were still at five points, waiting for a southbound train where there was actually a seat,or pulling overtime, or stopping at the store to get a few groceries, or picking up their kids from baby-sitters or daycare on the bus. Or waiting at the College Park station for a bus that actually had a seat. They never saw the broadcast.

Then she remembered why she did the work she did. Because lady justice could see very well, and she was class conscious too, and Morgan wanted to be the equalizer. She promised herself she will live through this.

Morgan saw the cabin. It was in the distance with soft light burning in it. The sky had darkened in the woods and she was glad to see the beacon. She wasn't sure how far it was, but she knew as long as she could see the lights, she could make it.

Steve sat waiting for his prey. He was excited with the prospect. Another death in the woods. He thought about Morgan, with her high class ways. A family that loved her.

Who did she think she was. Stopping his chance at success. All his life he had been kicked around and not wanted and put out and put around. She grew up, loved, cared for, educated. He was bright in school in the good days. When his parents loved him.

When he was younger, as he remembers, there were good times. For awhile. But everyone isn't meant to be a parent. He was a blond headed little boy, with a quick smile. His parents were nice for so long. Then the changes came. At first, it was subtle. His mother stopped working. She stayed home and at first did the June cleaver thing, you know, cooking cleaning, taking care of things. The slowly, the mailman started bringing the mail, personally, inside. The milkman.

One day, little stevie was going to see his mother, he was lonely being in his room all alone and he walked to her room. There she was on the bed legs in the big V with the paperboy. But instead of stopping the action because her little boy wandered in, she threw something at him, cutting his head, and screamed at him to close the door and go to his room. He sat in his room and cried. She never came to see if he was alright, and if his father hadn't come home, he probably wouldn't have eaten. His father took care of him for a while, then noticing that his mother was not interested anymore, he became disinterested in the boy and kept watch on the mother. That went on for years, coupled with arguments, down right fights. Stevie had to learn to fix sandwiches and later learned to cook. He learned to be slick, cooking when everyone one was gone, and cleaning everything up so that it didn't look like he cooked anything. They were usually drunk and sleepy when they got in and only noticed food missing when they decided to be hungry. His father still brought him a few clothes or got some from goodwill. Many a day he went to school, getting laughed at because someone's parents had thrown out the shirt he was wearing. Or the jeans he had on. They stopped buying clothes all together. Then one day, they just didn't come home. He was fine with it at first. There was still a little something to eat, and he worked at the market in the evenings. But then it got quiet and empty. The school found out and he went to live with some relatives who didn't really want him. They made sure he went to school and fed him, but didn't talk to him at all much. But he heard what a slut his mother was and how dirty she was and that his father was no good following that whore around. He decided then that, if his father had had him alone, without his whore mother, he wold have taken care of him. He hated women after that. His aunt, his mother, and all the whores that were out there, destroying a little boys life. But, he knew there was a difference between whores and other women. His friends had other women as mothers. They fed him sometimes, helped him with his homework and talked to him. But, he couldn't stay, he had to go home. Or anyway to the place he stayed. The first time he killed, it was a dog that barked at him. He had always kept a knife because he used it for things, but the puppy was barking at him and he picked him up, took him out to the woods and stuck him with the knife. When the puppy yelped, he felt an excitement go through him, making him feel tingles, sexually. He finished the dog off, and felt his dick harden and soften, leaving a wet spot on his pants. He liked the feeling. After that, all his pent up aggression went into killing things. He didn't start on people until later, after he was out of high school. It became easier with each victim and he felt vindicated. Now, the ultimate, the supreme death. Those hookers mean nothing compared to what he was planning to do to Morgan. If he had not met her as Renee, and she hadn't interfered with his plans, he could have spared her this. Her above all. She was basically a good person. But, she got in his way. And she didn't buy that shit about him trying to bust Amir, especially now. But that was more money than he had ever seen and he wasn't going to let any body take that from him, not even Morgan.

Steve heard a rustling outside the cabin. He turned himself away from the door, facing the filing cabinets.

Morgan had reached the cabin. Looking in the window, she saw a park ranger, looking at some files. Thank God, Steve hadn't made it here.

She opened the door and rushed in. Speaking fast and locking the door, she didn't bother to turn around, but went straight to the window to see if she was followed.

"Listen, sir, there is man trying to kill me. He killed my friend up the road, I need your help."

"Sure, babydoll, I got your back"

She spun around.

There was Steve, sitting behind the desk, smiling at her.

"And you are mistaken babydoll, not trying, I am going to kill you. Its off season, there are no rangers here and won't be until about—uh, October."

Morgan tried the door, and realized it was much easier for her to lock than to unlock. She did get it unlocked, but he was there, holding her from behind.

"Babydoll, just relax. We have a while to play. You don't want to leave yet. Trust me. This party is just beginning."

He turned her around and began to kiss her, deep and heavy. She pushed him away and he hit the desk.

He immediately jumped up.

"Look bitch, this can happen fast or slow. I prefer slow, but I can do it now. Don't fuck with me Morgan. I want to fuck with you for awhile. Don't make me kill you fast. It will take all the pleasure away."

He grabbed her and sat her down beside the desk.

"My plane doesn't leave until morning, so I have time"

"Plane? What plane?"

"Well, I guess I can tell you, you aren't going anywhere. I have a flight out of Cincinnati going to new York to get paid. The drugs should be there."

"They won't be there."

"What?!!! Say that again"

"They won't be there Steve, my people picked up your transport on 95 when I was near Knoxville this afternoon. There is no shipment, no money."

"You bitch."

He slapped her hard across the face. She fell back, but she stood her ground.

"That's right lover boy, no money. No drugs. In fact, we set it up to look like you double crossed them, and now you are wanted by them and Atlanta."

"well, babydoll, that's fucked up for you. That means I don't have to kill you until right before the fall. So, you fucked me, but you fucked yourself too. And poor Amir, died for nothing."

"My people know where I am."

"Bullshit. No one knows about this place but me. I grew up here babydoll. You know, I loved to hear your father call you that. You were a little babydoll. Now, you're just a dead bitch."

She played her card. Nonchalance. He wanted fear, but she won't give him any. Not this time.

"So, fuck you, kill me. I don't give a damn."

"Yeah, right. What about your dad?"

"There are plenty of people to take care of him. He will grieve, but once he finds out I died in the line of duty, buried in full honor, he will be so proud. So fuck you, Steve. You were a disgrace to your parents and now you will be a disgrace to the world."

He slapped her again.

"My parents were a disgrace to me, you bitch. My mother and all the whores like her. I was just a little boy that nobody wanted, don't you understand that? No, you wouldn't understand, everybody wanted you. You were left alone to take care of yourself or stuck in your room while your mother fucked everything that came by the house. You don't know me at all. Fuck them and fuck those whores. And tonight, fuck you."

"Oh save that bullshit for someone who gives a damn Steve. You aren't the only abused dysfunctional kid in this world. Its full of them. So don't justify your sordid behavior because of your parents. I am so sick of that. I was abused, I wasn't loved. Well, this isn't a perfect world you little shit. You are a coward. You prey on women who can't defend themselves, who, for whatever reason are out there on the street selling themselves to asswipes like you. You take advantage of the people who are disadvantaged. You are a plague on society. If you are looking for sympathy for your past, you sure as hell won't get it here. You were a police officer. Not because you enjoyed the job, but because it gave you power to do the dirty little shit you do. You knew you were a sick man, and you could have done something about it. You carried that abuse around like a badge, well you aren't the lone ranger. And how much money were you going to gain for this little venture you were on? Would the money buy you happiness or love? Hell no, you would still be the same little shit that you are now."

Steve stood there looking at her, raging inside. Morgan was afraid that she went too far, but she had to buy some time, she couldn't let him just kill her right out. She had to keep him talking. Slapping didn't hurt as much as that knife would.

"Well, Miss, I had the perfect lifestyle, maybe you are right. Maybe I took advantage of the fact that I hate women, to satisfy some perverse need. It won't help you any to know that now."

"Why do you keep saying that my world was so perfect? You don't know how I was raised. All you know is what you see when you go to my house. My mother didn't die of natural causes. She came home from work one day and saw my father in the bed with our next door neighbor. So don't you dare sit there and tell me about my perfect little world. You don't know nothing about what goes on behind these closed doors and windows of these homes. You don't know if those girls you killed had family somewhere. You don't know if anyone cried that night because mommy didn't come home. You just assumed they were thrown away because society said so. But you don't know for sure."

"Morgan, the bottom line is, your world is over. So all this means nothing."

Steve unwrapped the long knife that he had with him and smiled at it, his hand running along the blade. He walked to Morgan and held the knife to her throat.

"Lay your sweet ass on the floor, this is going to be so good."

Morgan started down toward the floor, and as she went down, she grabbed Steve by the balls and squeezed. He screamed and slashed at her with the knife. From the angle, the knife sliced into her shoulder and she didn't feel the pain at first. He doubled up and she ran for the door, remembering that she hadn't locked it back.

Out into the dark woods. She let her eyes focus and continued running down the path. Stay on the path Morgan, it has to lead to somewhere.

She ran, and could feel warm running down her back, she thought it was sweat but she was also feeling faint. You can't stop now Morgan, you gotta run.

"Morgan, I know these woods better than you, you can run, but I will find your sweet ass."

The pain in his groin was going away slowly, and he walked fast up the path, with his flashlight, following the drops of blood that Morgan was leaving in her wake.

Morgan followed the path as best she could. But she couldn't understand why she was feeling faint. She couldn't see and it was getting hard to stand. She fell to her knees, trying to work the dizziness off.

She fell. Darkness was closing in her mind. She couldn't focus. Morgan, don't faint, oh God, don't faint, stay awake.

Steve found her on her knees.

"Its a great position Morgan, but it won't do for what I have planned. Oh, I see we have a little cut on our arm. Too bad. Well at least with that one, the other won't hurt you too much more. My blade will cut you like a hot knife in butter. You won't feel a thing, trust me."

He lay her down and turned her on her back. Putting the flashlight beside them, he straddled her, and unhook his pants. Morgan was fading into twilight.

"No, Morgan don't faint, damn you. I want you to look me in the eyes when we do this. I want you to see me kill you."

He slapped her face to bring her too. Morgan felt the slaps, just barely and she tried to open her eyes. The sweet twilight closed in on her again. Steve slowly penetrated Morgan, it wasn't any fun if he can't see that look of surprise when he stabs her. As he brings the blade close to her heart, something happened.

The knife fell to the ground and Steve fell on top of Morgan, bleeding from a gunshot to the back. He never heard it.

Morgan saw a flash and heard the shot. It was the last thing she remembered.

XIV

When Morgan came to, she was in the hospital. Her father, John and the doctors, standing around, looking at her. She opened her eyes.

"I gotta get these contacts out my eyes. They feel like sand."

The doctor smiled.

"We will take care of that for you."

He called the nurse. They wet her eyes with a solution and the contacts removed very easily.

Her father held her hand.

"Why didn't you tell me the truth about what you were doing? How long have you been doing this?

"More than I should have. I almost bought it this time."

John spoke.

"We got to you just in time. Steve is dead, Amir is dead, we have the cocaine. The only thing we didn't get a chance to do was stop the bomb."

"what bomb?"

"Steve's diversion was a bomb at the Olympic Park. People were killed. It was awful."

"Damn, I forgot about the diversion he was planning. So, I guess he had the last laugh afterall."

"Well Morgan, gets some rest."

He kissed her on the forehead and left the room.

Morgan's father just looked at her.

"I guess I can't understand why you didn't confide in me. I could have been there for you and none of this would have happened."

"I can't tell you everything dad. It was my choice to do what I did. It wasn't something that you should have been involved in."

"But I had the man at my home, our home. We were buddies. And you knew what was going on and you didn't tell me."

"No daddy. I didn't find out until I was in my cover and I couldn't risk telling you. Your need to protect me would have been too strong and you would have taken it upon yourself to get involved."

He was silent. He knew she was right. The father in him would have come into play.

"Your mother would be proud of you."

"No she wouldn't. She hated police work. I do remember that. I also remember what happened to her daddy. It was your fault daddy."

"I know, Morgan. And if I could turn back the hands of time and change things, I would. I never meant to hurt your mother."

He sat on the bed beside Morgan.

"Morgan, I can't change the type of person that I am. I did love your mother, more than anything in this world. I didn't do those things because of who she was, but because of how I was."

"It was wrong daddy."

"In a perfect world, babydoll. But this isn't a perfect world and I am not a perfect man. Just a man. Perfection is a perception that is very hard to live up to. I am not saying that it can't be done, I am saying that I can't do it.

You don't look for perfection when looking for a mate. You'll never find one. There will always be something about someone that will make perfection hard to achieve. An attitude, an action, something. But you deal with how that person is. Your mother dealt with me. She knew how I was. Its what love is really about. Acceptance."

"You're saying she knew about you?"

"She did. She could deal with the knowledge, but not seeing it first hand. Your mother was a beautiful woman, in mind and body, and I do miss her. But, without saying too much more, she wasn't perfect either."

"what do you mean?"

"That's another story, Morgan. This isn't the place. What you have to do is go on with your life. All men aren't like me and Steve. There are some really nice men out there."

He kissed her.

"Stop running, Morgan. All men aren't like me."

BOOK TWO

The beginning

Morgan grew up in the suburbs of Atlanta, well actually in south Atlanta. Nice upper middle class neighborhood. Pretty houses. Manicured lawns. She and her friends rode their bikes up and down the street, not a busy street, mostly traffic from the people who lived there. Occasionally, people passing through. There were slumber parties and church on Sunday's.

Morgan's mother had wanted her to go to a private school, but her father would have none of that. Her father, a police detective with the City of Atlanta, wanted his daughter to see people and know that she was blessed to have it as good as she did because a lot of kids did not. Particularly in their area. It used to be a thriving neighborhood, but certain parts felt the blight of crack cocaine and they descended into the madness and despair that drugs take you to. The apartments, once nice, were slowly filling up with crackheads, crack hoes, crack dealers, and their children, mostly unsupervised, left to wreak havoc on other thrown away kids. Nothing to do all day, but sit around, most stopped attending school. There were a few good mothers still living there, trying to catch the bus first thing in the morning, working to support their kids, but not having enough time to supervise them adequately. But they did what they could do. Once in a while the night was permeated with the sounds of a mother dispensing punishment on a child who had gotten out of hand and who deserved the punishment. But mostly, they just ran wild. Morgan's neighborhood was still mostly untouched by the fracas. When school was not in session, Morgan's mother was home to direct her activities and give her things to keep her busy. She was not unsupervised and her mother wished that all mothers could say the same thing, but that was the way of the world. The haves and the I am trying to haves. The division was getting deeper.

But, she took her daughter to ballet lessons, and tennis lessons and they went shopping together and to the library. While her father worked. He worked late hours all the time, but he was always home for dinner at 6:30. Even if he did have to go back out to "handle a case" he was there in time for supper and conversations with his family.

Her mother generally talked about the high cost of things and how the neighborhood was changing. Couldn't East Point have more patrols on the streets. Can Atlanta help. Things like that. Her father talked about the criminals he had interrogated and situations that he had to put down. Morgan liked hearing about her fathers job. She wanted to be a cop when she grew up. Fight crime and help people. That was her perception of the police department. She felt protected that her father was a cop. She felt safe and that nothing would happen to her as long as he was on the job. Her mother adored her father and Morgan would lay in her bed at night and listen to the sounds of them in the bedroom together when he came home to sleep. Her mother would laugh and giggle with him and Morgan could hear him talking in that soft baritone that made her love him more each day. The laughing would be replaced with soft moaning and she could hear the bed moving rhythmically until finally, she could hear the snores of her father and she would go to sleep. On the days that her mother didn't have any activities planned, she and her girlfriends jumped double-dutch on the drive way and the boys played basketball at one of the numerous hoops that were in the yards. Every boy wanted to be Michael Jordan. Sometimes, she just stayed in her room and read books. She had a computer, but it was in her father's office and she didn't like it too much except for playing games and doing her homework. When she got into middle school, her tastes changes a little. She no longer jumped rope with her friends and they spent endless time on the phone talking about the boys they had seen and the new cheers they were going to practice so that when they got into high school they could be cheerleaders. Her mother and father were not so close anymore, and either, they didn't make those sounds anymore, or Morgan had learned to ignore them. She would lay there in her bed, thinking about boys and go to sleep. Sometimes, she would hear arguments between her parents about some woman who called or this and that. Lipstick or makeup on her father's shirts or other little things. She didn't pay them much attention anymore, she had her own life. Her ballet lessons over, she spent her free time more on the phone with her friends, or at her friends houses practicing the newest dance steps or watching videos. She always had to be home for dinner when her father got home, but now the conversations were less and less. She still enjoyed hearing her father talk about the criminals and her mother never said too much anymore. She just ate quietly and sometimes, she looked so sad.

When there was a ball or a party by one of the officers, her mother use to dress up pretty and go. She stopped going to all those functions and most of the time her father went alone, unless he asked Morgan to come. There was always some boy he was trying to introduce her to that was one of his fellow officers sons or some other guy. She didn't like those guys however. Most of the time, they didn't have much to say. They just looked her over and decided that she wasn't givin' up anything so they would rather not deal with her. And she wasn't. Sex was something she thought about, but never had the nerve to do. Some of her friends were doing it and she went with them to planned parenthood and they got birth control pills or condoms and they had sex with their boyfriends. Morgan didn't really have a boyfriend. She had friends that were boys that she had known since she was little and they came by and talked to her sometimes and she helped them with their homework or they danced and hung out, but they were scared of her father and didn't stay long. If he came home, they usually found a way to excuse themselves. She did hate that about her father. It seemed like the only boys he would be nice to were the boys of fellow officers, and he tried to intimidate anyone else who came over. Middle school wasn't a difficult time, but it became a very lonely time after the incident.

Morgan came home from school, as usual. She put her back pack down and looked for her mother, who was usually in the kitchen preparing dinner. Her car was in the garage, so she had to be here somewhere. Morgan went to her room, turned on her music, then walked through the house calling her mom. What was strange to Morgan was that there was no smells coming from the kitchen. Always, ever since she could remember, her mother would be cooking dinner because exactly an hour and a half after she got home from school, her father would come home from work. She would sit in the kitchen and watch her mother fuss over dinner. This time, the kitchen was dark and the breakfast things were still in the sink. There was some hamburger in the refrigerator and Morgan tested it to see if was thawed. She made a meatloaf, having watched her mother do it so many times before. She went to the garage again. Her mother's car was a little warm, but not like it just came into the garage. She had been somewhere. But she had been back for awhile.

She went into her room to gather up her dirty clothes and put them down the laundry chute. Then she walked into her mother and fathers room. Her mother wasn't in there and there was a different smell in there, perfume, a sweet perfume. She didn't pay it any attention and notice that the bed was not made, or rather it had been made, but it was messy now. Her mother always made up the bed in the mornings. She had stayed home from school one day and her mother had a routine about the house. She laughed and said she had a routine because the house was so big, she had to keep it neat in a particular order or she would never get it done. But the beds were always made. Morgan had to make her bed up before she went to school. Her mother said there was no excuse for not making up the bed and that it made them so much nicer to get back into at the end of the day. She gave Morgan a little leeway with her clothes because sometimes Morgan changed outfits right before going to school, if the one she had on didn't feel right. She walked around the room, the smell of that perfume in her nose was not appealing to her and she was turning to leave when she noticed the red panties on the floor. For some reason, they unnerved her. Her mother had nice underwear, but she would never wear anything like this. She looked at them and then went to her mothers amoire to put them away. There was no matching bra for them. And everything her mother had matched. If she wore a blue slip, she had a blue bra and panties. There were lots of pastels but no red. Morgan put them in her pocket and left the room, closing the door behind her. She went to the bathroom and put the towels in the laundry chute and put out fresh towels. Things her mother normally did. She did the same in the guest bathroom, throwing the towels on the landing to the basement where the laundry room was. She would go get them later. She could smell the meatloaf cooking and went back into the kitchen, washed her hands and finished off the meal. Mashed potatoes and gravy was what her father liked best with meatloaf. She made three salads with fresh lettuce and carrots, and radishes. Took the bacos out of the cabinet because her father liked bacos. There was no ice tea in the refrigerator and they always had iced tea with their meal so she made a pitcher and put it in the freezer to cool off faster, her father would be home in half an hour or so. She dusted off the things in the living room, then when she heard her father's car drive up, she set the table. Her father came in and came straight to the kitchen. She got him a beer and he asked where her mother was. Morgan told him that she wasn't home when she got here so she made dinner. They ate, but this time it was quiet. No conversation. Someone was missing. He saw the clothes on the landing and told her that they would do the laundry for her mother, she must be out with some church friends. But Morgan didn't think that because her mother usually left a note with instructions saying where she was going, when she was coming back and things for Morgan to do while she was gone. Morgan told her father that the other things were down the chute and she would start a load. He smiled and said he would help her and together they descended the stairs. Morgan opened the laundry room door for her father because he had the towels in his hands. As he walked in, he tried to backstep and stop Morgan from following him, but it was too late, Morgan was standing there beside him, watching her mother swinging. She had hung herself.

Her father dropped the clothes and grabbed Morgan and took her upstairs and called 911. Morgan sat in the living room. Numb. As she sat there, the house became very crowded with people. When the 911 call was received, the police, recognizing the address also dispatched some cars, and some Atlanta cops came too, because they knew Morgan's father. And Morgan sat there.

They descended into the basement and took her mother down. While they were bringing her out, Morgan's father took her into his bedroom and sat her on the bed. He closed the door and went back out. The smell of the perfume was killing her and she pulled the red panties out of her pocket and looked at them. When her father came back in, she stood up, looked at him, throwing the panties in his face. She screamed at him, these aren't mothers and she went into her room and closed the door.

When she finally realized that her mother was dead, it was late into the evening. There were still lots of people around and she stayed in her room. He father kept knocking on her door and asking her if he could come in and she said no. She lay on her bed and realized that her mother was not coming in to kiss her good night and she cried quietly all night. She tried to figure out over and over why those red panties made a difference and she knew that somehow they did. She didn't quite no why, but she knew they did.

She awoke and judging by the sun it was late morning, someone knocked on the door, a soft knock. It was her auntie. She quietly asked if she could come in. Morgan let her. She liked her auntie. She was different from her mother even though they were sisters. Her auntie was a little more loud, a little more fun, her hair, cut really short was straight and blond. She had curving hips and wore tight jeans and boots with open front shirts and gold chains. She had bangles on her wrists and rings on her fingers. She always wore ruby earrings and had ruby tattooed on her leg, even though her name was Patrice. She always said she felt more like a ruby than a Patrice. She sat on the bed with Morgan and held her hand. Her perfume was nice, not sweet like in the room. She asked Morgan what was wrong why didn't she want to talk to her father. She sat up and she told her auntie about the red panties and how wrong it felt for them to be there and that she felt there was a connection. She saw her aunt change the look on her face, she asked Morgan if she was hungry and if she could get her anything. Morgan said no and her aunt said she would be back later to bring her something to eat.

She closed the door when she left and Morgan turned on her music. She turned it off because she heard loud voices in the living room. It was her auntie.

"You had another bitch in the house, in your wife's bed, you black bastard. That's what happened to my sister. She saw you, and Morgan found the whores panties. Fuck you, you are an asshole."

She could hear her father trying to say something, but he couldn't get a word in between the verbal onslaught that her auntie was giving him. She called him more four letter words than Morgan had ever heard. She stormed back into Morgan's room and told Morgan to pack a bag and that she was leaving. Morgan was hesitant about leaving.

"Who will take care of daddy now that mother's gone? I can't leave him. He doesn't have anybody."

Morgan and her auntie sat on the bed and cried for a long time. She didn't see her anymore until the funeral.

The funeral was surreal to Morgan. There were lots of police and lots of crying. Morgan, standing beside her father, while he held her hand, was unemotional. This was not real, it was a dream and soon Morgan would wake up and they would be going shopping together and hanging out together. The preacher talked for a long time about her mother and she didn't realize that so many other people loved her too. Her auntie, stood in the back, tears streaming down her face, looked at Morgan and when her father turned to see who Morgan was looking at, her auntie turned her head away from him. She left before they put her in the ground.

Morgan was ushered away to the waiting limo while her mother was being put in the ground. A soft rain began to fall and Morgan wondered if that was because the angels were sad. If her mother went to heaven, they should be happy. She would make a good angel. The tears wouldn't come. She waited for them. But she couldn't cry. She watched her father. He looked kind of lost. Not sad, but lost. She would make sure that he would not be lost. She would take care of him. Her mother would have wanted her to. The funeral possession slowly made its way back to their home. She sat in the living room while people bustled around her and past her, offering her food and kisses and tears. She looked at them, but she didn't see them. She just saw her daddy's lost face and the red panties. The people put money in her hand and signed a book and Morgan kept looking for her aunt, but she never came. Morgan got up and went to the patio, it was quiet back there and she sat and looked at the flowers that her mother had planted. Red, and green and white. Her mother had told her that those were Christmas colors and if you kept them around all year long, your house always felt merry like Christmas. The birds were in the trees, but the seemed strangely quiet to Morgan. She could hear them, but they sounded far away. Eventually, Patrice came to the patio, but not through the house, from the gate. She said she knew Morgan would be out here. It was where she always went when she was a little girl. She asked Morgan if she wanted to stay here or come to Savannah for a little while during the summer just to get away. But Morgan would not leave her daddy. She gave Morgan a kiss, and looked up to see Morgan's father standing there. She told Morgan to call her anytime, and she left, through the gate, not speaking to Morgan's father. And she drove off. Morgan listened to her corvette going down the road. It had a distinctive sound. She whispered good bye Ruby and let a tear fall.

Morgan's father came and sat beside her in his big chair that he had special made for him for his patio. He looked at the flowers that her mother had planted and he looked at Morgan.

He held her hand and she took her hand out of his. She looked at him, kissed him on the cheek and went inside to her room, closing the door softly behind her.

II

Time had stood still around her. She had found the red panties in the trash after the funeral and she took them out and put them in the back corner of her closet. She didn't know why.

Her father had taken her out of the middle school she had been attending after some classmates were whispering about her mother hanging herself. It didn't bother Morgan, it was what happened, but when she told her father what she had heard, he took her out of the school and sent her to a private school. She didn't have to live there, but she rode the bus and wore a uniform. Most of the time, she didn't ride the bus because her father made sure that he took her and picked her up. Except on the days that he was busy. He would give her cab fare but she didn't want to take a cab. She liked being in the train station in her uniform. It felt grown up to her. There were other girls there and they tried to make friends with her. But Morgan wasn't really into friendships right now. Her mother had been her friend and she was gone. She didn't want to lose anymore, so she talked a little with them, but she didn't have much to say and after awhile, they stopped trying. They would speak to her and whisper about her and her mother, but she never told her father.

She didn't know where he would send her if she told him again. Sometimes she called her auntie in Savannah, but she would try to talk her into leaving her father and Morgan couldn't do that so after awhile, she just stopped calling her.

Her father always came home at the same time and she made dinner for him. Some nights he would eat, but most nights he would tell her he would eat tomorrow and that he was going to take her out to eat. They went to all the restaurants in Atlanta, East Point and even Fairburn, but it wasn't like being home. He would try to talk about his day to her, but then his eyes would mist over and he would look lost again. But Morgan made sure that he had his uniform clean and kept the house clean for him. He never smelled like perfume like he use to sometimes. It wasn't until Morgan got into high school that she realized that her father wasn't seeing any women. He never talked about them, never looked at them. When the church ladies would offer to come by, he always made up excuses. When they went grocery shopping, the women would flirt with him and he would ignore them. Not outright, but he would say hello and keep going. Never giving them any attention. One day, Morgan asked him why he wasn't seeing women. Her mother was gone and that was over. It was time for him to move on. He looked at her with tears in his eyes and said he would never again. She thought it was because of her and she told him that it wouldn't really bother her if it was the right woman, and he told her not to ever mention it to him again. It wasn't her fault, it was his. He was wrong and his wrong cost him the only woman he ever really loved. No one could take her place. He ranted and raved about being a stupid fool and that he would never forgive himself for that, and he cried. He broke down and cried and Morgan stood there, watching him, the red panties laying on the floor in the bedroom coming into her view, and she put two and two together. She realized that she didn't hate him, but she didn't feel for him either. She couldn't help him with that pain and she let him feel it. Morgan didn't speak of women to him for a long time.

Once in a while, when Morgan was drifting off to sleep, she could hear her mother moaning softly in the room with her father, or so she thought. When she got up, he would be sitting in the living room or on the patio. She asked him if she could move her room to his office and he move his office to her room and he agreed. He wasn't sleeping very well either and some nights, they sat together on the patio, not saying anything. Looking at the flowers. But he continued to work, just not as much.

He was at her graduation and bought her a car. A corvette, like Ruby's. She bet he didn't know it was like Ruby's but she knew. She was signed up for Georgia State and was studying criminology and psychology. She didn't take a break that summer although Patrice—who had changed her name officially to Ruby, wanted her to drive to Savannah and spend some time with her. She drove for a weekend and let her see the car, but she looked so much like her mother, she couldn't stand it and told Ruby so. Ruby understood.

Morgan decided to take some summer classes in the martial arts and found the diversion positive. She was shaping up and she loved the action involved with it. When school started in the fall, her father had semi retired from the police force and when she came home from classes,she would tell him what she learned. He had begun to open up again, although he was still not dating, but she couldn't fault him because she wasn't either. So they spent their time talking about criminals, and environmental versus economical impact and if criminals are born or made. If they are taught, can they be untaught. He really enjoyed sharing his wisdom and she enjoyed listening to him. It was something they shared and he was thankful for it as much as she was. They had begun having supper together again, in the kitchen, her father learning to cook. He had gotten cook books and pots and pans and she was treated to some type of gourmet recipe or another when she got home. He had begun doing racquet ball with some officers he knew and tried golf a little. He read his bible more and more and between the police discussions and his occasionally being called in to investigate or help with an investigation that was stalled, life seemed almost normal.

III

Morgan had begun taking a class in deviant psychology with John Atmore, a professor who use to be with the FBI in criminal investigations. He was very aware of who Morgan was, revealing later in their relationship that he had known her mother and her father back in the days. He was an older man, white, and he actually looked like what Morgan thought an FBI agent would look like. He screamed of narc. The other students found his class boring, but necessary because of their majors, but Morgan found it fascinating. He talked about the criminal mind. He taught them profiling, a relatively new technique and his pros and cons on the subject. They got into discussions on whether or not profiling was just stereotyping and he explained the differences. He taught them that profiling was finding a list of psychological imprints, while stereotyping was just parroting beliefs that were handed down generation to generation. There was nothing scientific about stereotyping, it was a learned and repeated misconception. Profiling a suspect or using to catch a criminal was investigating the criminals mind. How, some acts show what type of psychology people were dealing with, or how some crimes are committed can show what was really going on in a persons mind.

They talked about how two same age persons, living in the same environment, violent, coming from two relatively like households can have two different attitudes about the situation. While, the two persons are in the same environment, both desensitized to the violence, what is the difference between one or the other that makes one become violent, and the other recognize that violence is violence and go on to live a violence free lifestyle despite the environment. Is it home training, is it attitude? That fascinated

Morgan and she would pose these questions on her father who would just smile at her. He always said, I don't deal with them until the crime is committed, then I try to figure out why. She wondered. She had two friends she had grown up on this very street, one was in college also, up in New York, the other was doing a life sentence in jail for killing another young man. Same environment. Same upbringing basically. Morgan theorized that it was a perception of things that caused some kids to listen to rap, love the music and never let it turn them into a gangsta, while others emulate the rap and become it. Are they filling a void. Is there something that they needed? Of all the classes that she had, she enjoyed that one the most. She and Professor John as she called him would talk for hours in the bar on campus. Sitting at a table, drinking coffee or sometimes drinking wine if there were no classes. On the nights she stayed on campus, she always had to call her father and let him know. Sometimes he was pretty paranoid about her not coming home, especially when he had made a meal and there were no cops stopping by to eat. East Point police stopped by pretty frequently to talk to her father, taste his food or just chat with him while they were on patrol.

Rumors began floating around the school about her and Prof John, and they laughed about it. He was a nice man, and he liked her intuitiveness and her ability to grasp situations quickly. He would give exercises in intuition and profiling. Sometimes, she would go to his home. He had a nice home in Roswell. He and his wife lived very comfortably and his wife was glad that someone was around to listen to his police stories. She laughed and said she was tired of it all. She would make them a snack, call Morgan's father and then retire to the bedroom. In his basement, he had a shooting range built and they practiced on all different types of firearms. Morgan liked the 9mm the best, but she also shot rifles and standard police issue. He taught her how to shoot targets, moving and not moving. He taught her how to throw knives and how simple objects could be used as weapons. He encouraged her martial arts and had her come and practice in his weight room. She laughed that the FBI must have paid well. He never talked much about what he really did with them but he would use some actual case studies minus the identifying information in his study groups at school. He was a good teacher and she was an apt pupil.

IV

Morgan was learning very quickly. Once in a while, there were other members of their little group who came by to add their slants on Prof John and Morgan's discussion. There was Michael, who was training for the CIA. He knew John when Mikey as John calls him was chasing girls with spit balls. There was Thomas and there was Sheila. They sat and had lengthy discussions on the mindset of serial killers and how they choose their victims. How to tell if a person is acting on a stress related deviation or how much is actually related to the psyche of the person. Stress makes people do things that they wouldn't normally do and in this time, stress is a factor in many of the impromptu murders. Road rage, getting fired. All these stresses led to related assaults. But what about the guy who transitions into society, being a model citizen, with the thoughts of murder deeply imbedded in his mind. What triggers his responses? What turns a seemingly normal person into a killer? Are people normal anymore?

Sometimes their discussions would go on to late into the night. John's wife, always the perfect hostess, would appear magically with sandwiches and cokes. Just when everyone was needing it, even though they didn't know it. She was great about it. She said it kept him out of her hair.

One evening, after a discussion when every one else had gone, John posed a question to Morgan.

"I am have been running a small agency that helps the police department solve crimes. It involves some hands on investigation and most of my operatives work undercover. Would you be interested in working for me?"

Morgan was excited about the suggestion, but she didn't know if she was ready for something like that.

"You have the skills, you just have to learn to put them to use. You have to be able to forget who you are and be someone else to get the job done. Go home and think about it. I will have to ask you not to speak of this to your father. If you have to go away, we will make sure that he knows nothing of your assignment. It has to be that way."

"But he is a cop."

"And he was a good one, but we can't involve any more people than necessary."

He took a file out of the cabinet.

"Study this and let me know what you think. Get back to me by mid week, because Michael will be ready to leave first of next week and I want you ready to go with him. He feels you are ready to be with another person, not alone. And he is the best."

In the file, there were three sections, one on Michael's character, and her character, the suspect they were trying to apprehend and the things they will need for the assignment.

Morgan looked at John. He just smiled.

"you're ready. Michael has the same file, study your part well and get with me soon okay. Time is of the essence, this man has eluded us for years. We need to catch him."

"Who do I work for, the CIA?"

"You work for me."

Morgan drove home through the streets of Atlanta. Looking at the lights shining on the freeway, the lights in the homes as people did their routines for the evening. It was pretty late for a Saturday night and there were lots of lights everywhere. The city was alive with Saturday night card games, house parties, couples getting ready to make love, people coming home from the club or kids just enjoying Saturday night in Atlanta.

The weather was cool since it was the fall and although you couldn't really see the seasons change unless you went to the mountains, Morgan could feel the slight chill in the air. The hot days were over for a while. She cruised 85 south, heading home. Watching the planes lining up to get into Hartsfield. Some of them were so low it seemed you could almost wave at the people. She wondered where everyone was coming home from. Where had they been? Where were they going.

Morgan touched the file on the seat beside her. She had no idea that John was anything more than a professor. He didn't explain his whole purpose or what he had in mind, but in the file was a little booklet. It had her name on it and the stickynote attached said 'read this first' and it was signed by John.

She drove home, listening to her Michael Franks c.d. It seemed to fit the mood of the city tonight.

Morgan got home and her father was sleeping on the couch. She tried to be quiet, because, even though they were moving and living like normal, he was still having trouble sleeping sometimes and she would find him on the couch in the morning, her mother's picture laying on his chest.

He awoke instantly as she came in. And sat up.

"Late night? Was you on a date?"

"No daddy, just studying."

"You study too much. A nice looking girl like you should be out on a date."

"you should too."

"I'm too old for that foolishness."

She smiled to herself, at least he didn't get mad at her and she didn't press the issue.

"maybe I will find a good cop and get married."

"someone like your old man, huh"

The temptation was there,the temptation to bring up his infidelity, but she denied the temptation.

"yes daddy, someone just like you."

She kissed his forehead and headed to her room. He lay back down on the couch and fell asleep. He turned the lights off as she closed her room door. She knew she would find him there in the morning. Morgan undressed and stepped into the little shower that her father had put in when he was working late. He didn't want to use the one in the bedroom and wake her mother, but he didn't know she was always awake, waiting for him. She put on her night shirt and sat at the desk and put her reading glasses on. She had begun to use them when she started school because the studying was giving her bad eye strain. She read the booklet first. There was a note clipped inside.

Morgan—

If you are reading this, then you have been chosen to join our group. We are a select few who are employed to catch those people who live outside the law and the law can't for whatever reason, catch them.

Our objective, to catch them and bring them to justice. Most are criminals with international crimes, wanted by interpol, and other agencies. They contact me when they need a team, and I supply them the man power or in some cases, the woman power. Being an African-American, you can be of special interest to us. You can infiltrate where Caucasians cannot and you can also make a situation seem normal. No one would suspect you. The deeds you have to do, which will be part of your job, will include sex occasionally, and I don't know what your moral fiber dictates, although I hate assuming, I will take a chance and state that you were raised in a religious environment. Don't get me wrong, you won't be typecast or stereotyped as a hooker or any of the demeaning professions that blacks are generally set in, unless the situation calls for that and many of these do not. These are criminals with money, class, and these are the hardest criminals to catch. But sex, I have found is an important part. It is used to test loyalty and it is necessary. You will be protected at all times as we have foreseen any scenario that could possibly arise.

You are perfect for our organization, the missing piece so to speak. I hope you accept this invitation to join us.

—John

Morgan looked through the file. There was an envelope in there, plain, brown, sealed. She opened it and there was $10,000.00 in cash. The sticky note on this said, payment.

V

Steve was born to a truck driver and a blond in the hills in Kentucky. The neighborhood was quiet and small. Most people in the town worked somewhere else. Steve's mother, pretty and young, didn't really want kids. It just happened. She told him that time and time again. They gave him the room off the kitchen, which looked more like a closet than a room. When his father was gone, his mother basically ignored Stevie. She kept hot dogs in the house and when she felt like cooking some she did, but he was use to eating them raw. Steve was left alone by his mom most of the time and he loved it when his dad came home. His dad always had something that he brought from the road. Last time he came home he gave a blanket for his bed. He brought him clothes and shoes and jeans and jackets. He brought his little boy toys and even a gold fish, but when his dad left and Steve wanted to feed the goldfish, his mother flushed him down the toilet and said that that's where all little kids belong. Steve use to cry when his mother did things like that, but later, he learned not to cry. Crying didn't help and it didn't bring his father home any sooner.

He went to kindergarten with the other kids in the neighborhood, but their parents had taken the time to try to teach them something before they went to school. Steve couldn't read or write his name. The teachers tried to help, but Steve couldn't stand the kids laughing at him, so he was usually sent home for fighting and his mother kept him in his room. He could hear the men coming and going and he realized that these men weren't not his father. Once, he ran out of the room to see who it was. His mother smacked him in the face and put him back in his room. But the man was nice and went to the dairy queen and brought the boy back some ice cream. He never came back to see his mother again and she blamed it on Stevie.

Stevie struggled through kindergarden and then through 1st through the 6th grade. In the sixth grade, his father got a job at the new gas company that was built and he was home more. He did a lot of things for Stevie and his grades improved. His father would walk him through the woods and show him things about plants and animals. But when they came home, his father would try to talk to his mother.

She didn't have much to say to him most of the time, and he tried all he could to get through to her.

They would go into the room and do things that the other men did but Stevie didn't have to stay in the room when his father was home. He just knew he had to stay away from his mother. She hated him. Stevie never could understand why she didn't like him. But he knew that she didn't. He tried to do nice things for her. He brought her flowers from the woods and she would take them and put them aside. He tried to keep his room extra clean for her, but she never even came in there. At night, when his father was home, he would hear them fighting about her. And she would always blame Stevie. Stevie was the cause, if she didn't have Stevie she could have a real life. She never wanted to be a mother. Then his father would come in the room and hold him. Tell him stories.

Stevie went to school every day, like he as suppose to. The other boys use to fight him all the time and call him stupid. He wasn't stupid. He could learn if he wanted to. But he didn't want to. He would think about his mother and why she didn't like him. He made good grades for a while. From the 3rd to the 6th grade he was a straight A. But his mother didn't care. His father did. He would give him money for his grades. Stevie tried the best he could to make things right. Sometimes, he just sat in his room. Mad. One afternoon, he decided to go for a walk. There was a dog barking at him as he headed to the woods. He ran in the house and got a piece of meat and lured the dog to the woods. As the dog ate the meat, he watched him. Then, he took out his knife that he had begun carrying after the last time he got beat up at school and he stabbed the dog. As the dog yelped and cried, he stabbed him more and more, thinking about his mother as he did.

He buried the dog underneath a log. When his father lost his job with the company, and took back to driving a truck. He had began to leave Stevie again, but this time, Stevie was older. He would talk to his father before he left and his father would give him money so that he could eat and go to school. His mother would stand in the doorway, looking at them. As his father drove away, his mother closed the door and locked it, but Stevie had fixed his window so that he could get in.

He didn't care anymore that she didn't like him. He didn't think about her too much, but when she had men over at night, he would sneak out his window and stand there peaking in the window, watching her be with those men.

And everytime she did, he would find something to kill.

His father came home from the road and one of Steve's mothers friends was leaving out the back door. His father saw him. But he didn't say anything to the man. He went straight to his wife. In the room, Steve heard them fighting and arguing and he heard his father screaming at her. His mother told him that she needed to get out of here. She needed to go away. So they decided they would go on the road. But his father said he would be back. Steve was a junior in high school then. He didn't mind having the house for his own for awhile and his father left him plenty of money. It would be nice not to have his mother looking at him with those eyes. It would be very nice not to hear her in the night with those men. He would miss his father though. His father looked so old and tired by this time. He hugged his son, and Steve had the feeling that he wouldn't see him anymore.

They drove away. His mother didn't look back.

Steve was fine for awhile, he kept his grades up and he did like he was doing when his father was home. But he didn't manage the money well and it ran out. There was no food and the electric got cut off and the phone and the gas. He would go to Miss St. John's house to eat. She was a really nice black lady that lived at the edge of the woods. No one bothered her and she didn't bother anyone. But if someone needed some healing or some medicine, they would send their husbands to her. She fed Steve and he learned her to read.

On night, laying in the bed in the dark and cold house, he realized that his parents were never coming back. He got up and walked through the streets of the quiet town. He was going to go to see if Miss St. John would let him stay there, but he didn't want her to have no trouble. The race relations were not that open minded in this town and he would not like to cause her any grief. She was a kind soul and he really liked her. She treated him more like a mother than his own mother. He walked slowly looking at the lonely street light and the shops closed up. Up the street, he saw a shadow under one of the shops. It was a homeless man. The transients passed through here a lot on their way to somewhere else, because the cops wouldn't mess with them too much, as long as they didn't beg for money. He had a blanket on him from someone. Steve sat beside him on the curb, smoking a cigarette. The bum looked up and asked for one. They sat and talked for awhile and the Steve told him he had some liquor stashed in the woods if the man wanted some. The man gladly followed him. They walked and talked for a while. Steve had his hands in his pockets, fingering the knife he had. As they got to the woods, the man stopped walking and asked Steve where the liquor was. Steve, smiling at the man, took him to the log where he buried the dog,and had the man sit while he went behind the tree. When he came from behind the tree, the man stood and faced him and Steve stabbed him. Holding him close to him, he stabbed him. The man looked Steve in the eyes and all Steve could see was the men that his mother was with in the bedroom. He stabbed him for a long time after he was dead.

Miss St. John had an old shed in the back of her place and she told him that he could stay there. She would fix it up for him. She was sorry about his parents but she told him that people can't choose their families, and if his didn't think enough of him to hang around, good bye to them and hello to steve's world. He could be what ever he wanted and she would take care of him until he decided to move along.

He went home and got his important things. His little things that reminded him of his father. The sheriff met him as he was leaving and told him that he had known his folks were gone but that he was a big enough to handle himself. The sheriff didn't necessarily like the fact that he was staying with the black woman, but he said most white families was stugglin anyway and if it didn't bother him, it didn't bother anyone else. Steve told him that he stayed in a shed in back of the place and that they didn't live in the same house and that he wouldn't be eating in the house with her. That was important. You talked to them, but you didn't sit down to eat with them. The Sheriff told him what a good boy he was.

Steve went to his new home. Miss St. John had fixed the shed up nice. She put curtains on the little windows and a table and chair in the corner with a lamp. He had a cot to sleep on and she put one of her hand made blankets on it and gave him a little plant. When she cooked dinner, she brought it out to him and he ate, alone in the little house. He continued to go to school and he noticed that the kids didn't treat him so bad anymore. He could feel that they felt sorry for the boy whose parents left him and had him living with the colored woman in the woods. He didn't care about those people. He also continued to kill.

When the fall came, Miss St. John got him a little space heater to keep his place warm. He had tired of eating alone and when it got dark, he would go into her house to eat. They would sit at her table and eat in silence at first. Then eventually, they would talk about little things. He continued teaching her about current events and things. She taught him how to cook and do basic medical things. He chopped the wood for her stove and helped her around the house. He asked her where her children were because he could never remember seeing any black kids in town and how she came to be here.

She said that she was here before the white folks started moving in. When the mines opened, they let black men do little tasks and paid them a little bit, but they couldn't live in the area with the whites so her husband built her a cabin out here. He went to work in the mine and she stayed home and kept house. One day, they sent him in the mine to take some water to some of the white men down there and there was an explosion and they never found them. She never remarried, never left and never changed her life. Steve couldn't understand how someone could just let life pass them by and not change after all these years. Miss St. John told him about when the white folks started moving in. They wanted her to move but she wasn't because her husband built this house and she was staying put. They tried to burn her out and she showed him the part of the house that was rebuilt by some townsfolk later after their fathers had burnt it out. When she was a younger woman, she cleaned up some of the houses but most of the folks lost their money when the mine closed up and she took to hunting for little game and growing her own vegetables. She had a bible that looked like it was a hundred years old, but she could never read it. When Steve taught her to read, she was thankful and read her bible for the first time. When he graduated high school, she gave him a 10 dollar bill that she had "just layin' around" and he was so touched. He made sure that her house was secure and chopped enough wood to last her awhile before he started off for Atlanta. The night before he left, she sat him at the table and talked to him.

"It ain't none of my business, but you need to stop killin' folks. I knowd you was doin' it fo' along time. I seed you once, but it ain't my business to tell folks. Bein' mad at your ma ain't gonna justify takin' those lives to God, my son, you need to pray. But I owes you for teachin' me to read my bible and I won't say a word. You be careful in 'lanta"

He fixed her dinner that night, lacing her portion with sleeping pills so that she would sleep soundly. He went to his shack and got his things together. Went back into the house and smothered the old woman while she slept. He cried the whole time and it was the only killing that he regretted. It hurt him to do that to her, but he couldn't take a chance on her telling on him. He placed her bible in her hands and kissed her brown forehead. Then, straightening up her home, he locked the door behind him, put the key under the mat and headed for the bus station for his new life in Atlanta.

VI

He arrived in Atlanta late afternoon and walked out of the bus station downtown. The city was alive with activity and he quickly found a residential hotel and put his stuff there. He got a paper and read about the jobs going on and noticed that they were having a hiring drive for Police officers. He signed up and went through the training, the background checks and everything else.

He didn't have a record anywhere and he passed with flying colors. When he graduated from the academy, he was officially one of Atlanta's finest.

He moved from his little hotel room and got a nice place over near Buckhead close to the Lindbergh train station. There were quite a few Mexicans living around the area, but that didn't bother him. They just went to work and came home. He was assigned to the Stewart avenue area which was perfect for him. It was the part of town notorious for hookers and drugs. He watched the people milling around all the time, with no particular place to go and nothing to do. It was strange to him. Everyone he had ever known had did some type of work. He realized that drugs and prostitution was the work that they did. And it was more than a nine to five job.

Once in awhile,he would remember about the dead people in the woods he left behind. And the black woman who treated him so well that he had to kill her. But those days were long gone. He was Steve St. John, Atlanta Police officer. He met some nice ladies that he hung out with and a really nice older police officer who had a daughter that he talked about all the time. Apparently, he had lost his wife and his daughter had been taking care of him. They played racquet ball together and he saw his daughter once or twice. She was a beautiful lady and he hoped that if he played it nice with the old man, he would be invited to partake of his sweet daughter. And although the dark times were behind him, his appetite remained. He wasn't killing as often as he had as a younger man, but the need was there.

He liked doing things with his cop friends, but their circle was small. They did everything together. In a cop group, cop wives, cop cousin's friends of cops. He cultivated his relationships outside of the cop realm. He had lots of lady friends, black and white. It wasn't because he was overtly good looking, it was because he didn't sweat them for sex. They liked him enough to give it to him, but he never had a girlfriend and didn't really know how to do the relationship thing. But they enjoyed his friendship and they always had a good time together. He laughed because they actually though the was gay. One evening, he got a call from his Beverly, one of the cuter black women he knew. She was going to this party at a swank uptown apartment building. The party was in the penthouse. She wanted Steve to go so that she could go and not be alone. Steve was the perfect escort. They always had something to laugh about. She liked to smoke her weed and when he was able to get a good weed bust, he got her some. She was one of the few women who didn't mind the fact that he was a cop. He didn't act like one. She picked him up and they drove to the downtown apartment building.

When they walked into the place, he was amazed at how nice it was and when he found out who owned it, he was incensed. He lived modestly as a protector of the people and this man lived like a king. He wanted to live like this. Beverly introduced him to the man who owned this place and Steve realized that the drug game wasn't all Stewart avenue, but it had a hierarchy all its own. This man was the head honcho. It impressed Steve and Steve wanted in and he wanted it in a big way. He decided to ditch his cop friends and began a relationship with this black gentleman. His name was Amir. Steve did his best to ingratiate himself to Amir. He let him know when busts were going down so that he could pull his guys off the streets. He let him know what was going on in the project houses where his boys hung out and told him what attracted the cops to watch them. He discussed the advantages of dealing in powder weight as opposed to dealing in the street level. The street level game was good for those who couldn't do better, but now that Amir was living the posh life, he had to distribute to the posh set. Dealing in weight keeps the traffic flow low. Most of the dealers in the projects had houses full of hangers on and women, who, in a fit of jealous rage, would call the cops and turn the guys in, steal their money, and take freebies until the profit margin is all but gone up in smoke. Don't deal in crack. Crack creates the problems. The crack heads buy a lot, but they cause problems. You get into dealing with stolen goods, robberies and assaults. Crack houses get robbed more than residential homes. Each crack dealer trying to cut the other one out.

After their first conversations, Amir invited Steve back. They sat on his balcony, overlooking the beautiful downtown hotel district of Atlanta, watching the limousines move in and out of traffic. Steve pointed to each one. Those are the people you want to deal with. Not the street people. Amir listened intently to this cop. He didn't really trust cops, but the man was making sense. They began to frequent the upscale Buckhead nightclubs as opposed to the neighborhood haunts that Amir used to frequent. His clientele changed and the money rolled in. He cut Steve in for some of the profit. His thanks for showing him the way. The headaches of dealing with the street dealers was gone. No more lost merchandise, no more anything. If the weight purchasers wanted to crack it down to the neighborhoods, it was on them. Amir was out of that loop together.

He and Steve were around each other a lot and he began to trust him just a little more. Steve enjoyed the trust, but more than that, he enjoyed the time he could spend with the upscale people of Atlanta. A cop's life isn't all that pretty, but this cut into Amir's life had put him straight on the road to the big time. And, it left him still able to cruise the crack hoods and get his prey. Once in a while he had to be confronted with the division, questions about things. But Steve kept his homelife to a minimum, something that looked like a cop salary. And even though he always had money, he said it was because he was low maintenance and that he didn't really have any hobbies to spend his money on. The cops eventually believed him. He drove a beat up white older model cop car, a narc-mobile as the street people called it and he had a junk white car that looked similar. The latter was the car he used when he was trolling. And, on those nights when he wasn't partying with Amir, or he was just feeling that way, he made the trek to the Stewart avenue district and picked him up a thrill.

On this particular night, he was angry. The captain was changing his area and giving him a partner. He didn't want a partner and had to fight not to have one. He stated that his connections with the drug busts depended on him being a lone wolf. That's what the people in the neighborhood were use to. If they see him with someone, it would blow it for him and the arrests would drop considerably. After much arguing, he talked them down, but it left him irritated. He drove through the district, late. They had just busted most of the locals and they were away for the week. They would be back. He saw a young lady standing against a darkened building. She was kind of pretty Steve noticed after she got into the car. He drove her around a while, then decided on a price for a blow job. He drove her to a secluded area and she began. It was a good job. She did her work well. Afterwards, she told him that she could give him good ass too. She tried to talk him into going to a place she knew, but he knew a better place. Off near the Chattahoochie. He had never really done this before. Finding his spot, he lay her on an old blanket he kept in his car. Finding his condom, he lay on top of her and penetrated her anally. As he slid in and out of her tightness, he pulled his knife from his back. As she moaned, he stuck it in her, hold his hand over her mouth. She writhed and moaned and the feeling was so intense for Steve. He had never felt like that before. He came as her last breath left her body. He took great care in cleaning his crime scene. There would be no DNA evidence here. He left her, nude, on her stomach, on the dry grass.

Sex and death. What a perfect combination Steve thought as he went home. Sweet sex, sweeter death. She would give no more blow jobs on this earth. As he returned home, his phone was ringing. It was Amir inviting him over. Steve turned him down and took a raincheck. He was weak from his experience tonight and also energized. He wanted to lay still and remember the feeling, over and over again.

Amir understood Steve's wanting to rest. Or so he thought. The party scene was getting more intense with Amir making more money than he could have hoped. He now had time to purchase art and enjoy the fruits of his ill gotten gain. Dealing in weight was a good deal and he wondered why he hadn't thought of it himself. He looked at Steve in a different light. It was the second time in his life a man not of his race had helped him along by showing him the ropes.

VII

Amir was born in the projects. His mother was a quiet lady who lived on the 15th floor in this large building. She worked at the Chinese market down the street. The market in the black neighborhood that blacks never ran. It was always someone from another ethnic background. Right now it was the Chinese people. His mother worked hard for Change the shop owner and she was the only black in the neighborhood that he trusted. He even let her handle his cash. She kept his books and occasionally he gave her little bonuses. When she first started working there, Chang's wife was there. She was an old frail looking woman and she sat near the cash register, carefully watching Amir's mother making sure she didn't steal. But the woman died and left Chang with no one but Amir's mother. Amir would come and visit his mother at the store when he was little. Chang kept him in the back where he lived and Amir watched t.v. ate rice dishes and things like that.

Before Amir's father left home, Amir would lay in the bed and listen to his parents having sex. They were loud and rough and he would hear his mother crying sometimes during the deed. He would peek in the room and see his father doing things to his mother that he couldn't understand. He would slap her around and pull her hair, then make her get on her knees and put him in her mouth. All the while she was crying. Afterward, she would hold him and kiss him and he would tell her how much he loved her. His father use to say that you can't have pleasure without pain.

One day, his father left and he never came back. His mother went into her shell and didn't say a whole lot to anybody. Some nights, after she got home from the store and had been drinking, she would beat Amir, then hold him to her breasts, her nipples hard in his face.

Some afternoons, when he was supposed to be home cleaning up the house and staying out of trouble, he would sit on the stoop and watch the drug dealers and the pimps hanging out in the streets. They had nice cars and nice clothes and they treated him really nice. They knew his mother worked for Chang, she was one of the few women who actually worked in the neighborhood and they made sure they kept an eye on him. This particular afternoon, Amir was sitting there, one of the other young men came up to him. He told him that he wanted him to take a package up to a theater off 42nd street. Amir knew where he was talking about because his mother had taken him shopping there all the time, sometimes they just went to walk around. Amir told the man that he wasn't really allowed to leave, but the young man told him that his mother would be busy at the store for a long time. It was the first of the month and it was a busy day. Amir took the package and headed to the theater. It was an X rated place and when he got there, he went around back like he was told and met the owner Mr. Cavetti. Mr. Cavetti took the package and looked at Amir. He remarked at how young Amir was and that he shouldn't be doing this, but he paid Amir and Amir left and headed home. He got back just in time. His mother had left the store and although she was coming up the street toward him she didn't notice him. He ducked through the alleyway and found the young man and gave him his money. The young man paid Amir 50.00 for his troubles. More money than Amir had seen in his life that was his alone. He went up to his apartment through the back way and met his mother coming down the hall. She had groceries and he opened the door for her. She asked him about his day while she made dinner. He saw the bottle of gin hidden in her purse and knew what kind of night it was going to be. He took the 50 dollars and stashed it in a coffee can in his room. Amir was 13 at this point and his mother had been doing the same thing to him for years. He got a perverse sort of pleasure from it, but he knew it was wrong.

This night, she came into his room, cussing incoherently and she slapped his face hard. He stood there, looking at her and she took him into her arms. Holding him, she tried to put her nipples in his mouth and this time he refused. He hugged her back and told her that he was too old for those games anymore. She sat on his bed and cried for a long time. After that night, he began hanging out with the young drug dealers and filling his coffee can with 50 dollar bills.

Some nights, he would come in between runs and check on his mother. She would be sitting there, drinking quietly to herself. He noticed that she looked old and haggard and he wanted to fix her up. Afterall, she was still a relatively young woman and yet, she looked like she was 70. She only did her hair when she was going to work and she never went out on a date or had men in the house. She just sat there, collecting dust like all the furnishing in the house. She never opened the curtains anymore and didn't cook too much either. Amir would cook her a meal and make sure she ate something. He noticed that she didn't look him in the face anymore. Shame was in her eyes and he didn't want her to feel ashamed. He knew that what she had was a sickness and he that she needed to be loved. He tried to fix her up with different men that he met in his rounds. Even bought her nice dresses, but they only came by once in awhile. They told him that she was a nice lady, but he knew inside she missed his father. She missed him for years. If it wasn't for the store, she would probably never leave the house. Just sit here and waste away to nothing, like so many women.

Amir continued to deliver packages to Mr. Cavetti. He had the privilege of going to the man's house now. Not meeting him at the seedy little theater he ran. Mr. Cavetti lived uptown and had a nice place there. It was full of art work. Paintings, sculptures and art magazines. Mr. Cavetti, an avid art fan would tell Amir about the pieces and where he got them and how to know the difference between real and fake art. When he had parties, he had Amir there to serve his guests. He told Amir that white people were impressed when you had coloreds serving. Personally he didn't dislike any group of people, but the coloreds just seem to always come up with the short end of the stick. It was just the way it was, Mr. Cavetti told him. But he liked Amir and taught him everything he knew about art, throwing lavish parties and other social graces. He instilled in Amir, a love for beautiful things and the knowledge to help him achieve those things. Amir didn't want to be a drug runner all his life.

Before Mr. Cavetti had began tutoring him, Amir had dropped out of school and was destined to be a child of the streets, but Mr. Cavetti taught him the importance of getting an education so that if he achieved success, he would know how to keep it and not end up rotting away in some prison, all his ill gotten money gone. No body likes you when you're down and out, Amir, is what he use to tell him. Intelligence will help you keep what you got and get out of the game. That's the trick to doing illegal activities. Knowing when to get out, take the money and run.

Amir had moved up in the large underworld in this big east coast city. He knew all the major players and had his own territory. He kept Mr. Cavetti as his client however, even though Mr. Cavetti was part of another territory. But it was understood by all that he was exclusive to Mr. Cavetti and because Mr. Cavetti spent big money and had big friends, no one bothered to question or challenge the situation. He went on art trips with Mr. Cavetti sometimes, as his personal assistant. They flew to Paris, Rome and met with people in Atlanta. Amir liked Atlanta. It was a beautiful city and he never thought for a moment that he would live in Paris or Rome, he knew that eventually he would move to Atlanta. It would be conducive to his lifestyle and blacks had wealth in Atlanta. No one would think it an odd situation.

II

By the time Amir was 18, he had 30 coffee cans of 50 dollar bills. His mother had come through her crisis period and was dating a man who was a lot like his father in certain areas. Areas that were important to his mother. He hadn't lived at home for a couple of years, but he kept his key and was always welcomed. One night late, he had stopped by to check on his mother. He could hear the sounds coming from the bedroom. Familiar sounds of pleasure and pain and he knew his mother would be alright. He decided that now was the time to make his move to Atlanta. He slipped out of the apartment and went home, stopping by to pick up one of his many women friends for a little fun. He had lots of women who came by his house for his unique kind of love making. They liked to be abused and he enjoyed abusing them. Pleasure and pain. He had learned well.

He went to see Mr. Cavetti a few days later and told him of his plans to move to Atlanta. Mr. Cavetti was sad to lose him, but he gave him the names of some people to contact and to keep him in the underworld activity. There was a lot of activity in Atlanta, but you had to know the right people to be a player in the game and Mr. Cavetti made sure that he would not have to start at the bottom. He reminded Amir to remember when to get out of the game. "I would hate to find out you were rotting in prison somewhere Amir. You have a noble name and you should be living up to that name. Don't be a stupid boy, do the right thing."

He always thought it was funny that Mr. Cavetti always called him boy. But he knew it was because of how he was raised and never held it against the old man. Amir was on his way to Atlanta.

The bus trip was long. But Amir didn't want to fly. He wanted to look as the city was behind him. He had said good bye to his mother and left her some money. He didn't say goodbye to his friends. He wanted them to think he was in prison. Kept them from asking questions. He won't miss the mean streets. He looked forward. Forward to his life in Atlanta. A few more years in the game and he can forget this life. Live in the fast lane with the people with the money. He thought about his mother's little apartment and the projects. He thought about the girls he ravished in his place. He thought about why his father left. As the bus rolled down the road, he let all those thoughts fly behind him, like the exhaust from the bus. He would find a nice woman who would share his bed and the world he was going to create for himself. He would collect the best art and show his art collection. The High Museum was in Atlanta, and it was beautiful. He could go there and see the beautiful things and get into the art community. And no one would ever know he was just a drug dealer from the big east. He thanked God and Mr. Cavetti in his silent ride to freedom.

He arrived in Atlanta in the morning. It was going to be a hot one, the sun already burning the mists out of the sky. He could see the skyline as he approached the city and felt an excitement inside him. Mr. Cavetti had arranged for him to have an apartment in Midtown, to give himself time to get established. He wasn't sure where he was going, but there was a man waiting for him when he arrived. He took him to his place. The man talked on about how Mr. Cavetti highly recommended him and that he better be worth the praise. He told him to get settled in and that there was a party tonight that he should attend. He would send a limo to pick him up around 8. He smiled at Amir. After the party, the business would begin. He didn't have to wait to be initiated. Mr. Cavetti's word was enough and he would be set up after the weekend festivities. For the time being, Amir had time on his hands. He walked around the hotel district, there was plenty of excitement, people around and about, restaurants open. He walked past that, past the Peachtree center station openings and on toward five points.

At five points, he saw people going and coming. He got a seat on the mezzanine and watched the people, the real Atlantans. People getting off from work, or trying to get to work, kids riding the train home after hanging out. There were uniforms of all types, Picadilly's, Church's Chicken, Popeyes, Woolworth's, every burger joint you could imagine. Hotel employees, all cooks wore the same pants. It was the women who dressed differently. He could always spot the cooks. Those standard issue pants always giving them away. There were men sitting around drinking wine out of the bag, and hustlers selling gold chains or watches or what have you. There were makeshift booths and real booths setup where you could buy fruit or juices, peanuts or candy, magazines, sandwiches and anything you didn't see, he was sure you could ask for it. He wondered if they had any idea what was going on at the Ritz. He wondered if they cared. There were people sitting at a small Chinese restaurant, eating fish and drinking beer, talking and laughing. He walked in and looked around and then went back outside. He wasn't hungry. He just wanted to see everyone. There were ladies with gold teeth and lots of hair. Hair in braids, hair piled up and sprayed so that it wouldn't move. Purple hair, blond hair. He smiled and wondered what was the deal with blond haired black women. Was it true blonds had more fun? The men looked hard, some of them. Like life just kicked them around and this was there only outlet. The huddled close to the women, looking at him suspiciously. He was much too overdressed for this crowd. They wondered if he was there to steal there street business, but they didn't have to worry. His clientele was bigger than that.

Amir got on the train and went to the Arts center station. When he walked out of and stood on Peachtree, he was looking directly at the High Museum of Art. He was impressed. It was closing at this time and he made a point that he would come here tomorrow as soon as it opened. There were restaurants down the streets with tables set up outside so you could eat and take in the ambiance that was Atlanta. He knew he would love this place. Upscale all the way. He saw people heading somewhere with coolers and back packs and things. Groups of people so he followed. They were heading to the park. Amir could hear the music playing and walked with the crowds of people.

III

Piedmont Park was having a jazz festival. Headliners and local talent was the attraction and the park was full of partiers. People had their grills out cooking, laying on blankets and hanging out. It was a hot day, but no one seemed to mind. You could catch a whiff of weed floating above the throng. People on roller blades and any type of food you wanted if you didn't want to cue your own.

Amir walked through the park, dodging the bladers and looking at the lake. The sounds and rhythms of the music were everywhere. It looked like an oasis in the city. The tall building circling the park like protective icons, watching its people below, central park with southern hospitality. He saw all the beautiful women, black and white and he was entranced. This was definitely the place to be.

Morgan and her father were sitting in the grass under a nice full tree. There were 3 other families there, bbq grills going with the smell of ribs and chicken all over. Her cooler full of wine coolers and her father's pint of spirits, they sat and enjoyed the music of the jazz festival. There were children running and playing and having a good time. Couples holding hands and walking, people throwing Frisbees to their dogs. Morgan sat back and enjoyed it all. Tito had not begun playing yet, but the other bands were just as enjoyable. There was an afterparty going on when the festivities in the park were over. She would try to ditch her father and check it out.

Steve was on patrol for the park festivities. He rode his horse around watching the people playing and he could hear the music over his own thoughts. He couldn't enjoy this time at the park, his mind preoccupied with what he felt he needed to do this evening.

There were no potential victims here. But there were lots of beautiful women here. There was a young lady walking by herself. Enjoying the music, in her own world. He wondered about her then saw her little boy run toward her with a huge glider he had just caught off the wind. He smiled at it, but wouldn't approach her. He watched the people skating and walking, throwing Frisbees. He could smell the marijuana in the air and was trying to find out where it originated,but it was too hard to tell in this amount of people. Little kids came up to him to pet his horse, eyes wide open at the wonder of it all. He wanted to take them all for rides, but he couldn't he was on duty. He did wish they didn't try to feed him. He was on a strict diet and these little treats were not good for him. He was on patrol also. A four legged patrolman for Atlanta Police dept.

Amir didn't want to think about business today, but he noticed that there were plenty of places where you could hide out and handle your business. He chose an area off the parks main drag where there were just a few bikers and skate boarders. People trying to park on the busy street had to walk this way, but they were concentrating on getting to the music. They didn't even look at him.

Amir could still hear the music getting heated up so he decided to wander a little closer to the band stand, the Latin rhythms moving him inside. Yes, he was home.

Morgan and her father headed toward the bandstand where a new band was performing. They were right in the front, enjoying all of the concert with no interruption. The view was great, Morgan wished she had her camera with her. It was fantastic. There were people dancing with those Latin rhythms that Morgan wished she had. Her father was dancing with a beautiful Hispanic lady and he wasn't feeling any pain. His pint almost gone. She didn't know he could dance like that. The crowd loved watching him. She hadn't seen him have this much fun since . . . well, she didn't want to think back to that. She would get him home and try to get to that after party. Maybe some sexy Latin man would show her how to move like that.

As she stood there moving to the beat, a very nice looking gentleman took her hand and began dancing with her. He had that Latin rhythm and she laughed because she didn't. He said his name was Amir and he was showing her some steps, out in the grass, in Piedmont Park. The night was warm in so many ways.

Steve had turned his horse in at dusk and was walking back through the park to get to his car. He watched the partiers dancing to the Latin beat and could see people dancing at the stage. There wasn't a concert he had ever been to that you could be that close to a performer for free. He stood for a moment, watching an older gentleman dancing really great with a young lady. To look at him, you wouldn't have thought the old guy could move that way. He watched and smiled to himself, but the smile was short lived. He had to get to his car and get to where he really wanted to be. Searching for a victim.

When the music was over and the park was darkening, Amir headed back to his car. He remembered his party that he was invited to tonight. He thought about the young lady he was dancing with and laughed to himself because he didn't even get her name. He watched her walking off, holding the old dude up. That man was feeling no pain. But he had a real good time.

The lights were all aglow. He wanted someone to be with him tonight. The party was at the Ritz Carlton and was invitation only. He had decided to forego the Limo ride and enjoyed the walk through the downtown area. Atlantans were dressed in their best nightwear and he paused more than once to watch the sexy southern women go by on their way to some party. He hoped they were going were he was going. Amir made a note to contact Mr. Cavetti to see if his pull could get him an apartment in this area. He wanted to be here.

Morgan helped her father to the car. The after party was out of the question. Her father was just too intoxicated and she knew that she would have to stay and make sure he was alright. She drove them through town, looking at the lights and wondering what the real single people were doing tonight. She wanted to be out there, but her father was all she had and he had nobody but her. She couldn't leave him alone. If she could get him to date, then it would free up her time and she could date too. But for the time being, they had each other. She wondered what it would be like to have a man hold her and make love to her. She wanted it so bad. Her father was snoring lightly in the seat beside her. He kept mentioning her mother's name periodically like he was talking to her. She glanced and could see a tear roll down his face. He cried a lot in his sleep and she could hear him on the couch sometimes. Heart breaking sobs that would make her want to cry also. But she never did. She held them in and was ready to deal with him the mornings following that. He was always so subdued and quiet then. She usually made breakfast then, so he wouldn't have to try.

She pulled into the driveway and into the garage and helped her father out the car. She would get the cooler in the morning. She took him to his room, knowing that when he awoke, he would get out of there, but she put him there anyway. She wanted to sit up and read a little and she didn't want to do it in her bedroom. It just reminded her of how she was spending her Saturday nights and she didn't want to get any more depressed than she was already.

She turned on the track lights for a subtle lighting and sat down on the couch. She thought about the cops she had met and she didn't really want to date them. The guys in the organization were interesting when they were on assignments, but not otherwise. They talked about their work and although she enjoyed busting the bad guys in her clandestine organization she did not really fit in to their social pattern either. Did she fit in anywhere? Would she ever fit in? She always felt so out of place in this world. Maybe she wasn't meant to be in it. She laughed about being from another time and another place and just woke up here one day in the body of a little girl called Morgan.

It was like that as long as she could remember. Never quite fitting in. Always feeling like she was on the outside looking in. She was much better when she was in disguise playing a character when she was working. But for herself, she didn't feel like she belonged anywhere. But the night was so fun, she wouldn't depress herself thinking of what an outcast she was, she put the music on softly and read her book.

Steve drove down Stewart avenue. The strip was hot tonight. He was in a car that would not stand out in a crowd. He didn't want to be remembered. He wanted to anonymously get in, get his victim and get out. People would simply remember that it was a white car, or a brown car, nothing flashy. No identifying marks. He had taken the license plate off one of the cars of his friend who had a junk yard and replaced the license of this car he was driving. There was no sting in progress this month, so he wouldn't get caught up in that mess. Being a cop, he was privy to information that the average john wouldn't know. Like when the undercover cuties would be put out as bait to catch the unsuspecting Johns looking for a cheap thrill. They should be able to recognize the plants however, he always thought. They looked so much more well kept than the real hookers. They real ones looked like they were hookers, with hard life emblazoned in their eyes and their skin and the cheap makeup they wore. They always looked a bit downtrodden. You had to watch those things. If a hooker looked too clean and neat even though she tried to look otherwise, you knew she wasn't the common whores that hung out. She didn't look abused enough. Inside.

He slowed down toward a side street where there was a rather thin looking young girl standing almost in a bush. There was a dim street light above her and she was just standing there, watching the strip. He circled the block and came up the other side of the street from her. She turned and looked at him and tried to smile. You could tell she didn't want to be here, but she sauntered over to the car anyway.

Steve smiled at her and she looked at him. Then she backed away from the car. He looked too much like a cop. He got out of the car and walked over to her, explaining that he was just out the military and that he wasn't a cop. He could tell that she didn't trust him, but he talked her into it anyway. Inside his mind, he thought the she should have listened to her instincts. They were very good. This would be her probably first and only trick of this evening. And she would have nothing to show for it, and no one to tell about it unless spirits talked. She tried to direct him to a spot that she knew and he talked her out of that and drove to his spot. The farther they got away from the city the more worried her face became, but she didn't fight him, just rode in silence, watching the street signs disappear and trying to get a mental bearing as to where she was going. She didn't know the area and he could tell.

When he got to his spot, she was reluctant to get out of the car and he had to pull her out. She began to cry and tell him not to hurt her. It was her first time out on the strip and she was just doing it to make some extra money. Steve held her hand and pulled her along to the woods. As he started to take his clothes off, she relaxed a little and took her clothes off. As he got onto her and began to penetrate, the knife also began to penetrate and she tried to fight him when she realized what was happening. But she was very thin and he held her hands above her as he completed what he needed to do. She spit at him as she took her last breath. He never saw anger in the eyes of his victims before. And this girl was angry. He laughed at the irony of her leaving as he was cuming.

Steve carefully got dressed and picked up her clothes and any other thing that might be construed as evidence. Her hands, still above her head where he had pinned them, the blood looking obscene in the dark.

He found a large piece of log and laid it in front of the body and covered everything with brush and leaves. He kept his lights off until he had reached a safe distance and continued toward his home.

IV

Morgan had fallen asleep on the couch and she was awaken the smell of bacon and eggs. Her father survived the night afterall. He was dancing a sort of tango, cha cha thing in the kitchen, some Latin jazz playing on the boom box that she had put in the kitchen to help her set the mood when she decided to cook.

She wiped the sleep out of her eyes and headed to the bathroom to freshen up before she hit the kitchen. She was hungry and she was remembering the park and the after party that she didn't get to attend. As she headed for the bathroom she heard her private cell phone ringing softly and she knew that John was trying reach her. She detoured to her room and picked up the phone.

"Good morning, how are things?"

"Fine John, what's happening?"

"A nice assignment for you. Or shall I say for Amoire."

Amoire was the identity she assumed when they were trying to catch someone who had a fancy for exotic women. Amoire was a dark-haired beauty with green/blue eyes, who Morgan created from a dream she had. She liked the Amoire character because it allowed her shed all her inhibitions. The nationality of her prey, she would find out later, but if they were calling her in, it meant that he had a taste for women, and men could not penetrate his inner sanctum. She would make sure she kept herself fascinating to the gentleman.

The packet would arrive shortly after the phone call by courier, and she knew that the plans were made. She would go to Holland, and posing as one of the many exotic prostitutes of the land, would make her self available to the prince who was a leader in the heroin trade, and just never got caught.

Morgan made her way to the kitchen, the smell over whelming her and she sat and ate with her father. She told him that she had a modeling job which would take her to Holland for a little while and that she would stay in touch with him.

"That's what the phone call was about? I heard your cell phone, how come you don't let them call on this line?"

"Well, dad, I keep the phone with me so I just have access to any jobs that our available. Sometimes, if they have to leave a message, by the time I get it, they would have assigned someone else to the shoot, and I hate to lose assignments. So I have to be readily available at a moments notice. The time between a message left and a lucrid assignment, is too costly."

"You don't need the cash, why do you do it?"

"I just like it Dad. It is exciting, and who knows, I may be discovered and actually make a good living at it, so that I can postpone my journey into the world of police work for a while."

She kissed her father's face

"besides, some rich man may discover I am a natural beauty and sweep me off my feet."

"He doesn't have to be rich, baby doll."

The Package arrived fed ex. Morgan looked at the paperwork as she was heading toward hartsfield. She would read the rest of it on the plane.

She arrived at her flight early, and checked in. Taking her seat on the plane, she began to thoroughly analyze the sheets. He was a white man, of European ancestry. Probably a little Greek in him also. Very attractive. Greenish blue eyes, thick dark hair. Complexion not quite olive, but he probably tans very well. She was set to be delivered the red light district. The plans were arranged to have her stay at one of the better houses. The house that he was known to frequent. He had a reputation of being a kind, but somewhat aggressive lover. The girls liked him because he tipped generously and was known to take a girl to live with him for a while in his palace as his personal concubine. That was her plan, to be picked to hang out at the palace.

They were to keep her on ice until he arrived and then present her as the new flavor of the month. They weren't sure when he would arrive, but they know he would be there. Morgan chilled out and explored her new digs. The place was very lavishly furnished, large comfortable bed. She put on one her silky night gowns, putting perfume in the sensitive places and waited. She didn't have to wait long.

He showed up late on a Saturday evening. They told him that they had a special treat for him, and buzzed her room. He arrived. The picture did not do him justice. He was absolutely beautiful to Morgan. He had a style and grace that she couldn't place, must have been the royal breeding. He looked at her and smiled.

"Amoire is an interesting name"

"my favorite piece of furniture."

"furniture."

"yes, where you keep all your beautiful things locked away inside."

"and do you keep your beautiful things locked inside, Amoire?"

"just my heart."

He walked over to where she was sitting on the bed. He placed his hand on her leg and rubbed it softly. Morgan felt an involuntary shudder go through her body, like electricity. His hand was so soft and smooth. Like chocolate cream.

"you skin is like silk."

"so is yours."

"How would you like to come and play at my palace Miss Amoire? We can have so much fun together. I will dress you as my African queen."

"Well, I am not sure."

"You are so timid. Talk to the other girls, while I make the arrangements. They will tell you, I am not a monster."

He departed and 2 of the Swiss girls ran into the room. They spoke with accents, and Morgan loved the song quality of their voices.

"you going with the Prince, yes?"

"he will be good to you, yes."

They touched her hair.

"Soft hair, much body to it."

Morgan smiled.

The prince came back into the room. The Swiss women smiled at him and exited, looking back at Morgan and smiling.

"I have obtained permission for my African queen to accompany me for an extended weekend."

"I'll get dressed."

"no need."

He went into the hall and came out with a fox coat. Full length and beautiful.

"put yourself in this. My car is downstairs waiting."

The fox felt absolutely famously on her body. She wrapped it around the little outfit she was wearing and suddenly wondered if she could keep herself focused on the deed at hand. The man was going down, and she had to take him there.

But, he is wonderful. Was she really ready for this assignment. She hoped she could keep herself focussed.

They walked out of the building and into a waiting limosene. He opened the door for her and she slid into the plush interior. It felt like a silk stocking on a fresh shaved leg. She sat back and he motioned the driver to go. The sun was just setting and the view of the windmills and the tulips was spectacular. They drove down winding lanes and out into the countryside. He watched her every expression and she tried to act like she was sophisticated and use to this panoramic view, but her awe was showing. He smiled at her.

"where are you from?"

"Chicago."

"Chicago, land of the bulls."

"and Daley politics"

"yes, that too. How did you get into this business and way over here in Holland?"

"I was walking the streets one night, a very nice man saw me and took me off the streets. He brought me here and I haven't seen him anymore."

"just like that? Did your family miss you?"

"I didn't really have any family. My mother left us a long time ago, and when I got older, my daddy walked away and left me with my older brothers and sisters. They were into their own thing, lost the house that we lived in and we went our separate ways. I went to the street because I had no where else to go."

"Do you like what you do?"

"its a living that I had to make, that's all. I don't think about it too much. If I did, I would cry all the time. Having different men all the time. That's not what I thought my life would be."

"and what did you think your life would be?" He had positioned himself closer to her, looking into her eyes. Morgan closed her eyes to him, and looked down at the fox she was wearing, wondering why the ride was taking so long.

"I wanted to get married, have some children and raise my family while my husband went to work and I baked cookies and made lunch and cleaned house."

"Like June Cleave?"

"who?"

"you know, the beaver's mom. That t.v. Show, beaver."

Morgan laughed.

"You mean June Cleaver. Yeah, sort of like that."

Finally, the journey ended. At the end of a long country road, with trees on both sides was a chateau. Large and spacious with a pool that was enclosed. There were tulips and flowers everywhere and a large field where they were horses to ride. Morgan stood and took in the grandeur of it all.

"come my African queen, you can see all this later, you will be here for a while."

"how long is a while? I really should get back soon."

"back to whom? Or to what? The few things you do have are on their way here."

"My things are coming here?"

Morgan quickly went through her mind to see what it was she had exactly with her. Anything that can be gone into or looked at. She took stock mentally of what was at the house and what was safely at the hotel. She took a breath and relaxed. She didn't make any mistakes. She can't think about mistakes right now. She had to go along with this joy ride. It was what should have happened.

He walked her into the house. It was so spacious, she could hear her footfalls echo as she headed to the winding stairwell.

"go and take a nice hot bath, we will have supper together."

She ascended the stairs and in the long hallway, there were many beautiful rooms. She picked one that was done in a sort of African bush motif. There were large as life giraffes and zebra, a white skinned rug, a fireplace. She went into the room and he followed behind her.

"This is a nice room, my queen, but not for you. You will stay in my room with me. My man has laid out an appropriate dinner dress for you. Get comfortable and dinner will be soon. I will leave you after I take you to the room, but I will be there in time for supper. My man will come and get you when it is time."

He walked her down the hall to the last door. Or rather doors. It was a double set of doors. In rich mahogany. He opened the doors for her and it was as if she stepped into a palace. There were gold lame chairs, queen Ann style, sitting on either side of the door. Glass and brass covered every wall where there wasn't a Picasso. Through another doorway was the bed itself. Huge. With white satin comforter, red satin pillows, and a balcony. There was an Amoire, red cherry. Morgans favorite piece of furniture.

She smiled at it.

"Yes, I have one amoire, but it doesn't breathe like you. Its beautiful to look at, but I like to touch."

He kissed her naked shoulders as he helped her take off the fox. On one side of the bed was a white evening gown, sheer white with diamond studs all over. Little tiny beads of light. It was low cut in the back and the neckline plunged very deep.

"I don't think I have enough cleavage to do that justice."

"you have plenty. You will see."

He showed her to the bathroom, where are large, sunken tub was filled with bubbles. There was a glass of champagne on the edge table, with the bottle cooling in the ice bucket.

"relax my queen, I will see you later at dinner."

He exited the mini palace and closed the doors behind him. She heard the lock turn on the large doors.

Morgan looked around her surroundings, hoping she could pull off this assignment. She was not accustomed to such riches before and she was unsure how to take it. She sat on one of the chairs and just stared. She said to herself over and over that this man was a criminal. A criminal that must be taken down. She went to the settee and went through her things. They had been neatly folded and packed for her and everything was there. Except her cell phone. The beautician had fixed her hair very good, the soft curls holding up in spite of everything. Her makeup bag was undisturbed and she opened it. Everything was in place. In her small valise was her cell phone, but the battery had been removed. It was useless until she could get to the hotel. She wondered why she was locked in. Well, better enjoy this while I can, she said to herself as she undressed completely and got into the bath. The water had a satiny feel. Not like the hard water in Atlanta. She slid and almost slipped into the large tub. She laughed to herself. She lit the fragrant candles that were on the sides of the tub, and taking a large comb clip that was sitting on the side of the tub, she pulled her hair up and let the bubbles come up to her neck. Closing her eyes, she relaxed for a moment, thinking about how to do this case, without falling in love with the prince. She had to keep a closed mind. Not let this get to her. Morgan wondered why she couldn't find a man like this in the real world. Then she smiled again, unfortunately this is the real world. Prince charming was usually above the law, just a tad. Soft, jazz music began playing around her and she opened her eyes for a moment to see the prince standing there watching her.

"My business didn't take that long. You look so relaxed. Mind if I join you?"

"the tub is big enough for two."

He took his clothes off slowly, watching her watching him. He had a fantastic body, not the over grown muscles of a workout freak, but very toned. And he was not built extremely large in the other department. Morgan was glad of that. He behind her in the tub and situated her between his legs. He took the aromatic soap and began to message her breasts with each soapy hand. She could feel him getting aroused and he began to kiss her neck. Morgan felt herself stiffen involuntarily and he noticed.

"You are nervous? Why, this is your job isn't it?"

"my job is to do this in my room, quickly and quietly, not with all this romance. This is unsettling to me."

He nuzzled her neck.

"I am glad you are not use to romance. That means you have not been jaded yet. I can romance and love you and you will appreciate it. Most of the nice girls at the house can pretend well, but I always know when they are pretending. You are not jaded yet, and this is good."

He washed her all over and helped her exit the tub without falling. He lay her on the bed, carefully removing her evening gown, and lay himself on top of her. He kissed and caressed her body, to the point where she was wanting him to come inside her and take her there. She moaned in ecstasy at all the touches and kisses. She closed her eyes and a single tear fell from the corner of her eye. Morgan could feel him watching her and she was trying to make sure her contact had not swam loose in the fluid. She took her hand and gently pushed it in place. He thought she was wiping her tears.

"why do you cry? Is this not enjoyable."

"yes, it is, but, I . . . I . . . I am not that experienced. I know how to make money, but I don't know how to make love."

He smiled at her and kissed her face.

"I may keep you my African queen. You are not of the ordinary. You are so naive. I may have to keep you."

He got up and kissed her quickly.

"get dressed, we will sup now."

"but I thought . . ."

"patience my little queen. The night has just begun. This is the beginning of a long vacation for you. If not a lifetime. I have not decided the latter yet, but we have plenty of time to get to know each other. I will know you. You do not seem like a girl from the streets of Chicago. That is your story, and I won't pry, but you will tell me the truth. In your time. I will give you all the time you want."

Morgan went to the dressing table and began to put on her makeup. She didn't want hooker hard, but socialite soft makeup. She applied it carefully. There were some very nice scents in beautiful bottles on the dressing table and she put the scents in the most aromatic spots on her body. Then, she slid into the dress. It was a perfect fit. Even the top. It showed off her small cleavage very well.

Amir attended the party of the high rollers. It was an interesting set up. There were beautiful women of every race. He was glad to see the beautiful sisters holding their own against the blue eyed blonds that most men of power find appealing. He knew their line of work and was secretly pleased that if a black woman had to be in service, she could serve in this capacity instead of on the mean streets getting beat up and abused. He was escorted to a back room where there was a roulette wheel, 21 and craps. A private room. Still more beautiful women were in here, but only one sister. She had the skin of an Egyptian princess, the red tones making her look like a copper penny. He found out later that she was the head man's private piece of ass and no one, not anybody talked or touched her in anyway. He smiled his acknowledgment of her achievement and she smiled a quick smile and looked away. He remembered to himself to thank Mr. Cavetti for the hook up. This was going to be grand.

The gentleman looked at him quietly and the head man spoke.

"You have come highly recommended by my east coast rep. Mr. Cavetti thinks you would be an asset to us and I want to be able to count on you. You can have the clientele that, for whatever reason feel better dealing with an African-American as opposed to other races. The clientele you cultivate for yourself is yours. All we ask is hour share. We have changed your location to one more befitting your stature within the organization."

Then he called for a man to come out one of the anterooms. He was blindfolded and tied. He was sat down in a chair against the wall. A thick piece of wood was placed behind his head and a pillow in front. The head man made a motion and one of the larger men who were quietly standing around, pulled out a gun with a silencer on it and hold the gun against the pillow, pulled the trigger. Amir almost jumped out of his skin.

"this is what happens when I am doubled crossed. I don't ask questions nor do I require explanations. Right is right. You have graduated from a street hustler to a position that will amass you a great wealth, if you truly know how to play the game. If not . . ."

And he pointed at his men to discard of the body.

" . . . you are garbage and my mother always told me to take out the trash or your house will stink."

Amir wiped the beads of sweat that had accumulated on his brow. Did the temperature go up in here? No, he could still feel the cool air blowing, but he was sweating, none the less. He had seen guys killed in the streets. Shot down over this or that and it never bothered him before. It was the game. But this, this was entirely different. The ruthlessness was something that Amir never really experienced.

"I will have my driver take you to your new apartment. We are sorry that we had to put you in such shoddy accommodations but when you arrived, the place wasn't ready. We understood you love your art and I had a time finding all the pieces that Mr. Cavetti recommended. Now, enjoy the party and when you are ready to leave, just let me know."

"I am ready now."

"Are you sure? Yes, I suppose you want to get used to your new environment and your new job. Go home, get comfortable. Tomorrow, we do business."

They arrived at the high rise apartments that were just around the corner from the Ritz. It was beautiful and Amir hoped that his place was far enough up as to see the whole city laid out before him. His city. He was not to be disappointed. They walked up to the large building, past the guard at the gate and was met by someone who the driver called on the car phone.

"Mr. Cavetti highly recommends you to this place Sir. I understand you are to be a curator at one of his new museums he is opening up soon."

Amir was taken aback by the man, he had no idea what Mr. Cavetti told him.

"yes, I am. I need to be in the heart of the city. My clientele expect that from me."

"yes sir, we have a place with the most beautiful and spectacular view of downtown Atlanta. It was just recently vacated by business who was relocated to Panama, I think. You do understand that it is furnished with the basics"

"Such as?"

"you will have to see. I cannot describe it to you, I haven't been here in awhile, buy my decorator assures me that it should meet with your tastes, being an art curator."

"Thank you."

Amir loved the way this man was falling all over him. He would send Mr. Cavetti some Bulgarian caviar, his favorite, to thank him for the gesture. Mr. Cavetti, although getting on in years, still enjoyed his pleasures, as he called them, caviar, champagne and young fresh girls. Amir laughed because he knew that he would enjoy the caviar even if he wasn't physically able enough to really enjoy the young girls. He could look at them.

The walked into the doorway of the apartment. The foyer was spacious and he loved the peach tinted marble floor. Walking into the living area, there was a perfectly muted colored divan and 2 wing chairs. Neutral tones that he could build on. There was an oriental rug in the living area, and Amir made a note to replace that. Down the small corridor was the kitchen which was large and airy. The appliances were color coordinated to the dishes and things. They were black and gold tone, and liked that, here he wouldn't change a thing. The kitchen opened out onto the large balcony that overlooked the beautiful hotel district of downtown Atlanta. He could see the limousines driving here and there, people walking across the streets, looking like those small plastic figures you could by a long time ago. The cars and limo's looked like you could reach down and pick it up, move it to another location. Your own private playset. The other opening from the kitchen went into what the realtor called a play room. You could have parties and dance or set up a large table for dinner parties. It was a nice room to entertain in. Soundproofed and with a built in stereo system and a miniature movie screen, you could do what you wanted in there. It was not decorated because the realtor said, we like to leave the entertainment to the tastes of our owners.

Out of that room and semi-separated from the rest of the house was the master bedroom. Large and roomy, it had no windows, but very lavish tapestries on the walls. The bed was done in hunter green, and there was a wetbar and large bathroom with sunken tub. Amir would change this room as well, but he kept that to himself. Off the master bedroom was a smaller, guest room. It also had its own bath, but it was much smaller.

Amir was pleased. The realtor thanked him and stated that it was ready for immediate occupancy, that Mr. Cavetti had made all the arrangements. He gave him the necessary information and keys and pass keys. He told him goodbye and closed the door as he left. Amir sat on the divan and looked around his new place. Instinctively he went to the kitchen to get something to eat, forgetting that he had just moved in, however, in there was exotic cheeses, wine, champagne and a basket of fruit. Compliments of the rental association as a welcome home gift.

Amir walked onto his balcony to view his Atlanta. He had really arrived.

The task of redecorating the new palace was one that excited Amir. He had dreams of great art works and great pieces. He carefully went to the antique dealers and Phipps Plaza became a regular haunt of his. The stores had lots of exclusive pieces that, even though the people with whom he socialized would not tell a Picasso from a anything else, he would.

For the living space that he would make intimate for the occasion when he found the special lady to entertain, he changed the lighting to track lighting with muted tones of blue and yellow bulbs. The softest white rounded out the scenario. He brought vases from the dynasties of Ming, which he always felt would bring panache to any room. He had always liked the era of history and studied it whenever he got a chance. He changed the overdone oriental rug, to something a little less ornamental. A pale green Egyptian print with a little less busy-ness to it. He accented the room with different dried flowers and herbs, which gave the aroma of sweet spices. The kitchen he left alone, only adding a wine rack and some gourmet copper pots and pans to hang from his high ceiling. Amir had learned the art of gourmet cooking and when he wasn't out making deals, he was home, relaxing and doing the things he enjoyed. He often wondered when he would be able to get out of the lifestyle he was in, but couldn't think of an occupation that afforded him the luxury that he craved. It was a bad trade off he knew, but it was where he had the most knowledge. Street games, street money. He didn't want to take a chance on being turned down as a curator to a large museum such as the High. He didn't have the credentials to back up his knowledge and there was a limit to even what Mr. Cavetti could create, he was sure of that.

Amir planned his party to showcase his home, because unfortunately that was part of his business. To have his clientele access his home on occasion to let loose and enjoy themselves on the house. They would always be customers if he did that and bring in many more customers. Must keep that customer base. This was a supply and demand situation that had to be guarded carefully. If someone else put on the dog better than he, his business would migrate to them and take all their friends with them. Drugs are a word of mouth business and the better the party, the better the word on the street. People who ran in these circles liked the fact that they could feel part of the celebrity in-crowd, even if they were just two bit hustlers, pimps and prostitutes and some assorted businessmen, who had an eye for business but a nose for candy. When the bankers and financiers had clients in town who wanted to know the hot spots and where to get the best women for the weekend lay and party, Amir's name was the one that was mentioned. And now he had the showplace to pull it all off.

He changed his wardrobe to fit the new environment, Armani suits, tailored to his perfect body, silks and satin robes for lounging. Top of the line casual clothes for those occasional tennis or racquet ball sessions with his more athletic clientele.

He contacted a local woman he knew to do his catering. She was adept at taking the southern cuisine and embellishing it with more cosmopolitan treats. She could set a spread that made you want to go home to the country, and make you think you are in new York all at the same time. She told him she could have some ideas for him to look at later that evening.

Atlanta weekends were busy for Amir, and to try to conduct business and get the caterer squared away was tedious. But since he didn't have anyone who could help, he had to do it on his own. If only he had a special lady, who was not intimidated by his lifestyle, would not use his stash, and could be the perfect hostess. She should be out there, somewhere.

The weekend was getting ready for full swing. It was Wednesday and plans for Friday and Saturday nights in Atlanta were being made now. His pager rang off the hook for hours, with people trying to secure their party favors. People trying to make sure they were invited to his soirée, and businessmen with clients coming to town to party before the big pow wow on Monday morning. He ran up to Roswell and down to Union City and all points in between. His caterer caught him on the wing in East Point, and she hemmed him up long enough to tell him what she was serving, how much and how much she needed right now. He gave her the cash, she smiled and he knew that she would take care of everything. She knew the importance of having this man as her part of business clientele. He would recommend her to most of Atlanta if she could pull it off. She made sure that she did.

Amir finally made it home late Wednesday night/Thursday morning and slept until well into the afternoon on Thursday.

V

Steve found that through hard police work, he moved up easily through the ranks of the police officer and found himself promoted to detective. Narcotics. This gave him access to not only the best drugs in town, but the best women. He knew all the prostitutes, the drug dealers and most of the movers and shakers. But he wasn't in the top of the heap. He wanted to find out the big men in charge. He wanted to find the money men, the people who controlled the street rats. That's where his supplemental income would come from. That way, he could continue his lifestyle and no one would look at him twice. A detective, living in a modest neighborhood apartment, with very few friends wouldn't call to much attention, but with the extra money, he could take vacations and fly to different cities when his tastes led him to do so. He could continue to kill in this metropolis only so long. Eventually, so one would notice the hookers were dying. And someone would call the public to arms. After all, these girls had family some where. But so far, not a word. Just another crack hoe put out of her misery.

Steves cravings had taken him in some of the worst neighborhoods in Atlanta and he could see the devastation that crack had wreaked upon the people. Once respectable retired men and women, men who had nest eggs and took care of their homes, after working all their lives, fell victim to the crack pipe either directly, or indirectly by the young luscious bodies of the new crack hoes, coming to them in the night for a little cash. They gave these old men the sex they thought they had forgotten, and the men gave them their souls. The old women he had picked up at truck stops, trying to give head for whatever money they could get. Someone's grandmother with her false teeth in her pocket for better sensation. Grandmothers who should be baking cookies for the church bakesale. Grandmothers who, were caught in the crack struggle when their daughters dropped their children off to them and disappeared into the crack hell. Grandmothers who after being wore out from raising their children and their children's children, who couldn't drink anymore but couldn't do without, turned to crack to get that buzz that left them feeling no pain of their struggle. Their homes turned into crack dens until they are finally put out into the streets.

Some neighborhoods tried to fight back, have the abandoned buildings torn down, but there were just too many of them to get to and the city didn't care, as long as it didn't effect their tourist trade. Keep them out those neighborhoods and keep the neighborhoods far enough away from the main thorough fares that no one would see them unless you happen to know someone who lived there. The late night crack parties, the tired hookers looking for one more hit. The beer houses where you could go, buy beer, and possibly give the owner a little cash so you could go back and do your business in private and without having to share.

He enjoyed visiting the little make shift party homes. The people who ran them were usually good people, trying to make an extra dollar. Bought Beer and wine and whatever, fried chicken and sold dinners. Most were people who were hurt or disabled in some way and supplemented their income like that. Steve met many a wayward young lady, coming by for some beer and to see who she could pick up. Sometimes it was safer than walking the streets. He had a hard time getting at first because most of these people were from the old school and hated and distrusted white men. He understood, but eventually he made his way into the fold. And they laughed and said he was white on the outside. He talked about growing up in southern Georgia and being raised by a nice black lady who he loved dearly. Well, at least that part was true. He talked about his hatred for prejudice and even brought the beer in when they were running low. Smoked a joint or two and supplied some good stuff when he got his hands on it. He didn't dislike them, but he was there looking for prey. Like a good hunter, you have to know your prey.

Steve made sure not to make it a habit. He would be remembered and the only white boy there if anything happened and he knew his alliances would only stand up under pressure but for the time it took to say he was a white boy.

This particular weekend, Steve was feeling good. He had killed Wednesday night, a fresh crack head who came to town from somewhere Mississippi. She thought he was a john, and he turned out to be here last. His friend in the detective squad, the only real friend he had, or rather the friend he wanted to hang with, was working undercover narcotics and had gotten in really deep. So deep that he was now dirty. But there was this party at one of the big shots places in downtown. All the best of everything will be there. He wanted Steve to come to check out the real local flavor. The mainstream is cool, he said, but the upper echelon is much more appetizing.

Steve believed that the man was right. Hanging out in the mainstream was entertaining, but he wanted to hang out with the in crowd of the underworld. Where the money flowed like rain, and the drugs did too. He wasn't necessarily into drugs, but he liked the atmosphere it created. Not the poor crack heads who lived every day like it was their last. The crowd that didn't do crack, that did powder in long lines on glass tables with 100 dollar bills and diamonds on their fingers. The pretty crowd, with the pretty women. Not to kill, but to feel, and hold and caress. To treat any way your money would allow.

Steve chose his outfit carefully. Actually breaking down and going to Lennox to Structure to buy something that would fit with this crowd. He never put too much stock in clothes, but he would have to look the part. He stopped at one of the salons and had his hair done. He actually looked like he belonged.

He was very excited about this chance.

The arrived at the party, fashionably late. It was well after 1:00 but, these parties were notorious for lasting well into the morning. Where breakfast or brunch would be served to the remaining stragglers. The man had a reputation for his hospitality.

Steve and the other detective arrived and were ushered up the elevator to one of the several pentapartments. The traffic going in and out was like a who's who of Atlanta. There were stars that Steve recognized, rap people and their entourage. The wanna bees who followed them around. The beautiful black women of Atlanta, dressed in their fine slinky dresses, looking to meet Mr. Right but probably would settle for Mr. Right now, which always turned out to be the beast within. And depending upon the amount of alcohol consumed, how beastly they turned out to be. Some of them were hoping to snag the man himself. It was rumored that he was looking for a hostess to take care of his empire. And the most beautiful of Atlanta were here to try for the job. Steve marveled at the many shades of black that were in attendance from sweetpotato brown, and cinnamon stick to dusky silky black as the ace of spades, with beautiful almond shaped eyes, their real color hidden behind the tint of contacts. Hair done in so many different styles, it was like a smorgasborg. He was truly impressed. Steve had not realized just how beautiful black women really were. His thoughts drifted back to the most beautiful black women he had ever known, and how he treated her. She was old, but her heart was pure. It was still something that he never forgave himself for. He looked at these beautiful birds and wondered would time let them achieve the wisdom and degree of love that his mother st. john had achieved. He knew she was in heaven. Even though he sent her there, he knew that if there was a God, he would be happy to have such an addition to his flock.

His eyes misted a little and he shook the thoughts from his mind. Time to concentrate on the fun. There seemed to be music coming from every corner of the rooms, but Steve could not see any speakers or stereo. Their wouldn't be any room for it all. The place was shoulder to shoulder. He found the pleasure room off to the back where the lines and the joints were everywhere and the hedonists were in full swing, smoking, drinking laughing, touching. Steve did a line for each nostril and picked up one of the fat joints and began to smoke. He passed it on to a very beautiful bleached blond who could have used a few more pounds. But she was gorgeously made up and she smiled the smile of the damned. He walked past her and into the kitchen where the buffet was spread. There were all kinds of treats, and he took a couple of shrimp and headed to the balcony. There, sitting alone was Amir. He was sitting there quietly, smoking a joint, sipping on brandy.

Steve excused himself, he felt like he was intruding.

"I'm sorry, didn't mean to disturb you."

He started back in.

"you can sit here, I am just enjoying my view."

"you're the host of the party? Why aren't you inside?"

"I was inside, but this is better. Why are you out here?"

"just wanted to breathe a little."

Steve admired the view, it was beautiful. Up here away from Atlanta, but still a part of it.

"I want this."

"This place?"

"this place, minus about 200 people, and the view. I could do this"

"Yes, it is a lovely place. The party isn't bad, but its more public relations than anything else. In my line of work, public relations is key."

Steve smiled as he asked this question.

"you in advertising, supply and demand?"

"yes, exactly. Consumer goods."

"Well, my line of work isn't so nice. I am just a working joe, who happens to know the right people."

"It depends on how right they are, but if you are looking for excitement, this is the place."

They were silent for awhile. Steve wanted in so bad, he could taste it.

"well, if you ever need a partner, you let me know."

Amir stood and introduced himself to steve.

"Stop by sometimes, lets talk about that."

Morgan was in a situation. She couldn't get to the hotel to call John, the prince had her locked into the palace and she couldn't find a way out. He wasn't mean to her. He made love to her daily, nightly and in mid day when he came home from his rounds. She had occasion to look around and found a door that stayed locked. She wanted to get in there.

The prince bought her all kinds of things and she lay around the palace, alone most of the time. On weekends, there were the parties and he dressed her like his African queen in bright prints and colors from actual African nations. She was displayed and admired by the throng of party goers. He Kept her right on his side the whole time. Feeding her and providing her with drink. He paraded her around the palace like she was a queen.

And at night, when the parties were over and the guests were asleep, he would run her a warm bubble bath and together they would bathe and make love. He would sleep with her under his arm, when she tried to move, he would awaken, and hold her closely. She couldn't get a moment to get away.

One particular afternoon, she walked down the stairwell toward the door. She could hear voices in the closed door just off the foyer. She stood by the door, listening to his angry voice talking about a shipment that has yet to arrive. That, it should have been there yesterday and he hated to have to wait until the end of the week. He stated angrily that he would wait no later than Friday afternoon. He would be at the same location, Yes, he said, the house. Just ring the bell, the madam would tell him what to do from there.

Morgan heard the phone hang up and started toward the door. Quietly and determined, she had opened the door when she heard his voice behind her.

"Is my little queen trying to leave me so soon?"

"No, I was going to walk the grounds a little. Maybe ride the horses."

"I don't want you out there alone. Don't ever go out there unescorted my queen. I would feel bad if something happened to you."

He took her by the arm and led her back into the house. They sipped wine before he made love to her this time. The wine made her feel groggy and she barely stayed awake during this session. When she came to, she was chained to the bed by a leg chain, which was long enough to reach around the room.

He was sitting on the settee, watching her.

"you sleep like an angel."

"why am I chained up?"

"I have to go away for a few days. I don't want you to leave. You seem as though you don't like it here, like you are trying to leave me, shall we say, prematurely."

"But chains?"

"My man servant will make sure you are fed, and you can reach everywhere in this room that you want to. Unfortunately, you cannot leave this room. I am sorry, but you see, I am not ready for you to leave me yet. I have not tired of you. You, however, seem to be preoccupied with something or someone else. I cannot ascertain which it is, but my feeling is that you would not be here when I get back, and I cannot look for you. It would make me angry and I would never want to hurt you out of anger. I have a notorious temper and could, shall we say, inflict much damage to my beautiful queen."

He sat and stared at her for a what seemed to Morgan like a long time. Morgan, sat on the bed, tears falling down her face. It was involuntary. She was more angry than hurt, and she was trying to think of a way out of this. Her mind was telling her how she had botched this assignment and she had to get word to John as to the pick up going down on Friday. There was a phone there, and she remembered the office number and the code she should use. Hopefully, it will not be monitored.

"Do not cry my little queen. You will see that this is for the best. You give me such pleasure. I was hoping that I did the same for you. But no matter, you are my property for as long as I wish. No one will look for you in your Chicago town and certainly not here.'

He touched her face.

"we have much more time to spend together. The time will pass quickly until my return."

He kissed her passionately and made love to her again. The chains clinking softly.

"you arouse me so. I cannot think about anything but you. I cannot let my business suffer, but when I return, I will be needing you so badly. I must ensure that you have not taken wing and flown away."

He packed a bag and started for the door.

"please, prince, please don't leave me like this. I won't leave, I promise"

Morgan pleaded with the man.

He smiled, closed and locked the door behind him.

VI

Steve went back inside and joined the party. The girls were lively and lovely. He stood against the far wall, sipping his drink, the cocaine he had used was wearing off and he decided to get another toot or two before he left. Besides, it was free and it was flowing. He wondered if Amir had taken his suggestion. But he wouldn't worry about that now.

He made his way back to the real party room and sat down at the table where all the pretty lines were. He sniffed his fill. A really nice blonde walked up to him and handed him a drink, which he took. She smiled at him and Steve smiled back. Steve thought that she probably had mistaken him for one of the real movers and shakers, not a police detective, and underpaid one at that. When he didn't take the bait, she staggered away to more fruitful adversaries. Someone who could put her where she belonged, in their bed with a silver spoon under her nose at all times.

As he made his way to the door, Amir stopped him.

"let me check up on you abit, we can see what we can do together."

"I'm just a dirty cop Amir, no shame no game."

Amir was taken aback at the honesty and smiled at Steve.

"See you at the next party."

"I'll be here."

Steve was feeling no pain on the outside, but the pain on the inside was unmistakable. He thought about Miss St. John, again, she was on his mind. He couldn't figure out why he could not forget what he had done. He had forgotten all the others. They were just pieces of paper thrown around in the wind. But her face was staring at him sometimes. In his sleep he would wake up because he would hear her calling him to supper. He drove the highway, past downtown Atlanta, through the southside, heading for his favorite pick up place.

As he rolled down the avenue, he got a strange feeling. The girls were there, but they didn't look like the real set of losers. Something was wrong. He circled around and then made his way back to the freeway. He drove for a while, then exited at 10th street. Midtown. He didn't understand why he should be in Midtown, he had never picked up anyone in midtown, but he cruised anyway. It was dark and the park was closed, but he parked his car and walked through anyway. The lights from the area shining. The park was strangely illuminated as he walked. Maybe it was because his eyes were used to the darkness was his rationale. Steve marveled at how different the park seemed when there was no crowd there. The dogs were gone, no Frisbees. There was the faint sound of a commotion across the lake and he could hear the tinkling of bottles tossed onto the black top. Winos, hiding out drinking. He knew also that this was the pickup spot occasionally when a man wanted another man. He had never felt so inclined, but tonight, with the cocaine pulsing through him, he decided it would be something he could get into this once.

He made his way to the point and was not disappointed. Sitting on the side of the bench was a young man. He was white, very thin, but he didn't look thin like he was infected, more like the delicate thin of some of the gay boys. It must be a prerequisite. He has seen the black gay men with the same body type. He walked past a little and sat down on the next bench. Smoking a cigarette and staring at the reflection on the lake, he pretended not to notice the boy noticing him.

After a few moments, the boy sat down beside Steve.

"can you spare a smoke?"

Steve handed him a cigarette. His hands were shaking and dirty. Steve felt his stomach turn a little, but he continued.

"You a cop?"

"do I look like a damn cop?"

"yeah."

"well, cops have to have their fun too, or didn't you know?"

"yeah, I know. Is that what you want? Fun?"

"I don't know."

The boy stood up and walked away.

"I ain't doing no time for doing no cop man. I don't make that much money."

Steve motioned to him.

"c'mere man, I'm not on duty. I just want a little fun."

The boy walked back to Steve, hesitantly.

"I want a bottom, you a bottom?"

"when the price is right."

Steve took 4 twenty's out of his pocket.

"here."

"You settin' me up?"

"stop talking and lets go have some fun. Maybe I think you're going to be worth 80 dollars."

"I can be."

They walked back to Steve's car. The boy said he knew a place, but Steve said he had a place off of Peachtree Industrial.

"cool. I don't know anybody over there."

The boy sat silent as they drove.

They pulled up in back of one of the industrial building and behind a dumpster. Steve went to his trunk, to get a blanket he told the boy. He got the blanket and his tools.

The boy lay down on his stomach and Steve looked at the frail body. He couldn't stomach penetrating him, so he laid on top of him and simulated the act. The boy didn't care and moved as if he were really getting laid. Steve felt an erection coming and lay flat out on the boy, using his position to reach the knife. As the boy moved under him, Steve stuck the knife in his side. The boy tried to scream and Steve grabbed his head by his mouth and stabbed him again. He wanted to cut his throat but he couldn't. As the boy's body twitched in death, Steve lay on him and worked off his erection. He still couldn't penetrate, but the objective was achieved. He pulled the boys body under the dumpster which was sitting on a platform that was up off the ground enough. From the trinkling of water he assumed a sewer was under there. Must have a lot of water waste in this plant. He wiped the knife off on the boys clothes, bound them up to dispose of later and got back into his car.

As he drove away, he felt the bile rise in his throat and as he pulled onto peachtree industrial, he pulled the car over and vomited. From his position he could see the headlights of a vehicle approaching and the lights came on. A cop on patrol.

He walked up to Steve's car. Steve pulled out his detective shield.

"Hey man what you doing out here?"

The cop was a very large black man with a nice face. He looked at the shield and smiled.

Steve tried to smile, but again had to throw up. When he finished he notice the officer had backed up alittle.

"you okay detective?"

"yea, officer, I was at a party this evening, was way to drunk to drive, so I came over here where I knew their wouldn't be much traffic to puke my guts out and sleep for a minute."

"I understand man. Glad you didn't try to drive home. And usually there is no one over here, but I saw your lights and wanted to make sure. Sometimes people like to break in over here."

"No robbery officer, just a drunk ass detective trying not to get detected."

"hey man, I never saw you. Be safe man."

"thanks for not running me in, man."

"no problem, just wanted to make sure you were alright."

The officer went back to his car and went down the street always and turned his vehicle around and drove off. Steve was grateful that he was nice man. He didn't get his name, but he was a good cop. He could tell. The bile rose again and Steve lay his head back on his seat to ride out the feeling. He didn't know if it was the cocaine or the boy he did in, but he knew he wouldn't do that again. Not the boy anyway.

Amir wandered around his party. The guests were starting to thin out. There were just a few women left, hoping they would be the one. He knew that. He went into his kitchen. Didn't eat what was left on the trays, but fixed himself a sandwich from the refrigerator. As he turned around, there was a blond standing there. Petite and pretty, but she must looked very coked up.

"what's the matter? Don't like the food here?"

Amir smiled at the way her speech slurred.

"well this is my house, I can eat what I want, don't you think."

"this is your house?" her eyes lit up with surprise. She walked into the kitchen and took the bread and the meat from him.

"let me fix you a sandwich. Don't dirty your hands doing this work. This is women's work."

He smiled. She was kind of small for his tastes. Didn't have the great ass that sista's have, but she was willing. She would do.

"let me get rid of my guests."

She smiled at him and he walked away and gently began throwing people out.

Steve spent the next day recovering. His head was on fire and his mouth tasted terrible. He remembered the clothes in the car and what had happened the night before. The experience was not as fulfilling as it was with the prostitutes. He realized that he wasn't into the boy stuff and he wouldn't do that again, not sexually anyway. Steve checked his answering machine, took a couple of aspirins and went back to bed. It was 1:00 in the afternoon.

Amir made love with the blond woman all night. She was very good at what she did. But she definitely had too much of coke habit to be his hostess. However, he enjoyed her pleasures and never let her know that this would be the one night stand of her lifetime. As long as he kept the lines on the table, he could put himself in any hole that was available. And he did. He didn't have to be gentle with her, she wouldn't have noticed. So he was very rough with her, biting her and slapping her. She loved it, or she was so numb, that it didn't matter.

By noon, he had eased himself out of the bed while she finally slept. The bruises and bites were starting to fade and he would run her a tub when she woke up, which had better be soon. He had work to do.

Morgan sat there for a long time. Beating herself up for the predicament she was in. She looked at the phone and watched the phone. When it rang, she jumped out of her skin. It rang once, then stopped. Then it rang again, like a signal. She didn't know why, but she picked it up. It was the Prince.

"hello my little captive. I was wondering if you would answer the phone"

"I was hesitant, but I did anyway."

"good, the signal was for you."

"I wasn't sure, I thought maybe someone was trying to reach you."

"No my queen, this is my private line. No one calls me at this number, but I use it when I have, shall we say guests."

"shall we say captives."

He laughed.

"You are the only one I had to actually use my chains on. No one else ever wanted to leave before. I was thinking about why you would want to leave and it occurred to me that maybe you aren't use to being treated like a queen. Its a pity, you are very regal. I am in Chicago right now and have instructed my driver to take me through the not so nice parts of town. There are lots of black queens here who don't realize they are queens. So, now I understand. If it never happened to you, you wouldn't understand, be suspect. I am sorry. But I am glad I had the chains. Well my queen, I am leaving Chicago in a little while, heading back to Holland. I will see you probably tomorrow."

"I want to go home Prince."

"Whatever reason would you want to come back here? There is nothing here for you. Depression and despair is all that I see.

You don't deserve this. I will make your life wonderful. You can't want to come back here, but I must go. We will discuss it when I return."

The receiver hung up. She put the phone down, then picked it up again. Dial tone. She called John on his regular number that he kept for emergencies. It was a chance she had to take.

"Morgan?"

"how did you know it was me?"

"each of my agents have their own hot line. Where have you been. Your phone is off."

"my phone is at the hotel and I am chained in the Prince's bedroom."

"chained? Does he know who you are?"

"no, I tried to leave his little palace to get to my room and he decided he didn't want me to leave yet. However, I won't talk long. The pick up is Friday in the red light district here. I don't know which house, but I know its at one of them. I overheard him."

"don't worry about which one, I can plant an operative in each."

"are you okay?"

"yes, he's going to let me go when he gets back, and I guess I can leave here when he's tired. But now I know that I can get to you."

"I will give you a different number in Holland. Call me there the next chance you get. I won't leave Holland without you. I am flying out now."

The phone disconnected. Morgan breathed a sigh of relief. At least he knew she was okay and hearing his voice made her feel safer. She took the paper that she wrote the number on and stuck it under the mattress. So she could get to it. The she picked up her chain and walked to the tub. She turned the water on when she heard a knock and then the key in the door.

The man servant had brought her lunch in a silver serving tray. She thought about jumping on him, but he was pretty big and may not have the key anyway. Besides, she almost had the prince, no since in trying to escape right this minute. He sat the tray down and didn't say a word to her. He stared at her a moment, and looking embarrassed, stated with his wonderful Dutch accent, "I am sorry little one, I don't have a key." He smiled a weak, embarrassed smile and left the room, closing the door and locking it.

Morgan smiled to herself. At least he didn't like this anymore than she did. She decided she would finish her bath before she ate. Dragging the chain which almost didn't reach as she sat in the tub, one leg hanging out. She had lain her head back enjoying the water when she heard the door again. The man servant had brought her a bottle of champagne and a glass. He didn't look at her this time. Morgan finished her bath and dried in the large fluffy towels that were there. Peach colored. She didn't have anything like this at home, but made a note to get some. She sat down and had lunch, drinking the Champaign like it was water.

Amir made brunch for the young lady and woke her up to serve her. She didn't look so beautiful now. Her eyes had dark circles under them and her hair was a greasy mess. She didn't look petite, she looked too thin. She sat up and looked at the brunch.

"bathroom"

Amir pointed to the bathroom and she ran into it, slamming the door behind her. He could hear her throwing her guts up into the toilet. When she came out, he informed her that he had called her a cab. She looked at him, ready to protest and he kissed her sour mouth and told her he would call her later. That satisfied her. She put her clothes on without taking a shower, ran a brush through her hair and touched up the circles under her eyes. He didn't even walk her to the door.

Amir took his phone to the balcony. The late afternoon sounds of rush hour drifted up to him and even though it wasn't dark, the view was still beautiful to him. He made his phone calls, did his deals and then decided to eat something heavy before he hit the streets. Shrimp and things were good, but a man needed some beef sometimes. The lady he hired to clean would be here soon and he left her 100 dollars on the table. She never asked questions, and was used by most of the people in the building. But she said he paid the best. He knew when he came back, his house would be spotless. Even though she was an older black lady, she enjoyed a joint now and then and he left her a sack wrapped in a pretty box, (so as not to draw attention to it and she could put in her bag) and she always left him a thank you note. In some ways she reminded him of his mother so he always tried to be leaving when she came over. A couple of times he was there and she talked to him about his lifestyle and her worthless crack head kids and the grandchildren she had to take care of since her daughter disappeared. He didn't like thinking about men not taking care of their mother. He always sent his mother money, even though she never called him. He would call her number and when she answered he was satisfied and hung up the phone. He wondered where her daughter disappeared to. Crack heads were always the victims of crimes that no one cared enough about to look for. Most cops figured, well let her be in someone's crack city for awhile Keeps them from having to arrest her time and time again for prostitution or petty theft. He wondered how anyone could have sex with a crack head. They generally were not clean. Forget about sloppy seconds, we're talking sloppy tenths depending on the time you got to them. Or how many other dicks were in their mouth before yours. If they were on it hard enough, they didn't comb their hair, didn't change clothes regular and bathing was a luxury that they couldn't afford and didn't care about. He remembered the day the old lady came up to his car at the light at Grant st. She told him she would do whatever he wanted for five dollars. He couldn't imagine someone's grandmother selling pussy. He gave her fifty bucks. Maybe it would keep her off the streets for a while, or maybe she would take too much and kill herself, keeping her off the street for good. He watched her smile her toothless grin and headed over to the truck drivers who were waiting for their goods to be unloaded. Amir watched and felts sorrow. He would call and talk to his mother tonight.

Steve woke up again around 2:00. The afternoon addition of the Journal Constitution was sitting on his porch. There was a story in the paper, front page about a body found under a dumpster near peachtree industrial. The boy had been stabbed. Damn it, Steve thought to himself. The first time he kills a white boy, the papers are all over it. Why didn't they cover the poor black girls he had been killing. Sometimes there wasn't even an obituary. He knows that they had found some of the bodies. Wrote them off.

He read the article carefully. The boy had not been identified as yet. Then he remembered the cop that saw him there, puking his guts out. He called the office.

"Hey, this is St. John. Listen, I was in the Peachtree Industrial area the other night. Yeah, I was puking my guts out because I was drunk from a party. Yeah, a patrolman saw me, I didn't get his name or badge number but he got mine. I am thinking it was about the same time, but I was too drunk to know. I don't remember seeing any car lights or anything. Find out who works that area during that shift. He can verify it. No problem, I just wanted ya'll to know."

He hung up the phone. Damage control. If it had come out about his being in that area and he didn't mention it himself, it may be cause for suspicion. This way, it looked as if he may want to investigate. Steve walked into the kitchen. He needed coffee, not food. His stomach was still reeling from the party. He fixed the coffee and it seemed like hours before it was ready. While he waited, he went into his bathroom and looked at his face. It looked like bad road, about 16 miles worth. Damn that cocaine makes you look bad. Plus all the alcohol he consumed. The coffee finally ready, he poured a cup. Black and strong. He sat on the sofa, looking at the article again and again, looking for any clues. They didn't know anything except that they had a body. He shut his eyes and waited for the caffeine to do whatever magic caffeine does to a hung over party goer.

Morgan sat patiently sipping champagne waiting for the Prince, or John, whichever arrived first. She noticed that the leg iron was making her ankle swell and it was painful. The tried to message it the best she could. She wondered if she would ever get lose. After a while, she heard the key in the lock and wondered if it was jeebs coming to collect her tray. She had eaten the delicious lunch and was pretty drunk from the Champaign. She had consumed the whole bottle. Nothing else to do.

The prince walked into the door and smiled at her, but seeing her swollen ankle he became alarmed.

"my queen, I didn't realize it was so tight."

He undid the chain and messaged her sore ankle.

"I am entertaining tonight to celebrate my business venture proving profitable. But I am afraid my queen can't attend, you cannot walk on your ankle can you?"

"Not really, but I am not spending another minute in this room. Carry me down to the party or have one of your servants to come get me. I won't sit here alone."

He went into the hall way and brought back a package. It was a gold lame dress.

"this is for you. Wear it tonight and I will have my man come and position you comfortably on the settee. You can observe the festivities."

"good. I'll be ready."

She slid into the dress and fixed her hair and her makeup. 20 minutes later, the man servant who had brought her lunch was coming to carry her down.

"are you sure I am not too heavy for you sir?"

He smiled and in broken English replied.

"you are as light as a feather, I am glad you are joining the party. I would hate to think of you locked away in this palace with no one to entertain you."

He picked her up easily. He was a lot stronger than he appeared. Morgan supposed the premature look of aging is something that happens to people. Like heredity. As he approached the party room, he stopped and announced her.

"The queen has arrived."

All the guests stopped and clapped as he carried her to the velvet settee. He arranged her dress and smiled at her and he rested her swollen ankle on a pillow.

The prince came over and stood by his captive.

"Yes, my queen walks regally but not among the rocks of my palace and she twisted her lovely ankle. We shall try to keep her amused."

Everyone smiled at her and brought her drinks and food like she really was royalty. Morgan sat there, enjoying the ambiance, when there was a knock at the door.

John, and several detectives and police walked in and gathered up the Prince, and a few of his guards who tried to run to the back of the palace. The warrants were served without any problems or muss. It was like these people were use to being taken down or their royalty did not permit them to make a scene. Some of the guests looked like they would loose their lunches, but the Prince assured them in his princely tone that he would return after this minor inconvenience. He was a good liar, saving face in light of unpleasant circumstances. A prince to the end. He looked at Morgan, sitting there and he blew her a kiss. Morgan was happy to see John, and she maintained her cover while the people were being roasted out. She may need to be Amoire again, and she didn't want any connection to her and John to be apparent. But she was feeling so relieved and at the same time she would miss this treatment. John took them all out and came back into the house. He looked around.

"Morgan, you are well? What happened to your ankle?"

"The chain that was on my leg was too tight and it swollen a little. I'm glad to see you John."

John looked at her like she was his only daughter.

"You did good work."

The man servant arrived and looked at them both. He didn't say a word but went upstairs and retrieved Morgans belongings.

He helped John take her out to the waiting limousine. He looked at her and smiled weakly.

"I knew it was just a matter of time. I shall miss you my queen."

And he walked back into the palace. As she and John drove to the airport, Morgan told him all that had happened.

"It wasn't hard finding the right house. Apparently he had a favorite haunt and we arrested the madam and several of the hookers also. They were indirectly involved, but we will take away their licenses so that they will have to find another line of work"

"or move elsewhere and begin again."

Morgan was glad to be home. She couldn't wait for her ankle to go down, apparently it was more damaged than she thought. The doctor had bandaged it for her and told her to stay off of it for a few days. Her father was annoyed.

"What do you mean you fell off the runway? Couldn't you see it?"

"Dad, stop going on about it, I was caught up in the action of the show, my outfit was gorgeous and I just walked off the stage, that's all."

"yeah, well. It doesn't sound to bright to me. Was you high or something"

"yes dad, high on the crowd and the music and the joy of the show".

But her mind kept going back to the prince and the time they spent together. She knew that she shouldn't have gotten personally involved and wondered if there had been more time would she had fallen in love with him. Morgan wasn't sure if she would be able to keep it from happening.

Her father brought her soup and sandwiches to her room and treated her like she was a cripple. Which Morgan hated, but it made him feel good and she didn't complain. A few days later she was walking around again, although very slowly, catching up on some reading, and wondering what she was going to do with the money she was earning. Morgan considered buying a large condo in Florida, but her mother was buried here in Atlanta and she wasn't going to leave her here alone. Besides, her father wouldn't move. Atlanta was always his home and he never wanted to leave. He had been called in to investigate a case since she was gone. Sometimes, they used him as a consulting on matters that were hard to find out. Either because the person was such a mystery or the crime scene left no clues. In the case of the boy found dead, there were no clues and it was hard to figure out who he was. He was one of those rare individuals that had no dental work. There were a few cavities, but nothing had been done to him to indicate that he had been in the service of a dentist. So, dental records were out. His fingerprints told nothing. There was no match on file anywhere. This boy had kept himself completely anonymous. There were no tickets because he only had an i.d., no drivers license. His i.d. Picture was put out, and no one called in.

But there was talk among the clandestine relationships that go on in the park at night. The boys who hang out there, waiting for their tricks for the night were wary. They talked among themselves and decided to try to stick together. The boy had been a loner and no one could remember his name. They remembered seeing him there, now and then. But he didn't talk to anyone nor did they talk to him. When he was picked up for a quick meeting, he did so, and usually returned within the hour. He never went far. He never stayed long. One or two tricks and he would disappear into the midtown lights.

Steve went to work the next day. Still feeling a little sick, but well enough to perform. He felt that he still had green circles under his eyes. He talked his superior into letting him handle the case. Steve told the chief that because he was out there that night, puking his guts out, instead of being aware, he felt that he should find out what happened. The chief couldn't understand why Steve was so adamant about it, but he let him. But he told Steve that if he hadn't got drunk at the party, he probably wouldn't have been in the area and it may have still happened. Steve's rationale to the chief was, if the patrol cop hadn't stop to see if he was alright, he may have been in the right place at the right time to stop the killer, instead of checking on a drunk cop. The chief conceded and Steve was on the case. But they were consulting with an experienced detective who was retired, but liked to help when he could. Steve felt that this was somehow a reflection on his police work. But after he met the man, he found that he liked the older guy. For days they rode around the crime scene, walking and talking. Steve smiling to himself about how different it looked in the daylight. There were no foot prints which Steve wondered how that happened. The ground was a little damp. There was, however, little pieces of blanket. When Steve saw it, he felt his stomach turn, but since he wasn't a suspect, they wouldn't trace it to him so he called attention to it. They gathered it up in their evidence bags and took it to the lab.

Talking to the man, he found that the man had one daughter and that his wife was dead. He remembered hearing stories about a cop whose wife hung herself and he wondered if it was his wife. He wouldn't ask him though. His daughter was away modeling in Holland some where and from what Steve could tell, the older man was lonely. He started inviting him out to the racquet ball courts and the older gentleman had taken to making them breakfast. They had a lovely home and Steve made sure that whatever decisions were made on the case, he was apart of it. He still kicked himself for killing that boy. He should never pick white victims. Someone always investigates white victims.

Steve had also begun hanging out with Amir on the weekends. He went past his apartment one afternoon after racquetball and found Amir home. That sat and talked for a while. Steve again approached him about getting some of the action.

"What's a cop like you do trying to get in my business? Am I going to have to shoot you? Are you setting me up?"

"Man, if I was setting you up, I wouldn't have told that I was a cop. The general idea is to ingratiate yourself to the person you are going to burn, but you don't identify yourself or blow your cover. Don't you watch television?"

"No, not really. But if I do, its not police shows."

They laughed together.

"I can't believe you didn't watch detective shows when you were a kid."

"I was a street kid. Television didn't make me any money."

Steve reminisces about his childhood.

"Yeah, I was a street kid too. Or more accurately an abandoned child."

They talked a little more, and Steve told him he had to get back to work, but he would talk to him this weekend. Amir told Steve that there would be a private party this weekend. Just a few loose women and some close friends if he wanted to come. Steve said he would be there.

Amir was apprehensive about Steve dropping by his house. He didn't trust the man, after all he was a cop. They talked and although Amir was not totally convinced, the man made since. If he wanted to bust him, he could have just hung out at the party and not said he was a cop. But he didn't try to hide the fact. Amir knew that there were bad cops. Just like with anything else, you have good and bad. But this guy seemed like he just wanted some money.

They had similar backgrounds, growing up alone, but something about the way Steve had said it made Amir feel really bad for him. Amir had never been really alone. His mother was always around, but Steve was just abandoned. Left to fend for himself. He wondered what type of parents could walk away from a kid like a dog or cat walks away from their offspring. And in some neighborhoods, they don't do that. You see generations of kittens and cats just hanging out. There was something about Steve that itched in the back of Amir's mind, and although it wasn't a nagging itch, it was there. He would watch Steve before he put him in on anything. He would have to prove himself some kind of way.

Amir rolled a joint and smoked. He didn't do that often. Looking around his surroundings. He was so proud of his home. But Amir was lonely. He wanted a woman to share this with. Although Atlanta had its share of beautiful women, there was always a problem. He had taken out this secretary who worked downtown. He met her one day when he was walking through the hotel district. He had left his apartment and decided just to walk awhile, check out the flavor that wasn't in cars driving by. She was sitting in the park. It was a late lunch, because most of the women are in the park around noon. She was sitting there quietly, reading and smoking a cigarette. He watched her hide her pack and pull out one cigarette at time. The bums who slept in the park were as bad as the pigeons when you threw food on the ground. They would flock to the food and the bums would flock to the lady and bum cigarettes off of her.

It must have happened to her once before because she was very careful. Occasionally a man would walk by and ask for her short and she would look at him crazy and tell him that there wouldn't be one. Cigarettes were too expensive to save any of it. They got the message and walked away from her. Amir sat on a bench not far from her. He didn't want to approach her right away. She saw him, smiled and continued reading. As she got up to leave, he could see that she was a slim goody. Not drug slim, and she had nice hips and a bright smile. He approached her then.

"Enjoy your lunch?"

She was startled then looked at him.

"its a lunch. But I like being in the park"

They walked a little further.

"what's your name?"

"Sharon Lee"

"Hi Miss Sharon Lee, my name is Amir"

"Hi Amir."

She walked back to her building and went in side. She turned and told him good bye and he said good bye and let her go to work.

He hung around a little longer, then decided he would be back tomorrow to see if she was there. He saw her the next day and every other day he could when he wasn't working. Sometimes, he surprised her with lunch and she had given him her work number. Eventually they went out. She wanted to go to the Crows Nest and he took her there. They danced and drank and partied and afterwards he brought her back to his place. She loved it as much as he did. But when she realized what he did, she decided that he must have been dealing the type of weight that made people get killed and she didn't want to get involved in that. It scared her. So, he let her go. He didn't want someone that was afraid to relax in his place and she was. It was beautiful she had said. He liked that because he thought it was beautiful too. He missed her. But he understood. She would have been a nice addition to his place.

VII

Steve was living a double life and he enjoyed the feeling. He was a crack detective by day and a member of the elite social status at night. Amir's home was the gathering place. He had never seen so many good looking women in his life. He partied and danced and sniffed cocaine. Amir had taken him into his confidence and they were rolling together so to speak. He didn't actually ride with him, but he was in on what's was going down and even got to make a few deliveries for a nice sum. He could play the good cop during the day, hanging out with the old man, having breakfast and playing raquetball. The old man noticed that his serve isn't as good as it was. The drugs were taking control of his physical being. He used to be in good shape, but its hard to work out when you are up all night.

He wonders what the outside people see when they see the crowd of party folks. The in-crowd. During the week while people are going about their work day business, party people sleep, rest and talk among themselves about the next party. They may have jobs, but nothing that will interfere with the party life. Most of them are young people, lost in a world of drugs and drink. Living the life of a movie star without actually being one, rubbing elbows with the stars who come to these little soirees'. And they do come. The young women, looking for that chance to meet what they think is Mr. Right. Someone that is high profile, someone that can give them something for nothing. But Steve loved it. Its an aphrodisiac of epic proportions. When you walk into a room and the girls throw themselves at you, give themselves to you without even knowing your name, its powerful. Steve couldn't understand sometimes why it happens that way. A sort of pool of lost people. With men like Amir, showing them that this is the way. He couldn't entirely blame Amir, but, you had to find a scapegoat for this type of behavior.

Steve wondered where the parents of these children were, and most of them were children. Not even 18 or just barely. Made up life fashion models or rap video stars. For them not to be working, the clothes they wear are expensive, not necessarily tasteful, but they have to find somewhere to get them. Steve remembers going to a rooming house in midtown on a call of someone dying on the residence.

He walked into the house and it was owned by an old man. He had used the house to raise his children, nurture his wife, and be a family man. But the children moved away, the wife died, and the man started letting the young people move in, and pay him a little money. He didn't need the money, the house was paid for, he got retirement money. He was lonely. At first, as the man explained, he let a couple of the kids move in because their parents had put them out for whatever reason, no boys, just girls. They treated him okay, cooked dinner sometimes, took care of things. Once they got use to being on their own, they met other kids in their situations, and girls attract boys. The next thing he knew, he had a sort of flop house situation. When Steve went up into the room where the dead boy was, there were 15 kids living or sleeping in this one room. It had a smell of dirty clothes, rotting fast food containers. The boy was in the bathroom. Apparently they had a drinking party and he drank too much. Steve asked how they got the alcohol and one of the younger girls spoke up. She said that all they had to do was stand outside a liquor store, and the bought it for them. Especially when they had their own money. Even though there was a law against it. She was only 14. Steve made them all sit, some were trying to leave, saying that they didn't live there, they were just visiting, but Steve made them all stay. They sat on the couches and Steve just looked at them. Their ages varied from 12 to 17. The 17 year old, a girl who was half and half of something, was sitting there quietly smoking a joint. Steve asked her if she knew it was against the law, she looked at him and smiled, inhaling until there was nothing left but ashes. "If you can find any, lock me up." was all she said. You could tell that they all looked up to her. So Steve took her into the downstairs kitchen to talk to her alone. The other kids watched her go, and he could finally see a little fear in their eyes.

Downstairs, he tried to talk to the young lady. She wasn't cooperative, just looked at him searchingly.

"why do you even care, cop?"

"what makes you think I do?"

"you got that look like the preachers have. But you know what, I talked to a couple of preachers and they tried to take me to bed."

"really?"

"screw me in the name of the lord."

He was perplexed by this woman child. She was beautiful, but her spirit was bruised. It wasn't broken yet, but she was well on her way. One more trick, one more whatever she had to do to survive would take her there.

He asked her where she got the money for drugs.

"this is a capitalistic society cop, you don't need money. Whatever you have of value is what you sell."

"if its of value, why do you sell it?"

She smiled at him.

"Even the rich have to sell something sometimes."

Steve made her sit in the kitchen. He went upstairs and cleared out the room except for the occupants. There were actually only 3 including the woman child downstairs. The old man looked perplexed about the whole thing. Steve thought the man reminded him of his friend. Only in a different section of the societal web. He meant well with the kids. The throwaways. He told the man to relax and that he would make sure everything was okay and he could keep renting his rooms out. Loneliness was a pain. He thought briefly about the woman who fed him before he left home. She was lonely too. Until Steve took that loneliness away, in more ways than one.

The kids cleared out and the coroner came and took the body. No one really knew the boy except that his name was Jacob and he lived in the Greenbriar area of Atlanta. Steve would have to find his parents. He hoped he had some. He looked at the children leaving the house. All colors, all sizes. Acceptance. They didn't care about colors or anything like that. Throw always create their own families and color doesn't count. Steve went back to the girl.

She was sitting quietly in her chair, humming a song. He asked her about it and she told him it was "Antonio" by Michael Franks. She liked his music and tried to lift all his c.d.'s when she could find them. He made a note to buy that one and listen. Apparently, her mother had met a new man and felt threatened by the pretty young daughter that she had. So she put her out. Into the streets.

"I don't blame her exactly. I know how I am and if the opportunity had presented itself, which eventually it would have, I would have slept with him and he wouldn't have liked my mother anymore. You see Copman, youth in itself is an aphrodisiac. I am Aphrodite. I am love."

She laughed at herself. Steve listened to this intelligent young woman and wondered why she wasn't in school instead of wasting her life doing this. He must have looked at her that way because she answered without him even asking.

"you know, copman, in this world, you do what you can do. I wanted to go to college. I was a good girl up until my father died and my mother started dating again. Its hard to pick the right man when you have been with him all your life. Being without him is hard. At first, you question why he had to go. You make a pact with yourself not to ever date again. But the nights get lonely. You want to feel a man in your arms like you were use to. So, one day, you put on your party dress and you go out. First you go to the places you and your husband use to go. But the friends are different and they know you are alone, so they hold their husbands a little tighter and fix you up with people they know. Everyone thinks a widow is hot and full of money. She was both but she didn't know how hot she was inside. Until the first man. He would take her out to dinner then take her to bed. Casual sex is something a married woman doesn't have a concept about. Not if they have been married for any length of time. When she finds out its casual, she is hurt. Let down. So she stops dating, but sex arouses sexual needs. So she decides that she will be the hunter and not the prey. After half a dozen losers and you find one that you can tolerate, who makes you feel young, helps you spend your money but looks at your daughter like he can eat her up, you do what you must. The daughter must go. I go. Into the world. Not prepared, but learning really fast."

She looks at Steve intently.

"You think I am just a whore in the streets. Well, you are wrong. I plan to go to school, get knowledge and open a house just like this old man has done. To be the safety net for girls like me. I sell pussy because its a commodity. Not because I am a whore. I don't enjoy it, I am not proud of it, I was not raised this way despite what has happened. Survival is the need that does this to real women, not any thing else."

"If you had money, would you stop selling?"

"I tried to get work. But in the worlds standards I am unskilled. However, I will try to get something. This is not my way of life. Those kids up there, they need me. I am their hope. I am their mother and father. I don't let them sell pussy, I don't let them do dope. I give them money to get clothes, food, and help them treat this as our home. I try to raise them. But for so many kids to support, not to mention the old man, working in a fast food restaurant isn't going to give me the capital I need to support them all. I need big money and with my heritage, I command big money. I am a commodity, copman."

Steve was impressed and depressed by this woman child. He wanted to help her, but all he could think about was the old woman who helped him. She could have done a lot for this girl who hurts so much inside. He gave her some money, so she wouldn't have to sell herself. He paid the old man.

"make sure she goes to school."

"yes sir, I surely will"

Steve came out of his restrospect. Life just didn't work that way for most. Most people don't have anyone who gives a damn about them and they wind up selling cut rate pussy on a deserted street waiting to be picked off by a deranged person. He didn't kill tonight. He drove home slowly, looking at the women on the street. They weren't as noble as this young girl. They were just there. He knew that some of them had situations that took them there, but for the most part, they did this because it was easy. Crack hoes. He hated them all. They reminded him of his mother. Not caring, not feeling, just hoes. Crack or no crack. They would have been out here because it was easy. This is what he hated. Women who didn't care. He went home and slept, thinking about the young girl and the scholarship he could arrange for her to have. If he could get her to go back to school. It was what the black woman would have done, if she had the means. She really loved him.

VIII

Morgan lay in her bed, the Atlanta morning was a little brisk. She had left her window open last night. She curled under the blankets and warmed herself. The prospect of getting out of bed to close the window was too much. She could smell the breakfast her father was making. Beef sausage, coffee, cheese grits. The biscuits were almost done. But she didn't want to get up. Her mind was on the Prince. As an operative, she wasn't to get involved and she knew that. But he was special. She could see herself being his princess, but the chains were a different matter. She could have loved him. She could feel his kisses on her body and remember how they made love. Morgan wondered if that's how married people acted when they were together for so long. Was it was drove her mother to suicide? Thinking that her prince gave his love to another? Do men realize that women think this way? Do women think this way or was she just one of those women who dreamed of the castle and the prince. Happily ever after?

She could hear a voice in the kitchen with her father. Laughing together. His racquetball partner. She hadn't met him yet, but was not in the mood to meet anyone today. She heard her father coming toward her room after the silence. They must have eaten already. When he turned her door, she turned over and faked sleep. He looked in on her and closed the door quietly. Trying to slip down the hall. She could hear his footsteps because the floor was weak and he creaked no matter how softly he tried to walk. It was the nature of the house. Dampness crept into the floorboards. It happens. She could hear them laughing as they got into her father's SUV and she listened as they drove off, around the corner. When the street was silent, she got up.

Morgan got up, putting on her fuzzy slippers and her heavy robe. Walking down the hallway, listening to the floor. The coffee was calling her badly. She went into the kitchen, pouring herself a big mug. With cream and sugar. Morgan walked onto the patio. The morning in Atlanta was beautiful and clear. The fall was coming, she could feel it in the air. The coffee, making pretty white smoke in the cool morning, Morgan sipped. Letting the hot fluid flow through her veins. Warming her. The birds were singing and the neighborhood has not awaken yet. Not really. The children were off to school, but the housewives were still inside, cleaning the house, making the beds, making their list of things to get at the store. Probably talking to each other. Discussing the discussions they had with their spouses the night before. Did married women talk about sex? Did they call her mother and discuss the things that happened in the privacy of their rooms? She remembered the sounds and only realized now that those were the sounds of love. The kissing and holding and laughter. The soft laughter is what she remembers most. Did her mother feel like her father was her prince? Was it so hard of her to conceive of him with someone else that she hung herself behind it? The smoke rose in soft ringlets above her coffee mug. Her thoughts went back to the prince. Could she had loved him that way if the situation was different? He touched her so sweetly and in places that she didn't even know had feelings. She crossed her legs. The feelings coming back in vivid memories. Did her mother feel this way? Was she awaken in the middle of the night feeling lonely and helpless on those nights when father didn't come home because of work. Did she wait for him to come home and jump into her when they lay in bed. Like she did when the prince left and told him he would return. Did she feel the anticipation for her lovers return. The wetness in her. The longing? Did married women, older married women feel that way about their men? Does the desire wane with age?

Morgan drank her coffee, looking at her surroundings. Would they appear different if she had a man with her? Did she want a man? Did she need one. The prince showed her that she needed one, but did she want one. Would she end up like her mother? Would a man mean so much to her that she would commit suicide at his unfaithfulness? Men have had mistresses since the dawn of time. Its in the bible. Concubines were no less a part of history than the conquering hero. Sometimes as much as the hero. He always had his concubine somewhere close. She was there for him in situations when the wife was not expected to be. Was she more important than the wife? At times in history she was. Maybe she could be a mistress. An interesting concept. Waiting for her lover to come would still be the prime directive. All women wait for their men. Would she have a man to wait for? Did she want a man to wait for? She knew of some friends who had husbands who were there for them all the time. At their beck and call. They did things that made their women happy all the time. The women were happy most of the time, but she realize their conversations revolved around how they had their man wrapped around their finger. But in the end, their men had women across town. And they never knew. Their smugness made Morgan angry. Because it wasn't true. The only difference in these men were that they kept their homes together first. Just like her father.

Morgan missed the love making. Her body felt the fire like a Louisiana Sunday afternoon. Hot and steamy. Quiet. The quiet storm, raging inside her. There were men she could call that wanted to go out with her. But they weren't something. There was something missing with them. They were average men, and she didn't want an average man. She wanted the magic that came with the men she didn't know. And it couldn't be that way. Not in real life.

Her coffee finished, she went in search of the second cup. The grits had sat too long, the bacon was cold. But she didn't have an appetite for food. What she wanted was romance for want of a better word. Would it come. Would it come during one of her assignments when it was inappropriate. Could she help her self the next time. Morgan went into her room and looked at the contents. Hidden away in the bottom of dresser with the service 9mm, was the mysterious red panties. The panties that her fathers mistress had worn, and not for very long. They only smelled of perfume. She looked at them. Morgan had brought some dainty wear from Victoria's Secret to match the panties that she hid. She didn't wear them during her assignments, they were strictly for her private fantasy. She decided tonight she would go out. On the town, enjoy herself.

Amir scored the biggest connection of his career. A million dollar baby was born in his his lap and he was to inherit the spoils. He was elated. His Cayman Island bank account got the needed boost to get him closer to retirement. 3.5 million dollars in product, 6 mil in street revenue. He didn't allow a big cut on his stuff. His modus operandi was giving the high rollers the purest they could handle. If he was selling to the hoodrats, he would have made about 7 mil after allowing for the few who beat him, and the extra cut. But he didn't do business that way. If you got his stuff, you were assured of almost pure coke. No one could handle pure coke, but they like his. He would party tonight. A grand party. He would go to the jazz club called the Point of View. There he would pick up his group to party. It would be good. He called Steve and let him know what was going on. Steve was in the middle of a racquetball match with some old ass cop, but he told him he would be there.

Amir called his catering friends to fix up something to munch on. He pulled out his crystal for the party. It took him hours to get the atmosphere right and he had some neighborhood girls roll his weed into many joints. He paid them and watched them take joints and stick them in their bras and panties. But he didn't care. Tonight, he may meet miss right. It reminded him of the Great Gatsby. Having good parties and standing atop the action looking for the one woman who would be his. He called Sharon Lee and invited her. He hoped she would come, but you never knew about Sharon Lee. When she came, it was beautiful, but she would say she would come and not come. Sharon Lee was a different type of person than he had ever met. She wanted the good life, but she wanted her way. And she wouldn't compromise. She would let you be her friend, even sleep with you, but you always knew that you weren't getting inside of Sharon Lee, unless she let you. And she didn't let just anyone. He smiled when he thought about her. She would have been a great addition. She would watch your back, was willing to fight beside you if it came to that. The only problem was, she would let you make love to her then, get her stuff and go home. Not even telling you where you could reach her. Just disappear. He liked that she would have your back, but he hated that she could be so detached from people that way. She could turn you off without a second look. People that cold have been hurt really bad. But not bad enough to take her goodness totally away. He made sure she knew about the party. He knew she was scared to be with him, but that was because she had a kid and he understood, but Amir also knew she had a life that would make a party go. Plus, when she dressed in her after 5, she was awesome. Slinky black stockings, split, always a split, her hair perfect, she would add class to anything. He wanted to see her. He wanted to make love to her. What did old boy sing about . . . for old time sake.

His heads in the clouds, this would be his finest party. He wished his mother could be here, just to enjoy the ambiance. She would like that. She always enjoyed classy get togethers. When she was in her hey day, she went to the mason balls, dressed to kill. And she always had men wanting to bring her home. But she always settled on a cab. They paid her cab fare and she rode in style. In style to the projects. The dirty part of town, that, if she wasn't associated with the Mason's the cab would have never come. Hell the ambulance didn't come that often. Only after much hesitation, to make sure whoever needed them were dead already, that way they could get paid from the estate. If there was one. In his time of power, he thought about the people who toiled at the jobs where they only had 2 grand in insurance, working for company's that could afford more, but didn't. Charged them out their paychecks for the insurance that didn't cover a decent burial and left nothing to the family. Too many times he had attended funerals where he watched the family taking the food and wrapped it in foil to save for a later date. Hoping no one was watching. But not caring if they were. There was no money left after the funeral. Usually the insurance policies paid enough to bury the dead. But nothing more after paying on the same policy for 15 or more years. The insurance man coming to the house on Saturdays in his wingtips, talking like he was a family friend. Eating with the people. And they thinking that they had a real white friend. He would talk to the children, like he was interested, with his hand out to collect the money on those penny policies. The calendars hanging in many kitchens. This life insurance company or that. Or hanging underneath the picture of Jesus and/or Martin Luther King. His mother had one. Northwestern Life. It was a calendar from 1975. He remembers. She never took it down. It never moved. It aged with the apartment, like the furniture, the draperies, the mother. The dust that discolored and collected on it, collected on everything in the house.

But she never took it down. It was as much apart of the house as she was. And she never noticed it was there, but she would have noticed that it wasn't. It would have left a clean spot on the wall.

Amir looked at his place that he called home. There was no aging calendar on the wall. There was art. Art in the form of paintings, art in the form of vases and things like that. An oriental rug, beautiful drapes. A Divan, queen Anne wing chairs. Cherry tables. The lighting was muted, not dim like the hood. It was muted by choice. With the flick of a switch, he could make it as light as Christmas or as dim as a death. Romantic, or festive. He controlled the lighting, the comings and goings, everything. She should be here. Not just here, but living. He had room for her. There was nothing in it but things for her, and no one was allowed in their. He had showed Sharon Lee his room. She thought it was very well done. She said that if her son did this for her, she would live with him. But she also said that if his mother was like her, she wouldn't come. But she would appreciate the consideration. Some mothers want their child to do well and to move on. Not to look back to their beginnings. Maybe he had that type of mother. Her conversations always were good. Sharon Lee knew a lot and she was able to share what she knew. Damn, he hoped she would come.

With the finishing touches in place, the crystal bowl full of joints, minus at least 20, thanks to his hired help, the coke room ready, Amir put on the Rippingtons as his mood music and began to shower and get ready for the guests. He would hit the club first, then come back here. It would be a black night. Black pants, black shirt, black tie, black jacket. Gold around his neck and a diamond in his ear. Royal Copenhagen musk from someone he once knew, he always liked that fragrance, Amir was never into trends. That was what he liked most about Sharon Lee. She was a classic. In thought and deed and dress. And the classics never went out of style. Amir was elated and let down at the same time. He smoked his joint and looked out at his view. Tonight would be exceptional. His phone rang, not the private line, but his regular line. It was Sharon Lee. As he talked to her, he could tell her spirits were high. If they weren't, he could tell. She couldn't hide her emotions. And she was a moody woman. All was well with her, she would be there. He made sure he had enough eggs and things to make her eggs benedict in the morning. She liked eggs benedict and champagne for Sunday brunch, but never seemed to date guys who were in to that. He would make it for her. He would make her happy tonight. He hoped. If not forever, for the moment. And that's how we all live isn't it he smiled, moment to moment.

IX

Morgan walked into the Point of View, on top of the world in Atlanta's downtown district. The ambiance was striking and she loved it from the moment she came in. There were tables, but she wanted to sit at the bar. She didn't want to get a table to look like she was waiting on someone who wouldn't show up. Their was a band there, the Rippingtons and they had just finished their set. She positioned herself at the bar so she could see the people who came in. The men. She was on a mission tonight. Whether she could fulfill it it was her choice. Right now she was feeling frisky, but one never knows about the evening. She ordered a gin and tonic. Not Tanqueray. Tanqueray was strong for her and she didn't want the evening to end prematurely because she drank too much. So she sipped on seagrams gin. It was pretty early, which is what she wanted. To get a good seat before the crowd arrived. Saturday night in Atlanta was the best night in the world. The people partied and forgot their work week woes, and if they had to work Saturday, which was the case for many since this was a tourist town, they made it through thinking about what they were going to get into on Saturday nights. The people partied hard in this town. Atlanta was a Saturday night town. The best part was that every one partied. From the fast food worker to the stock broker. Saturday was a good time had by all. It was the charm of Atlanta. If you did nothing all week, you looked forward to Saturday. The beauty salons were full of women getting their hair done, the nail shops were full. She was lucky, she went early to get her nails done, before the party women got up. She did her own hair. When her father came home, she was almost dressed. This was a night for the little black dress. She put on her robe and met her father in the kitchen and told him she was going out. He was glad to see she was enjoying herself.

As she watched the door, a tall lady came in. She had an air about her. She was dressed in a long clingy black dress, with a slit up to her thigh. Her hair was in braids, long, she looked like ponchahontas. Morgan couldn't stop looking at her. She had keen features, a straight nose, thin lips. She walked over to the bar. Not really walked, floated. The barmen took notice and sat down a gin and tonic beside Morgan. She sat down. She smiled at Morgan but didn't say anything. Morgan commented on her dress and she commented on Morgan's. As they sipped their drinks, they talked to each other about little things. Hairstyles, dresses. Each liked each others dress. Her name was Sharon Lee. Morgan liked the name. The lady said it was because her father's name was Lee and he named all his kids Lee. Since she was a girl, Sharon Lee. She said she didn't really think of herself as a LeeAnne so Sharon Lee was good. They laughed. Sharon Lee said there was a party at a friends apartment. A penthouse and Morgan was welcome to come as her guest. Morgan smiled and thought okay. A party in the Penthouse. Good. The two hit it off well. Morgan admired her class and Sharon Lee admired Morgan for her class also. They were a match made in heaven. Sharon Lee went on to say that this man was a friend of hers. Heavy into things that she wasn't but she liked him as a friend.

"I do sleep with him once in a while, but you know how that is."

Morgan didn't want to say she didn't know.

"yeah, right."

"he's a good guy, but he's not my prince. You know the song, someday my prince will come. I hope he comes with more brain than money or an equal combination of both. Or hell, just brains, I could deal with a poor, smart man."

Morgan agreed. Everyone wanted a prince. Morgan had one, who chained her up. But the sex was fabulous.

They sat and talked for a long while, watching the crowd come in. Morgan liked this girl. She was hip, but she wasn't. She didn't talk ghetto, and Morgan could tell she had been around. And not with the average man. Morgan asked her what she did for a living.

"I am a secretary. I figured as long as I could type, I could work anywhere. That way, I can move when I want and not worry about finding a job. I type pretty fast and know all the new software. I will always be employed."

"Did you go to college?"

"No, I had a child and decided to work. I like working, although I would probably like college, but I like helping my child with homework. I can work 9 to 5, get home and not be tired. Have a life with my child. It all evens out."

"Good for you."

"actually, good for my child. After I get him in high school, I will decide if I want to go to school. By then, I will have time. My child will be old enough to stand time alone, you know."

"Not really."

"I would have taught him enough about right from wrong, sex and girls that I will be confident leaving him alone and I can concentrate on my studies instead of worrying about him. At least this way, if he chooses to have sex, I would have taught him what he needs to know, and if he doesn't, that's good too. But I will be there for him. By high school kids personalities are already set. His will be set in the right way."

"That's good"

"yeah, I hope so. I think you are cool. You are me, without the kid. You don't have kids do you?"

"No."

"I figured that. Don't get me wrong, I love my son more than my life, but once I imagined me without him and it would be you."

They smiled and bought another round. Morgan was captivated by this woman.

"Or maybe he is what makes me who I am. You know? He's a helluva boy and he will be a helluva man."

"Doesn't he know his father?"

"Sure. A nice boy. I was 16 and he was 15. What could a 15 year old do with a kid? So, I took over. His father was sweet and kind and I will always love him. But the government puts women in a better position to raise kids than men. He would have had to pay child support and he wasn't even working. You know? I didn't want to do that to him. So I did it myself. He had the choice, I always left the door open, but one day, I decided to move the door."

"did he follow?"

"no, he moved on too. Which is okay. He was young. Women are older than men in lots of ways. I have no hard feelings and never filed child support charges against him. We didn't need the aggravation. The door was still open, it was just that the door was in different locations."

Morgan smiled.

"You are a trip"

"No, I am a vacation"

They laughed.

"So, you will come with me to the party? I hate to arrive alone. Its always nice to have someone with you. And since I am short on girlfriends at the moment, you will do."

"Yes, Sharon Lee, I will go with you."

"cool."

Morgan was happy about her decision. She had met many women in Atlanta. Most were like her. Focussed, intelligent, looking for the right man, but Sharon Lee seemed free and easy, doing things that made her happy, whether she found a man or not. She was going to be herself. Morgan liked that. It wasn't that Sharon Lee wasn't focussed, she was just focussed on different things. Morgan wanted to be like her.

Amir showed at about midnight. The club was in full bloom. The Rippingtons were playing their smooth sounds and Sharon Lee and Morgan were dancing with some anonymous men. They were having fun. Morgan hadn't had this much fun in a while.

Amir walked in, and stood, searching for Sharon Lee. He hadn't really thought he would find her but he did. She was dancing on the floor. He walked up to the gentleman and cut in. Sharon Lee smiled and they danced. Morgan watched. Stepping off the floor with her partner who was pretty inept in dancing, she watched as Sharon Lee and her friend whirled around the floor. She had locked her hands around his neck and was smiling from ear to ear. She had a beautiful smile and Morgan watched them clear the floor. When the music was over, they walked over to her and Amir invited her to the party.

"My friend says you are looking for a good party. Come with us, we will show you a good time, won't we Lee?"

"Yes, baby, He always calls me Lee, Morgan. Oh, I am sorry, Amir, this is Morgan, Morgan, Amir."

They shook hands but he was captivated by Sharon Lee and merely touched her hand. He led them out of the club.

"Morgan, you want to ride with us or bring your car?"

"You better ride in your own car, Lee may not be leaving tonight. I don't get her out often."

Morgan laughed, but she was content to take her own car. She realized that maybe Sharon Lee would be tied up for longer than she wanted to wait. So she jumped into her vet, and followed them. She thought she was in for a long ride, but he lived just up the street. But it turned out to be a long ride, afterall.

Steve had changed clothes and was getting ready for what was going to be the blow out part of the decade. Amir and he had scored big bucks and he was celebrating. Steve wanted to kill. He could feel it, but not now. Not before the party. Maybe afterwards or sometime in between. Amir's parties were known to last well into the next day. He had time. But he was psyched and up. He hit a few lines of coke and was feeling good. His outfit, black, all the players work black except for this big country boy named John who wore gold. John always wore something gold. Gold leather in the fall, gold in the summer, gold. But it looked good on John. He was black as the ace of spades and the gold brought out all that pretty black. Steve sometimes wondered what it was like to be black. Something that you couldn't hide. Something that was always working against you, but you had to wear it. That John guy, tall and quiet, was a nice looking black man. If Steve looked liked that, he would have all the babes, black or white. White boys got black women, but only a few. Most had problems crossing the color line where white women did not. There were some that had problems but it was more economical than moral. Black women had moral battles with the issue. They either harbored a deep seated hatred stemming back from what the heard about the slave owners or they didn't care and went for it. The crack whores didn't have a problem. Black or white, money was green. He had heard it said that only white men buy pussy, but he knew that wasn't true. There were plenty of black men who paid for the pleasures of the night. He knew that they weren't the majority however. Coming in from their suburban outreaches to taste the forbidden fruit. They would have done better to wait for the pretty black secretary and see if they could get her. It would probably taste a lot sweeter. But they usually didn't do that. He found it depended upon how close they were with their fathers and how their father felt about the situation.

He thought about the black people he had met over the years. The one who touched him the most was the one he lovingly thought of as momma. Momma fed him and took care of him when his own mother wouldn't. And how did he repay her, by killing her in her sleep, with her bible in her hand. He still regretted that. She was the only woman who gave him a fair shake. She loved him because he was who he was. Period. Unconditionally. He took another line. Well. The others he met were okay. He didn't have anything against them personally. Steve killed crack hoes not because they were black but because they were accessible and no one questioned when a crack hoe got killed. One less problem on the street. That was the only reason. If they were white, they would have died too. He wondered about the women who looked at him with mistrust. The black women who worked hard every day. Coming home tired to feed their children. Hoping a man would rescue them. But not a white man. There was still a lot of distrust in the southern black women about white men. He found that usually they had come from smaller country towns where the whites ran roughshod over them and kept them at bay. This southern mentality was strange to him. The whites in his town just didn't deal with blacks but they didn't terrorize them either. They accepted them with a distant knowing that they were there, and that was it. And he couldn't get around it. Then there was Morgan and her daddy. The pillars of the community. There were still parts of Georgia that they couldn't venture into. Regardless of their social standing. That must be tough. He could go to any neighborhood. Almost. Especially in his official capacity. No one would dare stop him with his badge. His badge made it all worth while. The great equalizer. His badge and his service revolver. Although, the harder thugs didn't give a good damn if he was a cop or not and would have wasted him without a moments hesitation had he not found a way to get into their defenses. They thought he was a cool white boy. Which he laughed about. He was cool to keep from getting cooled. It was cause and affect. Nothing more. The victim of ones surroundings.

Amir drove with Sharon Lee on his side. It was going to be a great night. She, with her long legs and slim body. He was going to have great fun after the party was over. And maybe during and in between. Sharon Lee would let him have his way. She always did. It wasn't that he didn't like Sharon Lee. He did, but she was so nonchalant about the whole thing. If he did, he did; if he didn't, he didn't. It didn't phase her in the least. She was just riding through life, enjoying whatever bumps in the road would come up and riding out the hard times. He figured she was use to hard times. Being a single woman and all. He knew how hard it was for a single woman. Dating and trying to maintain. You put up with so much shit. He wondered why she put up with his shit. And he gave it to her. With both barrels. She let him hurt her, and she just smiled, went home and resumed her life. Like, nothing really matter. Maybe she didn't care. Maybe life had just burnt her out. But she maintained. Rode the ride. She probably knew that there was something else somewhere. She would find it eventually and that thought maintained her.

Sharon Lee rode along and thought to herself quietly. She liked the parties but she also knew that she was going to spend the night with Amir. Her son was safe with his cousins, so she had nothing to fear from that. So the night was going to be whatever. She was in the crowd. He was at the top of the crowd. She didn't want his money, or his fame, just wanted to see if being up there was worth all the hype and all the trouble. And it takes trouble to get there. Most people try it the hard way if they aren't born into wealth. If they go to school and struggle to get it, then, whatever it takes to maintain it, they will do. Including murder. Nothing makes you want to kill someone quicker then if you fought to get your wealth and this one person can instantly take it away. Or take it period. Then, there are the rich by accident. They hit on something successful and suddenly they were rich. It was interesting hanging out with them. They spend and spend, not caring if they have it tomorrow or not. It was an unexpected thing and they just enjoy it. But they usually lose it later. Most of them. There are a few who get wise and hang on to it, remembering their life lessons and settling in to enjoy without going overboard. Finding a nice wife, if they aren't already married, giving to charities. But the majority turn into hedonistic bastards who spend with no tomorrow and think the money changed the fact that they were always assholes. And the things they couldn't get as assholes they can now have and they appreciate it even less. Those are the ones who lose it all, talk about what they had and then they are divided into a subgroup who either continues to talk about it or tries to get it again. One scheme after another. They are the saddest because they never achieve that goal again. At that point, the rich and the poor know they are assholes and they are caught in that never never land of assholeness from which they never escape. People from both sides come to their funerals because they want to make sure the bastard is dead or they don't believe he died and they come to check it out for themselves. But there is no pity or remorse. Only the settling of a bet. Sharon Lee wasn't sure which category that Amir fell into. He was different about his ill gotten gain. He knows he probably won't have it forever and he is investing in a lifestyle that he enjoys. He either came from great poverty or middle class. Lower middle class. The upper middle class enjoy their status enough to help their children maintain it. Its like its grandfathered. Lower middle class usually becomes middle class. With the same problems and situations, just a little more of a means to take care of things. They send their children to college on the hope that their kids will become upper middle class. Not rich, but not middle either. Just a little better than their parents. Its a viscous cycle. Sharon Lee just rode the waves. She was neither middle or upper, not lower either. Her family was middle class only because of the number of kids they had. The money was definitely middle class but the number of children put them in a bind. Most of the people in the neighborhood had two children. There were 9 in her family. So the family of four scenario didn't quite fit. They were more like a family and then a few more.

She made good grades in school, but didn't try to excel. Most of the teachers knew her because they had her brothers and sisters. And her sisters children later on. They knew her mother and not much about her father. He didn't go to school much. She was in the click by proxy, because she was known. There were things that would not happen to her because the hoods had older brothers or sisters who knew Sharon Lee's older brothers and sisters. It didn't happen that way. Although she wasn't like them, their reputations had established a place for her and she held it. By being aloof. Hanging out with whom she wanted, in the click, but outside it. So she was riding around Atlanta with someone who was in the click. Not by proxy this time, but by herself. Her family didn't really know the company she kept. And they would not like it. But they were just people. People of their own created social standing, but it was a standing and accepted almost everywhere, like Visa. You could have a bankfirst visa, but if it had that visa on it, you were in the click. She knew that the sex would be rough. He liked it like that she didn't entirely not enjoy it. There were certain aspects that made her question why she was there. Her upbringing was not that way, but she chose to do it because she wasn't brought up that way. Just to walk on the wild side. Sometimes it made her sad, but you couldn't help your upbringing. She didn't forget it, remembered it always, but chose to ignore it when the feeling suited her and it did tonight. Tonight she would not have midwestern charm, she would be street slut, extraordinaire. When she did a character, she played it to the utmost. This would be academy award material, if she could get such a thing. For her performance. She wondered to herself why she was so noncommittal to anything in particular. Was it the fact that she had seen and been places where other people had not? Was it the fact that she had experienced so much that nothing surprised her anymore. Does a person continue to live that can't be surprised. Sharon Lee didn't feel let down, or hurt about her life. She took everything as it came, tried to read nothing special into situations. Just accepted them for what they were. But it was that very thinking that no one understood although they themselves did it, though not conscienceless. If you have been through shit, you learn to recognize shit, that's all. No matter how you tried to dress it up, shit was still shit.

Amir and Sharon Lee arrived at the place, Morgan not far behind. There were already people there, the parking lot was filling up. The security guard telling them where and where not to park. She saw John's vet in the distance. He was there. She liked him. Everyone liked him. He was so cool. She wondered which gold outfit he would be wearing. So like him, gold. Cold and shiny. What everyone wanted but only a few could have.

Amir parked the car in his spot, and Morgan slid her vet in beside them. They got out of the car and headed for the festivities. John was heading up the elevator when he saw them coming and held the door.

Amir smiled at the man.

"what's up man?"

John answered in his sweet southern drawl.

"same ol' same ol'. Hey Sharon Lee."

"John. How you? This is my friend Morgan."

"damn girl, you look fine."

He shook her hand and smiled.

"you flyin' solo tonight?"

"yeah man, woman on the rag and raggin' on me. Had to get a way, y'know. Plus, I need to discuss some business with you in a moment or two."

"ain't no drama man, you know you good for it."

They all got off the elevator.

"Hey morgan, maybe we can dance later."

"Sure John. Nice meeting you."

"Same here."

Amir stepped into his house and the few people that knew him acknowledged him and Sharon Lee. The others were just invited and they looked at him in awe. Women straightened their hair a little and when they saw Sharon Lee on his arm, turned away with their noses in the air. Everyone wants the head man. Sharon Lee took Morgan to the weed bowl and picked up a couple of joints.

"lets go to the outside of the party. The balcony is nice."

No one was allowed on the balcony but the closest of Amir's friends. They could see where someone had been out there. Doobies in the ashtray and empty bottles everywhere but in the trash can. Instinctively, Morgan began removed the refuse and Sharon Lee smiled and helped. They settled down in their seats to look at the full view of the beautiful Atlanta skyline. From up here, the limos in the big hotel areas were stunning. People getting out and getting in. The lights flickering and looking like stars that had come to earth to party on the Saturday night in Hotlanta. The traffic down peachtree was moving slowly, everyone taking in the view. People watching. They fired up their joints and inhaled. Deeply, letting the smoke fill their lungs, holding it a little then letting it out slowly. Morgan could feel the choking rising in her and she decided it would be in bad taste to cough until Sharon Lee did. They both coughed and laughed. Sharon Lee spoke in an exaggerated deep voice.

"Good shit huh?"

"No stems or seeds that you don't need."

"Acapulco gold is . . ." and together,

"Bad ass weed!!!"

"Okay, so we know cheech and chong"

"Well, my friends brother's did. We used to sneak and listen to their records."

"me too, Morgan."

"Its great having older brothers, huh?"

"Sometimes."

There was silence for a while as the each reflected on things. Morgan didn't have an older brother, but she wished she had let Sharon Lee think so. One of her girlfriend's brother was a cheech and chong fan and that's how she heard it. Sitting at the top of the stairs listening during while she spent the night because her parents were having a cop party. When people realize you have a cop in your family, they don't want to deal with you, so Morgan decided not to let the fact be known. Not to Sharon Lee. She liked her.

"Sharon Lee, are you in love with Amir? He seems to be in love with you."

"Morgan dahling, I have learned that love is fleeting in men. Amir likes me because he thinks I don't want him to. The more you push toward a man, the more he backs away. He's never had anyone who didn't get impressed by his ways. So, he doesn't know how to deal with me. That, in itself is the draw. He will try to find a way to please me, or he will give up. Most of them give up when they are so close."

"But you sleep with him."

"Sex is easy for a woman if she has the right attitude. Men sleep with women for purely physical enjoyment. They don't waste time on emotion, not at first. So, I have gotten to the point where I don't put emotion into sex. Instead of looking at the sex like most women do, as a show of love, I look at it as sex. Love comes later and its harder won than sex. So, I enjoy sex for what it is. Love is something that two people work towards. Its the little things, like candlelit dinners, or conversations in the wee hours of the morning that make me think of love. Or the Sunday's spent laying around, eating, talking, loving, watching movies, loving some more that makes a relationship. If I am physically attracted to a man, I can have sex with him. But if we talk afterwards, have a nice conversation, touch each other, I can fall in love. Amir has sex with me. He makes me nice breakfast—my favorite, eggs benedict. Not the way I make it, but its nice to see him try to please me. A man I was in love with told me that the one thing I want from a man, is the most impossible to get. I am holding out for the impossible."

"And that is?"

"Caring. Men have to care. Emotionally. I know that somewhere there is a man who will make love to me, and then, look me in the eyes, hold me. We will make plans together and talk together and do things together. It won't be about money or things. It will be about love. And when I find that, I will know he is the one."

"you're not material?"

"Sure I am, but not as a basis for a relationship. If I have to be with a man to secure myself financially, but cannot offer him the same, then its not a relationship and I will be sacrificing what I believe and feel to keep him happy so that the money won't be cut off. I would have to compromise."

"Oh."

"But Morgan, the money does get cut. Either the man finds someone else he wishes to be with, or he just gets tired of being your benefactor. Then the woman has to look for another benefactor. Amir has it going on, right now. But, he will get busted eventually, and then what does he have? The memories of when he had it like that, or the fortitude to get it back which will supersede everything else. If he loves me with his money, if the money is gone, his love of money will make him get it back and I will be just an inconvenience. If he had fell in love with me when he was living in the projects or something, he would love me after the money was gone. We didn't build this together. I want to build together. Not come in after its made."

"That sounds hard to achieve."

She sat quietly and hit her joint again.

"I believe (exhaling slowly), that there is someone for everybody. One day, or night, I will meet the man who is trying to have something and wants a woman with him so they can get it together. I know he's out there. And until I find him, I will endure the trappings that go along with this lifestyle with what Amir says is my detached emotions, have fun, so, in case I don't, I will have plenty of memoirs to keep me busy when I get old. Love is relative Morgan, life is real."

Morgan sat back quietly pondering this for a moment. Her mind wandering to the people below, the sky an azure with the stars twinkling in the sky. She loved Atlanta, and its people. And Sharon Lee.

Quietly they sat and enjoyed the night air. It wasn't too warm and hadn't cooled enough to make them put on a jacket. The music was kickin' and so was the weed.

"Well, lets go see the sordid group of partiers that have been attracted to the light like a moth to a flame."

"Sharon Lee, you have issues."

"Morgan dahling, we all do."

They walked back into the crowded place.

There was a woman on the dance floor who was doing her strip show, which, despite the crowd was focused on Amir. Everyone had stepped off the floor to watch her. Her eyes were focused on Amir and he was looking back with slight amusement. The light on the floor was showing all the blemishes that were hidden in the cover of the night. Her skin wasn't smooth and beautiful, is was worn and rugged. The make up on her face was fine, but she could have used some body makeup to cover the fact that she led a less than successful life. She continued her focus on Amir, until she saw him turn and walk away with Sharon Lee. Her eyes followed them until they disappeared in a private hallway. There was no reason to continue the side show and she walked off the dance floor to the coke room. The disappointment showing on her face like a flag. Morgan found a place in the back of the party to stand and watch the events unfold. It was fun but without Sharon Lee to talk to, she was once again the strange face in the crowd. There were so many people here, she couldn't believe the mixture. Black, white, and other colors. All partying together. Her eyes glanced over to the door, there was a man coming through the door. He was nice looking, but he looked like a narc or something, despite trying to look in the crowd. He went to the table, picked up a joint. Looking around the crowd, he glanced at Morgan and smiled. Then he headed to the coke room.

Steve arrived at the party when it was in full steam. The crowd was maddening, he had never seen so many beautiful people in his life. He looked around at the crystal bowls of joints and pills. It was a good night to party. He walked over to the table and picked up a joint and stuck it behind his ear. He glanced around the crowd. His eyes found a black rose hiding in the background. Steve thought she was very beautiful and yet she was hiding out. A flower shouldn't hide in the shade, she should seek the sun. He could be her sun. He smiled at her and she smiled back. He would find out who she was. She didn't seem to be part of the usual crowd. Well, that would be later, he headed for the coke room. It was time to get his party on.

Amir and Sharon Lee were finished with their private little party. He was in rare form tonight, Sharon Lee noticed. He wasn't as brutal as he had been with her. It didn't matter. She was just in it for the fun. Sex was always fun. Tomorrow she would be home. Maybe she and her little boy would go hang out in the park. Fly a kite or blade. He was getting better at blading. Sharon Lee watched as Amir got ready to make his appearance again at the party. She decided that she wouldn't go back out there. Nothing to see. Same group of hanger's on every time. Waiting for their something for nothing. She lay back in the bed, smoking quietly on a joint. Amir, ready to make his exit, kissed her and told her he would be back or something like that. She smiled at him, but her mind was saying 'whatever.'

Amir readied himself for his return to the party. He and Sharon Lee had a great time, but the best was yet to come. He wasn't really bad to her this time, too many people around. He knew she would be here for the night, leaving early in the morning. He always fixed her breakfast and she ate it, but he knew her mind was elsewhere. He watched her laying there smoking on the joint. She wasn't even here now. He wasn't sure if she was there when he was making love to her. As much as Amir wanted to be with Sharon Lee, her detachment made him angry. She never called his name, very seldom looked him straight in the eyes. When he looked at hers, they were not empty, but they were somewhere else. Could he ever get through to her? He really wanted to. He kissed her and told her he would return. She smiled, but she wasn't there. She was somewhere else.

Morgan realized that Sharon Lee wasn't going to be available for a while and she was suddenly pretty tired. Too much noise and too many people. Maybe she should have stayed at the jazz club. At least there the loud music was live. Oh well, she had had enough partying for one night. At least she got out of the house. Morgan realized she didn't get Sharon Lee's phone number. It would have been nice to talk to her again. Sharon Lee was one of the few women she had met that she actually liked. Morgan made her way through the crowd to the door. John had told her she would be getting a new assignment. With that on her mind, she started her vet. The quiet was wonderful. As she drove, she wondered where all those people would be after the party was over. Did they have lives? Did they live in these houses that were dark, except for the one light burning in a small window. The bedroom light? Did the men have wives waiting for them to return home? Wondering where they were. Would they have lipstick on their collars and red panties in their cars? She thought about it as she made her way down 85. Going home.

END

BOOK TWO

Beginning

Morgan played outside on her driveway with her friends from up the street. They lived in Forest Park, a southern suburb of Atlanta. Her father was a police officer and her mother was a housewife. Most of the girls or for that matter the other children of the neighborhood had stay at home mother's and fathers who brought home the bacon. Morgan was taught by her mother that this was not always the case, and her father inadvertently told her by Morgan listening to the conversations that her mother and father had in the wee hours of the night when Morgan was supposed to be sleeping. He would discuss his cases and the crimes that he had to investigate and her mother would listen and comment directly. Morgan loved the relationship that her mother and father had. She assumed that all the families had similar circumstances at home as well, no one really discussed what was going on in the bedrooms. It was not a child's place to discuss these things. Besides, they were happy with the way things were.

All the yards were manicured the same, it wasn't like those gate communities where you had rules and regulations to follow or you couldn't live there, it was more a conjoined effort by the people in the neighborhood. They took pride in their homes and their cars and the families that they built. There were neighborhoods like this scattered throughout Altanta and each had a pride within themselves.

Morgan's life was filled with friends, activities, her mother wanted her to have all the experiences that she wanted and she wanted many of them. She wanted to be a ballerina once, after seeing a play downtown. She wanted to write plays and act them out after having seen the Nutcracker. Her friends were eager to go along with her and the cummulative effort usually had them performing a play, complete with costumes in the basements of someone's home with family and friends togther.

Morgan's mother grew up in the small town of Madison Georgia and under the tutiledge of her mother and father, she was taught the ways of being a woman and the hard work that a man does. Her father did not want her to move to the big city, fearing that it would lead her down the wrong path, but her mother wanted her to go far from the quite country environment and see that there was more in the world than just cows, corn and cabbage.

Her mother met her father on a night out with her friends from college. They were attending Clark University and she was majoring in economics. It wasn't that she wanted to pursue a career in this field but her mother was insistent that she go to college and she felt that this course would be the less challenging. She knew she wanted a husband and she knew she wanted children. She was also sure that she would not live her mother's dream but her own.

Morgan's father came from a relatively rough section of town off Bankhead Highway. When he lived there, it was not as bad as everyone said, but then, reputation was always worse than the actual place. They lived like everyone else in Atlanta except they had to live it a little more hard. His father worked hard at the Ford Plant and his mother stayed home as did most of the mothers. The men in this generation did not want their wives to work unless lay offs or termination made them have to do so. There were a few people on welfare but it was not the norm back then as it was now. He had a way with the ladies and always wanted to be a police officer although he didn't tell his friends. The police were thought of as a nuisance but not an aspiration. They seemed to involve themselves in other people's lives either by invite or by tragedy. When they arrived, it was not because of something good. He watched the police when they came to the different houses who needed them, either an argument that went a little wild, or a fight that ended with a hospital trip. No one ever pressed charges which made the police not so willing to come out. But he watched them when they did. He liked their uniforms, their demeanor, their guns.

The sirens always made him chilled. The police didn't come as often as he would have liked, but enough for him to get the idea it was something he wanted to do.

They met at a mixer at Clark University. He was on the police force then, a rookie cop watching to make sure that none of the little college girls got into any trouble by having the wrong crowd invated their little dance. He spotted her across the room, not dancing, just sitting.

He watched her face while she was preoccupied with the excitement of the event. She was wearing a lime green two piece outfit which accented her skin. He laughed to himself that not too many people could pull off lime green. She didn't know that he was watching her which allowed her to be herself. She laughed, smiled and interacted but she didn't dance. He wished he could ask her to dance but he was on duty. He had to find out who she was. A young lady who was eyeing him passed close enough to him for him to smell her steamy perfume. The disappointment in her face was palpitable when he asked about the woman in the lime green.

"Oh, she's Sylvia. She is really a quiet country girl. Wouldn't you like a little more excitement?"

He did. Although he wanted to meet Sylvia, pretty women have always been a weakness for him. He'd get back to Sylvia now that he knew her name.

"What kind of excitement you talking about? And don't tell me one of those college kissing games, I'm not falling for that. If you aren't going to get down with it, stay away from it."

She smiled.

"Where's your vehicle? I never done it in a police car before."

He wasn't so sure, but he took her anyway. They spent a little time in the police car. He got what he wanted and she didn't know that he was pretnding she was Sylvia.

"We should meet again."

"We should, but we probably won't."

She pulled a piece of paper and put her number on it.

"Just in case you feel a need".

He tucked the number in his wallet for safe keeping. He would use it more than he thought. His one weakness and he cultivated it. It wasn't hard to get women. His uniform attracted most of his play and the others just liked his walk and his demeanor. He didn't mean nothing by it and to him it was just little diversions on an otherwise long road to nowhere.

He took her out a week later. Sylvia was shopping downtown in Atlanta and happened pass the police station. He was just going to get his car when he noticed her. She was walking like she didn't have a care in the world looking at the shops and the people. It wasn't like she was a tourist. He watched in amusement as she treated everything and everybody like she was seeing them for the first time. She didn't even notice when he walked up to her.

"You know, you should pay more attention to your surrounds"

She was startled but she smiled.

"Everytime I come downtown and feel this energy. Look at all the booths and items for sale. Everyone is so excited and glad to be here. I wonder if they are making money doing this or do they just like being downtown."

"Some of them make money, some of the are con artists. You have to know the difference."

"Spoken like a true police officer."

"I saw you the other night at the event at Clark. You had that same look of wonderment and joy on your face then. Is that how you see the world?"

"Everyday is new and exciting to me. I get to see everything for the first time every day I wake up"

Henry liked her attitude although in the real world it didn't work that way. He knew then that he wanted to make her safe and warm so that her world would always be as rosy as she perceived it. He knew then that she was going to be his wife.

He took her to dinner in the downtown hotel district so that she could sit up and look down at all the lights and the happenings. The shine in her eyes was so wonderful to him, almost like when he was a child and heard sirens coming. She ate quietly and told him about the way of life she grew up in. The country. Henry wanted to see the country. All his relatives were from the city. He had been in those little country towns with less reputable people, his longing was to see it from the perspective of a family that had a real life. Henry watched his bride to be and wondered if he would have to teach her anything in bed. He knew his experience level and it was evident to him that she was still untouched. That was the only thing that turned him off about her. He would have to be gentle and caring and sex to him was not like that. It had never been like that. He always made it fast and loose with the women who knew what to do. Teaching would be a different experience for him. What if she was unwilling to learn or worse, too scared to participate. His face clouded.

"Whats wrong? Your face just changed, very dramatically I must say. Don't you want to meet my parents? You don't have to you know."

"Its not like that Sylvia. I was just thinking of our future."

"Future? Already? This is our first date."

"I know, but my gut feeling tells me that you are the one for me. I know it sounds strange, this fast and all, but I am not a man who waits around and my intuition is very strong. I just don't know if you are ready for what marriage means."

"I am taking that to mean sex. Is that right?"

"Well, yeah. I don't mean before we get married but on the honeymoon. I have been around you know. I don't know about all that tender stuff that ladies like you are used to."

"I know what marriage means and even though I was saving myself for it, don't think I'm a prude who doesn't know anything. I grew up in the country. Sex was around us and a part of life. The animals, my parents. I didn't see them but I could hear them. Mom gave me a great attitude about sex, so don't think I'm one of those shrinking violets that are scared to get wet honey. I've been waiting for this a long time."

He smiled at her and she smiled too. He slid his hand under the table and caressed her leg.

"Just don't think you gonna get it with a promise of marriage, I won't let go of my virgin title until you give me the title 'Mrs'".

II

Amir was raised in the big city of Newark. He lived in the Weequaic section along with countless other folks. His neighborhood was full of pimps, pushers, prostitues, honest citizens, old women, church folks. All rolled into one big neighborhood. The bar was around the corner from their house and next to the school. He grew up in the streets mostly, although his mother was home. She did work.

She was a single mother which was no different from most of the children, the difference was that she did have a job when most of the other mothers were laid off or not working. The grocer she worked for knew her from when she was a little girl and she had come to him when she was pregnant and had no where to go. The Chinese man trusted her and gave her a job even over the objections of his wife.

Amir was nutured and loved by his mother while he was young. He didn't know that they lived in the 'hood. She never taught him that word and only found out later as he was working on his future as a drug dealer. It wasn't something that he wanted to be. It just happened that way.

His mother, young and lonely, dated the wrong men. Most of the time, Amir was left to fend for himself when those occasions arose that she had company and she didn't want them to know she had a child. He didn't hate her for that at first. It gave him the opportunity to play outside with the other boys when normally he would be in the house. It wasn't until he was in his teens that he realized his mother really did have a problem. Most of the relationships ended and he was back to his normal routine of being in before dark. It was as he was growing into a man that the tide of his relationship with his mother changed and he set off to find a quick and easy way out of his predicament. One night when he was sleeping, his mother came into his room.

"I know you are becoming a man and I need to show you what a man and a woman do together."

She slid in bed with him and on top of him. His body responded but in his heart he knew it wrong. He felt sorry for his mother so he kept quiet and let it happen. She left his room as quietly as she arrived but Amir lay their with his eyes wide open about what happened. He knew that nothers were not supposed to sleep with their sons. He also know that men usually did this thing to their daughters because he had heard some of the girls talking about it. He cried for his mother's pain and suffering. He thought to himself that she must be really sick to do this. He couldn't hate her for it, but it made him less inclined to come home. It was then that the streets called to him even more. He tried not to sleep at home.

"Amir, you have been gone for weeks. What are you doing out there, selling drugs?"

"No momma just hanging out, trying to make a living."

He gave her money. By this time he was in his late teens and the incidents that he tried to avoid with his mother at times would come back to him and he hated her for it.

"I don't want your money son, you know what I want from you."

She would walk close to him and hold him too close, rubbing her body against his. He hated that his body responded but it was mechanical not mental. This time, he would have none of it. He pused his mother away.

"Stop it. Stop it. This is wrong, and you know it. I'm sorry that you are my mother, I'm sorry that you touched me. I know what women feel like when they are violated. I hate you mother. I'm leaving and I'm not coming back."

She screamed a loud, ungodly scream like her insides were being ripped out.

"I loved you. I loved you better than a mother should. How dare you turn on me. I hate you too, I hate you too."

She fell down in the corner of the kitchen where they were standing.

"You think I didn't know it was wrong, what I did to you. You think I didn't feel sorry for you. You don't think I didn't hate myself for it. I did, I do, I always will."

She lay there, sobbing.

Amir left the money in the jar where he always left it, took a few clothes and left his home for good.

He walked the streets of Bed-Sty thinking about what he wanted to do. When he looked up he was passing one of the Italian restaurants where he knew the real activity took place but they didn't talk to the neighborhood blacks, just a couple that they had always known. Giovanni was stepping out the back taking out the trash.

"Hey boy, you, boy, come here"

Amir stopped and looked at Giovanni. He knew who he was and he didn't like that boy shit.

"What man?"

"Hey, you look like you leaving home. Where you going?"

"why you want to know?"

"Hey don't get angry, I seen you around hustling a little. I know your momma, she used to do my shirts. Nice lady, how is she?"

Amir felt a hot burn in his face when Giovanni mentioned his mother.

"She died."

"Oh, such a shame. Listen, you want to make good money, get out these streets? I can show you how."

Amir walked up to the man.

"Any why would your greasy ass want to help me? I ain't Italian and I ain't your boy. Whats in it for you?"

Giovanni grabbed Amir and took him inside.

"Listen smart ass, I ain't out to hurt you. If these guys knew I was helping you, they would kick me out. I'm doing it because my son is an idiot. You need help, and I liked your mother even if we couldn't get together, you know? Times ain't right for that type of thing. If times were different, I would have married her and taken you and her to a nice place in Atlantic Ciy. So, pay attention to me, and do what I say. Take your things to the little hotel up the way, check into room 112. Tell them I sent you. Wash up and stop looking homeless. I'll meet you there in a day or two."

He gave Amir some money.

"Go eat some chicken or something. Rest and lay low. Don't let me see you on the block until I say so. You're going to better than these street hustlers who are going to die right here is Bed Sty. Not you. I can't teach you how to be a rocket scientist, but I can teach you how to be the best dealer you can and live to make the choice to get out or stay in."

Amir thought about that. A choice. He didn't know of anyone who had a choice in the streets except kill or be killed. And this guy liked his mother. Amir wished that he had gotten to her before she had gotten to him. He still thought of her as dead, but he threw love into the mix with her and slept that night dreaming that Giovanni and his mother had married.

When the sun rose on Amir it was with a new outlook. He wasn't sure what giovanni was going to show him but he knew it was still in the life that he knew. He never had a real job anyway always hustling in the streets. The situation with his mother made it much more worth his while to hang out in the streets. He felt bad for the girls who had told him their dirty little secrets and felt worse because he was unable to tell them his own. Men were not victims they created victims. Those girls were victims of a man not the other way around. He held that in his heart for as long as he could. He would never be a victim again. Whatever was going to happen between he and Giovanni, he would not be the victim.

Giovanni showed up a few days later. Amir was getting worried because his money was running low and he was losing out in the streets. He needed to get his hustle back on before too long. However, when Giovanni arrived, he gave him more money and explained what he was going to do.

"Listen, you are not going to be a dumb drug dealer like these other guys, you are going to learn something."

He gave Amir three books. One was on great art, the other on wines and the other on great people.

"You read these things. The art will be easy, go to the museum and see the real art, the wines, also easy, each week come by and tell me what you learned about wine and I will give you the bottle to taste. Not to drink like an alley wino, but to drink and enjoy. The book on great people are explains the personalities of Mozart, Shakespeare, Homer. Read these. I don't know much about great blacks except Martin Luther King but you know enough about him already. Find books on Africa and read. Kings, Queens, civilizations. Read my boy, read until you cannot read anymore. This is the way you will become not a stupid drug dealer but an entrepreneur. Drugs are always going to be out there either legal or not. Don't feel the guilt of having this type of job. You do not bring people to you they seek you out. Learn, make enough money to have a life that you want, educate yourself and then get out of the business. Don't let it catch you up or how you say, get caught up."

Amir listened and it made sense to him. So he agreed.

Each day, he would run the drugs for Giovanni and each evening he would come by the room and ask him to explain what he read. Amir wasn't into wine but he read the book anyway. He went to the library and studied about the great kings of Africa and told Giavonni about them.

"I know that there were great black peoples. This land makes people forget where the come from and mesh as one. We are not one people but one group of different peoples. I am glad you are learning. My son doesn't want to learn. By the way, I saw your mother the other day. I don't know why you tell me she was dead. I told her what you said and she weeped. I don't know these mother/

son relationships but you did what you had to do I suppose. It is serious when the person who brought you into the world is dead to you. I don't want to know what happened but I will watch out for her for you."

Amir was glad about that.

"I could explain but I don't want to ever speak of it again. You watch out for her."

"I will. You cannot stay in Bed-Sty for ever, you will have to move on. She will be okay with me."

Amir felt good with that. He knew he was going to leave this area and go for bigger things. His education was not quite complete and he appreciated this man for teaching him.

III

Steve sat on the steps of the little trailer that he and his mother lived in. His father was a trucker and he was around once in a while. Steve listened to the man in the room with his mother. It was happening again. His mother had found someone to keep her company as she liked to call it. Steve was not stupid. He knew what was going on.

The trucker that lived with them was not his real father, he didn't know who he was and his mother did not talk about it too much. She didn't talk bad about him, just didn't mention him at all. The new trucker, Jimmy, was to be his step father. Steve knew that this man didn't want kids and resented that he was around. His mothe always stood behind her son when Jimmy tried to toss him out.

"He's my one and only and he has no where to go. I can't just dump him in the street."

But Steve was 6 then. He was almost 15 now and larger than Jimmy. The money that his mother received from the men that stopped by now went to her alcohol and not to Steve. She wanted him to get a job, but in the hills of Kentucky where they lived, there was nothing to do. No one was working but the truckers that came through once in a while and the ladies who worked the truck stops. He tried to work at the truck stop cafe, hauling and stocking things but the lady that ran the place always wanted him to stop by and see her after hours and he wasn't wanting to do that with her. So, she let him go. He was glad to go. She was wrinkled, ugly and old. So now he sits outside the trailer, waiting for something to happen.

He wanted to be a police officer and read books about it. But you had have a diploma and Steve hadn't been to school in months. He didn't have the clothes to wear to school, although everyone here was poor, his clothes were worse than others because he had no big brother to give him his hand me downs. The men that came by to see his mother left shirts and underwear sometimes and he would take those things and keep them for his own. But it wasn't the same and he hated school.

On nights with the full moon when the woods were illuminated, and Jimmy was at the house, he would walk. One night, Jimmy and his mother were having another fight about him. He heard Jimmy tell his mother that he wasn't going to come around no more if she didn't find somewhere to put Steve.

"He's a big boy and I ain't feeding him no more. You need to find somewhere for him to go. When I pull out, I'm taking you and not that boy so if you wanno go with me, you better think of something."

That Monday morning when Steve woke, his mother and Jimmy were gone. He had not heard them pull out. He walked around the trailer, looking. It was quiet. He didn't cry, he went to the refrigerator and looked for food. Nothing but 2 eggs and a little bacon. He made a bite and then looked for money. His mother used to keep money in the little cut in the mattress under the bed when Jimmy came home. He looked and there was roughly fifty dollars and a note. She knew he would go there.

"Steve, you a big boy now. I am sorry but I had to go. Take this money, go to a bigger city, Cincinnati or something. You can live."

That was all.

Stevie looked at the note and laughed. He was free. He wasn't going to no cincinnati or any of those other cities. He decided to go to the store and get something. On the way to the store, he saw and dog just walking down the road. Steve stood still and called to the dog. The dog came slowly, but he came. Steve petted the dog and walked him out into the woods. He petted him and played with him and lured him into the woods. He petted him more and the grabbed the dog. The dog began to fight with Steve, sensing he was in danger. Steve threw the dog into the tree and as the dog lay there unconscience, Steve picked up a large limb and beat the dog until there was no doubt it was dead. As he beat the dog, he felt excited and fulfilled. The harder he hit him, the more excited he became. His face flushed with excitement. When he was finished, he headed home, not to the store and masturbated until he fell asleep.

Steve's urges became uncontrollable. He would wake up in the morning looking for victims. Dogs and cats around the holler began to disappear. People were posting signs up for their pets.

Steve stayed in the trailer he called home. He had taken his mother's things out and burned them. As he was going through them he found ten dollars here, twenty dollars here. His mom had been hiding money all around their home and Steve didn't know it. It allowed him to stay in his trailer for a while longer than anticipated. No one came by looking for either of them. He never went to school and his mom didn't do much either except go to the bar. When he was in town and the locals would ask about his mother, he would say that she got a job in Frankfort and was making a little money. Let them assume what they wanted he didn't care. He was going to say Paducah but too many people here had family in Paducah, they could track his story if they wanted to. He knew they didn't. Steve continued to do what he was doing until one day he met a girl.

She was passing through hiking on her way to Tennessee. Steve spotted her walking and looking around. He knew he didn't look the best but he didn't look as bad as some of the other folks on the street. He walked up to her and had a conversation. She was walking to Tenneessee, going to start her life over and get away from her past. Steve asked her if she had a place to sleep and she replied the the woods belonged to God and were free and she would camp there. He took her to the little restaurant in town and bought her a burger and some fries. They ate and talked and he waved goodbye to her when he was sure everyone was watching. He set off in the opposite direction toward his home. Once he passed where anyone could see him, he doubled back through the woods and waited until it was dark.

When darkness fell, he walked, under the cover of darkness which now was not a problem with him, he could see like a cat in the woods. He could see the little fire light from the camp she had set up. He couldn't understand why a girl would like to be in the woods all by herself but he figured she was used to it. It wasn't good to put yourself at risk like that. She had and Steve was going to take advantage of it. No one would know that it was he who did what was going to happen. Being out in the open was an invitation for something to happen. It could have been a vagrant passing through.

He crept quietly through the woods. He could see her sitting there with her headphones on, her face in a book. A little light on her hat illuminated the pages. She didn't see him coming. He stood behind her, she was still unaware that he was there. Grabbing her from behind, he muffled her screams and wrestled her down to where she was laying on her back. Holding her down, he opened his pocket knife and laid her clothing open from the back like he was fileting a fish. She strugged but he could feel she was weakening. Maybe it was because he had her pressed into the ground cover. He raped her, from behind and as he was reaching his climax, he stuck the knife into her neck, feeling her tense as he did so. She struggled briefly and he lay the knife aside and put his hands around her neck, squeezing until he felt no more life in her. He lay there, on top of her for a moment, catching his breath. His face was wet with perspiration and the feeling he had inside was better than any drug he had ever had. He lay there, on top of her smiling to himself. When he caught his breath, he got up. Fixing his clothing, he looked around for a place to bury her. He didn't have to worry about getting rid of the campsite because so many people passed through and camped out.

Steve found a small ravine filled with leaves and debris. He removed her clothing and and piled it together to take with him. He dumped her unceremoniously into the ravine, jumped into it and covered her with the leaves and broken branches. Steve took a large branch and picked up her clothing. Walking backwards, he covered his tracks and headed home. He was hungry.

When Steve arrived home, he took the clothing and put it in a bag to burn. He stood in the small shower and washed himself. His body still tingled from the sex he had. He dried and dressed and went into the kitchen to make himself a burger. Yes, a burger would be good right now, with all the fixings. He decided he would go into town tomorrow and listen around, just in case.

Steve went to school for a while, just to make sure everything was normal. He was sure that folks knew his mother had run off, but most of the kids at school kept their distance from him. It was as it always was. He attended class and the teachers did say much to him. He wanted to make everything look normal. Sometimes he could hear them whispering about him, but they always did that too. It wasn't that he was dressed any different than the other poor kids around town, it was just that he didn't socialize. The kids assumed that his father was still driving rigs and that they would be back some time. A lot of the kids had parents, either one or both who drove rigs. It was the only job available after the mines closed down and that meant that a lot of them were left alone for some period of time. It wasn't something that made the law suspicious. They knew.

Dogs and cats continued to disappear and an occaional hitcher would come through. Steve stayed busy. He had racked up four kills and no one even wondered about the missing people. There was the two hippies passing through, the man and the woman. Steve had to be imaginative with them. He used his mother's sleeping pills that she kept everywhere and laced their food. He presented himself as a 'concerned citizen' and fed them a tasty stew that was powerpacked with sleeping pills. As the man slept, he lay his head open with a large piece of wood. The woman was sleeping through the whole thing. He took her and disposed of both of them. Steve found that the sleeping pills took the fight out of his victim and he decided that he would only go after lone women. Two was harder to kill than one.

IV

Morgan's life was going as normal for a suburban girl. But changes were in the air and she could feel it. She had good friends and her mother had enrolled her in ballet and music. She studied with her friends, taking time out to discuss boys or the newest dance that had come out.

Her room was filled with stuffed animals, pretty dresses, and all the trappings of a middle class young lady. Just as her friends had. Her mother cooked, cleaned and doted on her father, who had been promoted to detective some time ago.

There was a little tension in the household and Morgan could hear the converations at night about the women in her father's life. She didn't know for sure what they were talking about but her mother's tone was sad and frustrated. Morgan could hear her father trying to reassure his wife that there was nothing going on, but she didn't believe him.

There were nights on the weekends when Morgan was allowed to stay up later than usual, she would hear her father come in and run downstairs to greet him. He would have perfume smells on his clothing that Morgan could smell. It was faint, but it was there. Her mother wore only one kind of perfume and she only wore it when she went to church. The smells on her father's clothing did not match. At first Morgan was silent about it all, just glad that her father had made it home without a scratch. She watched the news and worried that her father would get killed by one of the many bad guys that were out in the streets of Atlanta. Her father always reassured her stating that he only went to the scene of a crime after the crime was committed.

One late night, Morgan heard her father come in and she ran to meet him. Wrapping herself around him when he picked her up.

"Daddy, that perfume on you is not mother's. Were you shopping? You know they spray that stuff on you when you shop. Did you get me something?

Her father looked at her and put her down.

"Yes, I was shopping for a gift for you and your mother at Macy's when this stupid lady sprayed this junk on me. And you are getting too big to jump on me like that, you will just have to find a more lady like way of greeting me when I come home. You're getting too big for me to pick up."

Morgan liked the fact that her father noticed she was getting bigger, growing up. She didn't question his reasoning about that although her father was upset with himself that he had been caught with the perfume of his lover on his clothing. He told her not to wear perfume when he came to visit but she always tried to leave a scent behind, like a cat.

After awhile, her father started coming home so late that Morgan was not awake when he did come home.

Her mother had begun to get depressed. Morgan heard her father say that word to his friend one day. Morgan started paying attention to her mother.

While they were shopping for Morgan's training bra and 'grown up' underwear, she looked at her mother. She did have a sadness in her eyes. She picked out pretty pink and yellow matching underwear for her daughter but the glow was not in her eyes. They shopped for tights and slips and frilly skirts for Morgan. Morgan wasn't so much into the frills but her mother enjoyed getting it for her. She knew she would have to wear them to church because her mother scrutinized her when she was dressing for church. School was different, her mother was so busy getting her father off to work and making Morgan's lunch that Morgan could dress they way she wanted to. As long as her hair was combed and the outside clothing looked good, her mother didn't have time to look harder at what she wore underneath.

Her father was showing an indifference to family matters. He had begun to not come home at all sometimes, saying he was on a stakeout or police business where no one really questioned him. Morgan questioned him in her mind but dared not to his face. The time he did spend at home was tense and weird. Her mother was very ingratiating and subserviant, trying desparately to engage her husband in any type of convesation, attention, whatever would work. She had even begun to buy lacey items from Victoria's Secret that Morgan discovered once when she was doing the laundry. Her chores were changing because her mother had stopped doing a lot of the household things that she once took pride in. Morgan had to cook the meals, wash the clothing and generally keep house. There were times when her mother would not come out of the room and Morgan would bring her lunch on the weekends and breakfast and dinner during the week when she had to go to school. It wasn't a hardship on Morgan, but she did wonder why her father was so changed. She knew it had to do with whoever he was seeing on the side and she was going to find out who it was. In the meantime, she had to keep the family together somehow.

V

Amir left Bed Sty just like he was told. He had progressed from a runner and doing odd jobs within his chose profession. He saved his money and watched his spending. Just using enough to get by. His goal was to make it to Atlanta, Dallas, or Houston. He wanted to be in the south and he wanted to be in a large metropolitan area with the largest gathering of black people but enough culture to keep him from actually residing in the hood where his roots were established. He did his research and Atlanta won out because at that time, there was a large migration of blacks from the north heading to Atlanta. If things didn't go well for him, he would go to Dallas next. He finished saving what he needed, bought a used car and headed south down 95. Amir had established a connection with a school mate and he had set Amir up in a small apartment in Forest Park. He bought a car because he was traveling with some goods to help get him in the market without stepping on too many toes and keep him out of the limelight for a while. He wanted to start out small time, and work his way up so that he paid his dues like everyone else. He had to make some southern friends. He knew too many people who went to Atlanta to get into the market by knocking out the southern competition but you don't go to someone else's house and then steal from them. They know all the ways in and out. All you get is trapped. He didn't want to end up on the wrong end of the 'county dumb' act. Antifreeze poisoning was an ugly way to die.

He arrived in Atlanta on a sunny, warm day, going to his school mate's house first to get his keys and get acclamated to his knew surroundings. His friend was middle range in the dope heirarchy and he was going to introduce Amir around at a social event that was scheduled for the weekend. All the big ballers would be there and some boys from Miami too. He would get Amir in 'on the strength'. Amir couldn't help but to trust his friend and he would get in and make his alliances later.

Amir checked out his new place. It was a step up from bed sty but it was not as good as you could get in Atlanta. He was satisfied with it however and its proximity to 75/85 and the airport would ensure that he could get his stuff picked up and delivered when he needed it. He invested in a small handgun until he could see what the other boys were playing with. He would rather have something and trade up than nothing and get caught without. Everyone had to have something.

His clothing was good enough for what he wanted to start however, he was interested in checking out the money crowd and needed to dress appropriately. He found that Phipps Plaza was the place he needed to go to connect with those folks and put it on his list of places to visit.

He sat back in his little world, and looked at his surroundings. He needed art objects. He wanted to start a collection and even though this place wasn't the grand ballroom he could at least put his touch on things. It was time he put to use what he learned about art and beginning slow was better than not beginning at all.

VI

Steve came home from school one afternoon to find that all the power to his little trailer was cut off. He looked around, shaking his head. To him, it was a sign that it was time to go. He packed up a few of his belongings, took the little cash that he earned and set off toward the south. He still had his dreams of being a police office and now was as good a time as any to get started. He didn't worry about his lack of education, somehow he would make his dreams happen. He didn't know how, but he knew he would.

He walked all that evening until the air got too cold for him. He spied a shack setting back off in the distance, the smoke rising from the chimney which to him meant a good meal at least. He knew that the old black lady who lived there was blind and she wouldn't mind having a friend to talk to. No one really messed with her, black or white. Some people you don't bother, no matter what their color. She was aged and wise. Some of the whites who swore they hated black people were go and see her for advice, a cure or just some conversation. It was said she made the best whiskey in the hollar. A descendent of freed slaves who first hid out in this region, she outlived any and all of her family. That alone, with this harsh life, was enough to give her hero's status. To have a family when the odds and the people are against you is proof that you have staying power in Steve's mind. He had staying power too and he was going to prove it.

He knocked on the door and he heard a sleepy voice tell him to come in. He did. The cabin was not lit very brightly but then she didn't need lights did she? But he did.

"Miss Eloise"

"Little Stevie"

"Yes ma'am, but I ain't little too much anymore."

"I kin tell by you voice. You hongry?"

"Yes ma'am I am."

"Go out back and wash your hands, food is on the stove. I know its kind of late so, if you want, you can stay back in the little shed back there. Got 'lectricity and heat. Folks don't like black n white eatin' together so come on back, git your plate. I knowd your momma gone, her and that trucker. Didn't know how long it would take you to get up outta there but here you is."

"Yes ma'am"

Steve went out to the pump and washed up. He wasn't sure what year Miss Eloise thought it was, but people stopped being weird about black folks and white folks eating together a long time ago. Racism wasn't gone but it had come further than that. Maybe she didn't like eating with white folks. People always assumed that blacks wanted to be with whites but it wasn't always the case. Miss Eloise didn't have to be with anyone she didn't want to.

He took his plate which was filled high with food, he thought that maybe Miss Eloise could see more than she let on, and went back to the shed. It was clean, dry and had electricity. A small cot lay to the back of it, a small table with a chair and a light to the front. In between was just space. He knew he couldn't stay long but he intended to stay long enough to get things satisfied so if he were to apply to be a police officer, he would have the necessary skills to get in. Most places didn't require much. He would study more later.

After the first few days, Miss Eloise didn't mind him coming to the house to read the bible to her

"I have long sense rubbed off those little raised dots for words. I was readin' so often. Rubbed it clear to the nuthin'. I have a Bible with words in it. You need to read anyway, man ain't nothin' if he cain't read or count his money. Bible is as good place to start as any."

So every evening when the dishes were done (Steve didn't mind washing the dishes for his keep, she didn't ask him for nothing else) he sat and read the bible to Miss Eloise. She would lay her head back quietly and hum a spiritual he imagined, not having been to church but he knew a spiritual just by the way she hummed and nodded, while he read.

Each evening, after he safely tucked her away in her bed, chopped a few pieces of wood for her fire to stay on, she was old and the damp night would probably kill her, he would go stalking out and about. There were more people traveling around these days it seemed with the summer ending, folks trying to get somewhere for the winter. He was able to take out two girls at one time this last trip. A black girl and a white girl. It worried him a little about the black girl because she didn't look like a tramp and black parents seemed to press the law harder to find their own—even if they have to play the race card. Some white girls just have more freedome. He worried over the black girl for a time. The crying didn't bother him. Well, it did, but it wasn't strong enough to chase away the urges that he felt. He shed a tear for these two because they may have made really good doctors or something. It was rare that he thought toward the future when doing his deed but something about that black girl . . . steve continued to go to school even though he didn't like it. He had just a little time to either graduate or to drop out and be able to get his GED. He opted for the GED although he would have liked to graduate with his small class but the obvious fact was there would be no one there to congratulate him. Miss Eloise probably would have gone but that would not have done. Not for the race thing just the fact that it would emphasize the fact that his mother was gone.

He stayed with Miss Eloise through the winter, making sure she had enough wood, food and whatever else she needed. People would stop by and see her and bring her things and he always made sure he was out of sight. He wondered how she made it so long by herself and in actuality she wasn't by herself but helped along by everyone. It was better that they didn't know he was living there. He didn't know why, it just seemed safe for people to assume that he was just on his own living somewhere, showing up at school occasionally even if he didn't have to be the topic of conversation at all the dinner tables, he liked to think that someone out there cared about what happened to him besides Miss Eloise.

He was feeling comfortable with his surroundings, even more comfortable than he had felt at home. That didn't surprise him any, he had long learned that sometimes black women were more nurturing than white women. It was why the plantation house always had a black women in charge of the inside workings. She nursed everybody, the wife, the husband the children even the dogs or cats that were inside. It was a sorry state of affairs for the black woman but it was perfect for the people who had her. Which was probably why slavery was very hard to get rid of. It wasn't necessarily the money that went with selling slaves, Steve surmised, but more about the nurturing that was given inside the house and probably why many people of wealth continued to have black women inside their homes until it was no longer well thought of to do so. Black people had come a long way and society frowned on that type of enslavement for blacks even though it was the Columbian or other spanish speaking people that took the place. Whatever is chic at the time, even if it involves the enslavement of people. Which is what it was even though there was a salary involved. It was never what the person was worth.

Steve also studied all the police books he could find. He was serious about being an officer of the law and knew that he had to endure this small bump in his life to make sure that it happened. No one really wanted an illiterate country bumpkin on their big city police force anyway. He didn't want to be one here in his little world, they made nothing and they did nothing. He wanted big city crime drama, drug dealers, prostitutes and other underworld figures. He wanted the excitement of that type of lifestyle. He had been a country bumpkin for as long as he could stand. He told himself every evening before he went to bed that he would have his life, the way he wanted. Patience.

VII

Morgan continued with her school work even though she had taken over all the chores associated with running a household. Her mother was just not into anything anymore and that bothered her. She wanted to confront her father about this and she knew that she would have to stay up late to do it. That was the hard part because she was so tired at the end of the day. She was determined however.

She set her alarm one Friday evening for two oclock in the morning so that she could get up and go to the couch in the living room and sleep there. She knew that eventually her father would come through the door. She wanted to be there for him. She had no luck ascertaining which woman he was sleeping with given her limited access to the outside world with all the things she had to do. But she did know that that was the issue. Police work did keep you away from home, but her father had been a detective for a long time and he had earned the right not to have to do as much as he said he did. She knew that.

Dozing on the couch, soft jazz playing in the background, just loud enough. She didn't want to wake her mother who was sleeping soundly upstairs. Her doctor had put her on medication to try to get her out of the depressive state she had fallen into, but Morgan knew what was the cause and the medicine could not cure a broken heart.

She heard the keys in the lock and sat up. Her father came through the door and was startled by her presence.

"Why are you up at this hour?"

"What is her name dad?"

"What?!"

"What is her name? I know its someone, I can smell the perfume on you. Mom is all depressed because she knows too."

"I told you you were too young for this foolishness, now mind your business and go to bed."

"Mom is my business Dad. She is wasting away to nothing and I am doing all the work around here, cooking, cleaning. I'm not a kid anymore because you made the situation that way."

Her father stood there for a moment and looked at his little girl, who was not so little anymore. He sat beside her.

"Your mother is ill, thats all. It has nothing to do with me, I promise."

"You lie."

"Morgan, grown ups have different things to deal with on a day to day basis. I can't think that you would understand, but I will try to be around more so that you can go back to having whats left of your childhood. Your mother understands what my life is like, she knew when we married that police work would keep me away sometimes."

"If it were police work daddy, I would understand, but I feel that its more than that. My feelings in my stomach tell me its more than that."

"Spoken like a good detective. But your intuition is wrong right now honey."

He kissed her on the forehead.

"Go to bed sweetie. I'll be around to help out more, I promise."

She looked at him and believed him. He was her daddy and even though she knew her guts were right about the woman, she also knew that he would be around more. If only for a little while.

She went to bed as she was told, but she couldn't sleep. Not well anyway. She tossed and turned until daylight shown through her window. The smell of bacon, eggs and pancakes encouraged her to stop pretending she was sleep and to get up. Going downstairs, she expected to see her mother in the kitchen as always but it was her father this time, cooking and humming a song. Her mother sat quietly at the end of the table, with a smile on her face.

"Good morning princess, your father decided to make breakfast this morning. Isn't that wonderful? I woke up and smelled breakfast. I thought it was you."

"No, I stayed up late on the phone last night, talking to Kathy."

She eyed her father and he winked at her.

"Kathy? Wasn't you supposed to spend the night with her this weekend, or was it last weekend? I have been so out of it, I can'gt really remember. When was it honey?"

"Oh mom, don't worry about that. Kathy has a new boyfriend and she doesn't have sleep overs anymore."

"Boyfriend? Oh my word is she old enough for that? You don't have a boyfriend do you? You are much too young for that foolishness. You should save yourself until you marry like your father and I did."

"of course I will mother. I don't like boys right now anyway. They are more into their video games and wrestling than they really are into girls. I want to study to be a detective."

"A detective like your ol' man, huh? Thats good."

"Well not exactly. I want to work more with the corporate criminals rather than the street punks."

"watch your language princess, you aren't a hardened detective yet."

They ate breakfast in silence. Morgan watched her mother smiling and couldn't tell if it was drug induced or if she was really smiling. She could feel that the tensions were gone right now, and her father was making an effort but this was just a few hours after their conversation, time would only tell.

Her mother went about her chores as usual and things for the day seemed to be a little normal. Morgan did homework on her computer and chatted with her friend Kathy using IM. Kathy was thinking about having sex with this boy and she was asking Morgan for advice. Morgan laughed at Kathy asking her for advice, she didn't think there was a boy worth losing her virginity for. She tried to advise her the best she could but what could she say really. She wasn't into those kinds of feelings yet and didn't want to be saddled with that type of emotional baggage yet. There would be time enoough for that later, when she had established her career.

The house seemed more normal over the next couple of weeks. Her father was coming home again in the evenings, having supper with them like old times. Morgan had started back taking her dance and music lessons, and her grades reflected the change in her household. She didn't have to assume the role of wife and caregiver and she was glad about that. She didn't mind doing it when she had to but her preference was to deal with the issues a teenage girl had to deal with, not a wife.

As the fall was settling into Atlanta, the rains began. Morgan hated this time of the year. The gloomy, rainy days and the wind blowing just made things miserable for all concerned. Her father had started staying out again, and her mother went back into her depression.

Once again, she had to take over the role of house wife, and even though she was glad to cease the after school activities, it was dark and wet when she got home, she didn't relish become a housewife again and told herself that when she grew up, she would never live this type of lifestyle.

One late afternoon, Morgan had come home from school. It was cold and cloudy, rain had fallen all day. She wanted to go home and sleep and was hoping that her mother had felt well enough to do something around the house or better yet, that her father was home or had called and was coming home. She went into the house and all the lights were on which was strange. Both her parents were into energy conservation and didn't believe in 'burning daylight', with the lights on during the day. They opened the curtains and let nature light the house. The curtains were still closed and the breakfast dishes, the breakfast that she had prepared before going to school were all still there, the breakfast uneaten. She went upstairs and dropped her bookbag, taking off her coat and changing into more comfortable clothing to begin to clean up and fix dinner. She peeked into her parents room and her mother wasn't there. Maybe she went out for the day with her women's club. It was thursday and even though she had not done that in a long time, maybe today, maybe.

Morgan gathered up the dirty clothing that was piled in the hamper and tossed them down the laundry shute, planning to start a load after she began dinner. Going into the kitchen, she threw out the breakfast food that had changed color sitting out all day in the house uneaten and loaded the dishwasher, throwing way trash and pouring the milk down the sink that had sat out all day. There was steak in the refrigerator that she had seasoned before she went to school and she decided to fry it up with onions and make gravy with mashed potatoes and green beans. There was cornbread in the cabinet and she thought that would make a nice filler along with some stewed apples to give the house an aromatic flavor.

While the stewed apples were cooking, Morgan heard the front door and her father came in. Surprised. He went to the bedroom, removing his revolver and other accoutriments to his job and came into the kitchen.

"It smells good in here honey. Where's your mother?"

Morgan grabbed the dirty kitchen towels and threw them into a basket she had waiting for her at the top of the stairs to the basement.

"I guess she went to her women's club meeting today, it is Thursday. She wasn't here when I arrived."

"Her car is still in the garage."

Morgan didn't hear her father, she was heading downstairs. She could see the lights were on down there too and that was weird. She walked past the bar that her father had built. She remembered the entertaining that used to happen when she was younger, all the cops coming over and partying in the basement with her father and mother. She sitting at the top of the stairs watching and listening when she was supposed to be sleeping.

As she entered the area where the laundry room was, the door was closed but the light was on. She could see it reflecting under the door. Stange.

As she opened the door, she heard her father calling her name loudly and could hear his foot falls coming rapidly down the stairs.

"Morgan, wait . . ."

It was too late, as she opened the laundry room door, there, above the clothing she had sent down the laundry chute was her mother, hanging from one of the rafters. Her father came in immediately behind her and grabbed her, pulling her out of the room and closing the door.

Before she had realized it, she was in her father's arms and he was taking her upstairs. He kept saying something in her ears but she could only see her mother hanging there. Her father lay her downon the couch in the living room. When he lay her down, she sat up, and he lay her back down and she sat up, staring.

"Morgan, baby, oh my God, I am so sorry, oh my God."

Over and over again he said that, trying to lay her down, and she sitting up. He finally gave up trying to lay her down and ran to the phone in the kitchen, calling the police, his friends, calling, calling.

Morgan sat there staring. Not comprehending exactly, but staring. The months replaying themselves in her mind ending up back in the laundry room, above the dirty clothing. All the lights on. She sat there through the flurry of activity, through the coroner and even though they took her mother out through the garage so as not to come past her, she could feel her leaving the house and it was only then that she got up off the couch. No one noticed her standing there looking into the garage where her mother's Mercedes sat, white, cold and quiet. Her father was distraught. He was walking in circles and clutching his hands. He looked at Morgan but he didn't notice her. When he did, he took her in his arms and took her upstairs, setting her on her bed like a suitcase, and closed the door behind him as he exited. Morgan sat there, in her room, in the dark. Staring.

When she became cognizant of her surrounds, it was somewhere near morning. The light of day was shining through her window. She realized that she hadn't finished cooking and wondered how she got into the room. Opening her door, the house was strangely quiet and she could hear movement in her parents room. She figured her mother and father were in there, doing what parents do behind clothes door and decided to make breakfast for them.

She went into the kitchen and saw that dinner was not put away, nor was it eaten. She realized then that she hadn't eaten either and wondered why not. It was in the middle of her cleaning the kitchen that she remembered. It hit her like a brick and she stopped what she was doing and sat down in the middle of the floor and began to cry.

VIII

Amir was moving quickly through the upper echelon of the Atlanta drug trade. He had made friends with some boys from Miami and had a nice network going. Powder and bud was flowing at an alarming rate and the city was ripe for the connection.

He had moved from his small apartment, into one of the beautiful high rises on Piedmont in the downtown hotel district, his view unobstructed by anything. He could sit on his balcony and Atlanta was spread out before him, the lights twinkling so many stars. He loved it.

He had begun quite and art collection, African and Contemporary, and his wardrobe was like no other. He didn't hang in the streets, appearing at clubs once in a great while just to keep his name on the lips of people who wanted to be in the it crowd.

He thought about his mother from time to time, she had passed away one night after working a double for the chinese man in his store. He Chinese man's wife had taken ill and she was helping him with things that she usually did for him. His friend and mentor called him to tell him the news.

His loss was not as profound as he would have imagined, losing a mother and all, but he did feel it. He also fell relief from the torments of his past, and when he attended the funeral he kissed her without fear of her waking and touching him in the inappropriate way that she did at times.

He never recovered from her touches and his sex life suffered because of it. He was a torturous lover, inflicting pain on his partners which somehow satisfied the pain that he felt with intimacy. He knew it was wrong, but it was the only way he could deal with intimacy.

Amir didn't have a hard time finding willing partners, in his line of work, everyone wanted to be a part of his world. Even the Atlanta police offices, not all, but some, were in his list of clientele and regularly attended his parties. He had to keep them paid, but it was worth it. Jail was not a place where he wanted to spend any time despite the business he was in. He didn't deal street level, remembering that his mentor had told him if he stayed in the street level part of the game, he would die street level. It was how it was.

Amir took trips to Egypt and Milan, picking up art treasures on his travels sometimes taking a good looking woman with him, sometimes not. He didn't really require the company of women all the time. Just when he needed a release or when he tired of sitting alone in some of the best restaurants in the world. It was on those alone occasions when he missed his mother, imaginging her sitting there enjoying the atmosphere, smiling. But the day dreams were always tainted with the ending turning out that she kissed him in a way that was not proper for a mother to kiss a son. It shattered like a mirror hit with a rock, pieces of his memories in small, sharp shards all over the floor of his mind. He would shake it off, holding a drink in his hand trying not to notice that his hand was trembling.

Those were the hard times for him. He never worried about being shot, or being arrested, and wanted peace in his mind from those memories. He wanted a wife, or a steady girlfriend that he could love in the right way. He didn't think about children, never really having a childhood, he wasn't sure he was prepared for that type of reality. Children required a home, stability and two parents who were willing to sacrifice it all to raise them. Amir knew he was not that type. Wanting instead a permanent partner to share his art and share his world. Someone who didn't like drugs, and realized that the drug game was just that, and like a game, came to an end eventually, sometimes abruptly at the end of a revolver or behind the bars of a prison cell for many years. He never thought that he was above the law and chose his alliances carefully, even the so called officers of the law. He knew that they could turn on him at any time. For the most part however, Amir was living the life he had envisioned for himself.

IX

Steve having completed his high school and was taking a correspondence course in law enforcement, was growing tired of his surroundings. Although Miss Eloise did not attend the make shift graduation ceremony, she did have a Bible printed for him with his name embossed in gold lettering along the bottm. It was the only gift he ever received.

People were also starting to talk about the disappearances of people around their town, having long suspected something was going on when their pets continued to disappear. People were into their pets more than the people, but the parents of some of the wayward girls were asking questions. Just like he had known, the young black girl's parents were in the media constantly in Columbus, saying that the police were not doing enough to find their daughter because she was black and that they were treating her like a common whore and runaway which she wasn't. She was loved and needed and missed and the girl that she was hanging around with had come to stay with them, sleeping in their garage because she was an outcast from her own family. Their daughter merely followed her to wherever she was going and was not an outcast. They demanded justice, but the trail was just too cold. The police were sympathetic but they could only go on what they had and right now they had nothing.

Steve knew it was time to go. He was still undetected at Miss Eloise's house, people thinking he was staying with relatives somewhere even though he continued with his education. He didn't answer any questions when asked by his classmates where he stayed and how he got to school, he just said that he made his own way with the help of trucker friends he knew. They didn't dispute that given his mother's reputation with truckers. His lifestyle aroused no suspicion and Miss Eloise never said anything. Even the Bible was mail order, not local.

On the last evening of his stay with Miss Eloise, he did everything he had done before. He cleaned her dishes, cut some wood for her. As he sat down with her in preparation to read her a bible story, she spoke to him about his future.

"Stevie, I know you getten' ready to go away from here. Its just a matter a time before people connects them killings with you. I knowd you was doin' it fo a long time now. That's yo business how you deal wid your pain. I knows you got pain because of what you mother did to you. I ain't judgin' you cause thats God's job."

Steve was silent.

"I cain't attest to you doin' anything 'cause I didn't see it, but I sho could hears you comin' into the shack in the wee hours. Peoples that cain't see can hear everything. I just prayed for yo' soul and hopes that you get better. You like a son to me, so, when you leave, rest assured that I ain't openin' my mouth. I ain't long for this here world anyway and it ain't my business. Just be careful who you makes as friends in your travels and try to get that pain outta your heart before it kills you or you gets caught."

Steve looked at the old woman and he felt bad for what he had to do. She was the only real mother he had. However, he couldn't count on her just remaining silent, especially if someone started questioning her about things. She was a holy woman and lying wasn't in her vocabulary. He knew that.

Steve read her bible story to her and tucked her in for the night. He went back to his shack and gathered the little belongings that he had, including a small diploma and a certificate from the crimial justice course he had taken. He also had the paperwork from his name change that he had worked on over the past year, not wanting to be associated with his mother or anything here in this area.

Under the light of the full moon, he crept back into Miss Eloise's house. He wasn't sure she could hear him, her sleep sounded so deep. He kissed her forehead and when she didn't stir, he took the large pillow off the chair that she sat in and smothered the old woman while she slept, holding her bible to her chest. It was the only killing that made him feel regret. Replacing her pillow to its chair, he listened carefully for the sound of breathing and watched her closely for he didn't know how long to make sure she was quite gone. The grip on her bible never loosened and he hoped that someone would bury her with it. He cried briefly and left, walking clear of the highway until he crossed out of Kentucky into Tennessee. There, along 75 south, he hitched a ride, heading to Atlanta.

X

The funeral for Morgan's mother was surreal. Morgan sat in her room as her auntie came and bustled around, arranging her clothing that she picked out for her to wear. Morgan had plenty of clothing to wear and her mother had brought her a black dress everytime she changed sizes 'in case something happened to your father, after all he is in a dangerous occupation'. Her mother wanted her to always be prepared for her father's demise but never thought about preparing her daughter for her own. Morgan sat quietly as her auntie chattered on and on about how her mother loved her and she would have to carry on. She mentioned something about coming to stay with her for awhile if she wanted and it was the only thing that Morgan responded to.

"No auntie, I have to stay and take care of daddy. Mom would have wanted that."

"Your mother would have wanted you to be taken care of sweetie, she was my sister and I know."

"You didn't know her. Not like I do. Daddy was her heart and soul and when she got sick, I don't remember any of you coming by to check on her."

Her auntie was wounded. But she didn't waiver.

"We didn't think depression was a sickness. No one in our family ever got depressed. Maybe it was being married to a cop that did it, but don't blame us. When we called her she always said everything was fine."

"Whatever auntie. I'm staying here with daddy."

Morgan felt bad for her tone and attitude.

"Auntie, once in a while can you come get me in your corvette? I think we can shop together and talk sometimes, if thats okay with you."

Her auntie smiled a big relieved smile.

"Sure honey, anytime you want you let me know. In fact, how about I call you from time to time to check on you, or better yet, stop by. I know I didn't spend a lot of time with my sister but she knew I loved her."

"I know auntie, I was just lashing out, I didn't mean to hurt you. You are my favorite auntie, and always will be."

Morgan put the outfit on that her auntie brought even though the outfit her mother had brought was hanging in the closet and was more to her liking. Her mother knew exactly what she liked and didn't like, what looked good on her and what didn't. She had given her a sense of fashion and a sense of herself in the short time they had together. Being a baby didn't count, it was the time that they could talk and share that made difference. Morgan would miss that. She also know that this had something to do with her daddy. The coroner said that the medication she was taking caused her suicidal tendencies and the news had articles about the antidepressant medication causing these types of reactions. But Morgan knew, and she lay the reason right at the foot of her father.

After the funeral, lots of police officers came by and paid their respects. They were a tight knit clan. Their wives brought food and kissed Morgan on her cheek and forehead. Morgan never had so many kisses from people she hardly knew. The neighbors came by in droves bring chicken, ham, sweet potatoes, potatoe salad. She appreciated it but no one volunteered to help her clean up the mess. Miss Flavors, the neighbor from down the block came in. Morgan always thought she was pretty. She leaned down to kiss Morgan.

"I'm going to help clean this place up after the guests leave, your mother would have wanted me to. We were good friends."

Morgan sat there puzzled for a moment. There was something familiar about her and she couldn' quite put her finger on it. She sat there quietly and then realized it was the perfume. She had smelled that perfume before. Where, when . . . . it hit her. That was the perfume that was on her daddy.

Morgan jumped up from the couch and went into the kitchen. There was her father and Miss Flavors standing way too close. How dare she.

"You get this woman out of here right now Daddy."

"Honey, what . . ."

"I mean RIGHT NOW."

She grabbed Miss Flavors' by her arm and began to drag her toward the door.

"Not the front door you whore, the back door, where you belong."

Morgan was feeling hysterical. She could feel it rising from somewhere deep inside her. As Miss Flavors struggled and her father tried to unpry the grip she had on her her, she yelled.

"This is the woman whose perfume I smelled on you every night you were late, this is the whore you were sleeping with and made my mother kill herself. Get OUT OF MY HOUSE NOW!"

Before her father could react, the whole house had gotten quiet. Miss Flavors face had turned dark with embarrassment and she headed under her own power to the front door.

"No, go out the BACK DOOR, stay out of my mother's living room."

As Morgan's father tried to hold her, she screamed and yelled at the top of her lungs making it impossible for Miss Flavors to have a quiet exit. All eyes were on her.

Her father took her upstairs but only after she had seen Miss Flavors sulk out the back door. Upstairs, her father sat her gently on the bed he shared with her mother.

"Morgan . . ."

"It was her daddy, you can't deny it. I smelled her. I smelled her on you all the times, she could have at least changed her perfume. I SMELLED HER ON YOU, I SMELLED HER ON YOU."

It was the last thing she remembered. When Morgan woke, the house was purply dark, the room was quiet. As far as she could tell when she sat up, the house was empty except for the voices she heard at the foot of the stairs. One of them was her fathers and she strained to make out the other one, praying that it wasn't that Miss Flavors. It was her auntie.

"How could you do that to my sister? She loved you."

"It wasn't like that, Morgan is just distraught, she's the one who found her mother."

"She's not distraught she's a detective like her daddy. She smelled that woman out. I'm taking Morgan with me in the morning. I won't leave her here with a father who didn't care enough about her mother to at least shower and rinse the bitches smell off of himself. You are a sorry bastard, and if you fight me for custody I'll put so much of your dirty laundry out in the air, you will think you are at a chinese laundry."

"Stop it. I won't let you take my daughter."

"Oh, and you think you can stop me, you sorry ass excuse for a man."

Morgan opened the door in the middle of their argument.

"go back to bed honey, I'll be coming back to get you in the morning, I'll bring my corvette and . . ."

"No auntie, I'm staying with daddy. Daddy needs me now that mom is gone. I have to take care of him just like she wanted me to. I'm alright now. You go home and leave daddy alone. He's got enough to deal with."

She walked out the room, feeling suprisingly grown up took her auntie's hand, leading her to the door.

"Go on home auntie, I'll take care of him. If I need you, I'll call. You said you would be there for me. Go on now, we are both tired and need to rest. I'll call you in the morning."

Her auntie tried to protest but Morgan was insistent.

"I'll see you in the morning."

Her father was still standing at the stairs, his mouth kind of open his eyes sad.

"Daddy, go to bed. Go lay down or something. I'm tired, you're tired and mother would have wanted you to sleep. She always worred about you sleeping."

He looked at his little girl, but instead of fighting, he went upstairs as he was told and closed the door behind him.

Morgan looked around the house and thought she could still smell that perfume. She opened the kitchen windows as she cleaned up the mess that the mourners made. The cool air felt good and it wiped out any remains of that perfume.

She stacked the dishes in the dishwasher, wondering why no one bothered to bring paper plates. Her mother would have brought paper plates, forks, knives and napkins. So that the family wouldn't have to wash dishes, they could just throw the remains of the day away and move on with their lives. She was thoughtful like that.

From that day on, Morgan became her father's keeper. The death of his wife had changed him overnight from a young vibrant detective, to an older, wisened man. He didn't come home late anymore, in fact, he didn't go out anymore either. When Morgan came home from school and started dinner, by the time it was done he was there. She could set his plate on the table and the food was still hot when he arrived. He talked about his day, watched the news and a few programs while Morgan did her homework. When she went to bed at ten oclock, he was in bed an hour before. She got up and made his breakfast after getting ready for school and sat with him while he ate before he dropped her off and headed to work. He became as dependent on her has he was with her mother, she ironed his clothing, cleaned the house and made sure he took his vitamins evey day.

Miss Flavors stopped by one afternoon on a saturday with a dish she had prepared. Morgan answered the door.

"Morgan, I'm sorry about what happened."

"I wish I could say the same, but I can't. Daddy doesn't need you to do anything for him, I'm taking care of him."

"But you are just a girl, he needs a woman to take care of him, to take care of you both."

"Miss Flavors, you are not the woman to do that. When my father starts dating again, it won't be you he will be seeing. Not as long as I'm around and I am not going anywhere anytime soon. You need to leave my property before I get one of daddy's revolvers and put you in the ground where you belong instead of my mother."

"Let me speak to your father."

Miss Flavors was adamant but so was Morgan. She told her to wait by the door and went to the cabinet where her father kept his weapons. Unlocking the cabinet quietly, her father was napping in the next room, she loaded the revolver full and went back to the door.

Leveling the gun at Miss Flavors, she smiled.

"Don't think I wouldn't enjoy shooting you. I am telling you once more, get off my property. Don't make me shoot you, because I will."

Miss Flvors back pedalled so fast upon seeing the gun, she almost dropped her covered dish. It made Morgan laugh to see her running up the street, the wind blowing her coat up enough to see that she wasn't wearing anything underneath. The whore.

They weren't bothered by her anymore. She didn't even call like she used to when she thought Morgan was sleeping. Morgan always answered the phone, her father didn't even hear it ringing half the time. He had napped through the whole ordeal, not realizing that Morgan had almost shot his used to be lover.

XI

Steve arrived in Atlanta at a good time. There was big recruiting drive going on for the police department. He applied and after a background check revealed no adversities which Steve was worried about, he became a paid recruit, going through the lessons on how and when to shoot, exercising like he was in the military. Steve was loving it all and excelled at every aspect of the police officers training. He rented a small apartment near Lenox square mall, bought an older car and cruised the streets of Altanta when he wasn't doing his studying or working out.

The streets of Altanta were teaming with victims. His urge to kill had not lessened, and in fact had worsened in all the stimuli. He could be sleeping soundly one moment and up prowling the streets the next. The crack game had put a lot of opportunity out there for him and he took advantage of it. The problem he had at first was finding a spot where he could put his victims without them being found. He knew the back woods of Kentucky very well but this was a new place althought he abundant overgrowth made it possible for him to hide victims during the summer months so that they would just be a crime scene when the foliage went away in the brief winter. By then, the humidity and rain had left nothing much behind and jane doe's began popping up literally everywhere. He was always careful about leaving DNA since this was the evidence of choice and was putting a lot of criminals who weren't already behind bars, in jail. It was also releasing those who were charged back in the days before DNA with crimes that they didn't commit. It was a good time for Steve. He was doing what he loved and doing whathe needed all under the cover of a big beautiful metropolis that kept his attention and kept him with victims. He thought briefly of Miss Eloise but read in his hometown paper that she had died in her sleep. He knew know one would question the death of an old woman who lived as long as she did in the backwoods. She was found by two hunters who had stopped in to get directions. She was laying with her bible clutched in her hands as the paper said "Like she was waiting for Jesus to come get her." Steve made sure that she was sent to Jesus prepared instead of being found laying out in the woods somewhere where any animal could have fed off of her. He felt good about that.

His first victim was a black woman who was ravaged by the crack demon. She was older than she appeared to be, living in the streets in the area of Little Five Points, selling her body or panhandling when she needed a fix. Her body wasn't in the best shape, but Steve wasn't into looks. This wasn't about that. He was trolling the city that night and just made his way down Memorial Drive to Moreland. Making a left on Moreland, he was looking through the neighborhood for any hooker or druggy that happened to be out on a night like this. It was raining and raw, and the streets were virtually empty. Coming toward Euclid in the heart of little Five Points, he had stopped in the Zestos to get a shake and a burger. Sitting at a booth looking out the window he decided that his urges would go unfulfilled tonight when she came into the store. She wanted a dollar for a bus ride she said. He gave her a dollar and the manager shoed her out of the store. Steve waited a moment, finishing his food.

"damn crack whores, they are a blight on the neighborhood, you know. The cops should do something."

"Its so many, its hard to deal with it all. Crack is a scourge like heroin was in the day."

"Yeah, I had a heroin habit, so I guess I understand."

Steve didn't want to waste too much time conversating with the man, he didn't want his little birdie to get away.

He jumped in his car and headed down Moreland, searching. He didn't have to look far. Turning left on Euclid, he saw her walking up an alleyway between some buildings where during the day, people hung out and played music. It was silent now. He drove slowly and she noticed the car, back tracking to come into his notice.

"hey mister you got a dollar . . . oh, I remember you from the Zestos"

"yea, where you going, home?"

"Sure mister, you wanna take me home?"

"You ain't no cop are you, trying to arrest me as a john are you?"

She laughed. She didn't have many teeth in her smile, no front teeth at all on the top.

"You sure you ain't no cop either?"

"C'mon and get out of the weather. I'll take you where you need to go."

"It will cost you suga', I ain't no cheap thrill."

"I knew that, that's why I followed you. You look like you may have been somebody once, before the crack."

"Oh, I can stop this shit whenever I want. It ain't got me like most womens. I just like the feeling but, I can get the same feeling with a good man, y'know."

"Yes, I know. I hope I'm that man."

"I don't usually mess with no white boys, but its cold tonight."

She got in the car. The stench of her body filled Steve's nostrils and he let a window down to keep from throwing up. He was sure no one would miss her.

She directed him to drive to a spot out past the city and past the airport. He wasn't sure where he was but the freeway wasn't far so he could get back. They drove off the rode down a path that was mostly trees and dirt. He wondered about his car leaving tracks but when the stopped, he could see that it was a makeshift dump for anything from tires, to washing machines and mattresses. There were plenty of tire tracks, some as fresh as his own. But he made sure to remember to buy new tires in the morning and burn these. He didn't want to be caught up on a humble.

She got out the car and asked for the money, which he gave her promptly. She lay on the dirty mattress but Steve made her take all her clothing off and put it in pile and he did the same. He took a blanket out the car and put it on the ground that he would burn with the tires.

Without the clothes, the smell diminished and he took her there on the blanket. As she was enjoying herself, he took his hands and put them around her neck and strangled her, his climax coming at the moment of her death. The bucking and kicking she did during the act made it that much more pleasant. She had scratched his back, and he hated that because he would have to remove her fingernails to make sure there was no DNA to get from her. Instead, he chopped her hands off, taking them with him. He put her clothing, her hands and the blanket in the bag he brought, throwing her body on the dirty mattress. He dumped some trash that he had collected from different parts of the city on top of her, and put those bags in his big bag. Putting it in the trunk, he drove off. Feeling ready for a good night sleep.

He arrived back at his home starving, he had stopped at the Krystals on the way home, in his neighborhood saying he was out because he couldn't sleep. The man who worked there knew Steve and they talked for a while. Steve was establishing an alibi, just in case. He didn't need one. It took a few days for the body to get discovered and it was written off as another Jane Doe crackhead. They knew she had been strangled and her hands removed but other than that they had no leads. It had rained that early morning the first day after and all the tire tracks were washed away in the red mud into the chattahoochie.

XII

Morgan began taking Criminology classes while enrolled at Georgia State Univesity. The Professor, John was a skilled criminal attorney who decided to teach about crime rather that fight it. He learned that a good lawyer, whatever the crime, could get someone off, guilty or not and that just didn't set well with him. He had gotten many a criminal off, only to find that they were back on the streets committing the same crime again, and he thought that was a useless waste of the justice system. In his class, he looked for the more intelligent of his class and had a special deal in mind for them.

John had a secret agency that took care of crime wherever it was, in the world. His team of criminologists, he stopped short of calling the crime fighters because it sounded too much like a comic book hero, took care of the scurge of society that society seemed to be unable to take care of.

It was his goal after he quit the attorney game. And to him, it was a game.

Morgan had great potential. He ran a background check and found that she was from a police family. Her mother had died tragically although it didn't say how, and her father was a longstanding detective with the Atlanta Police. A veteran, he would be retiring soon. John watched Morgan and she had great intuitiveness which is something that you cannot teach, along with a willingness to see things conclude the right way, with the criminal behind bars or dead, which ever was a more advantageous conclusion. She was also good to look at, which would help with the infiltration needed to catch some criminals. She was african american but she could be egyptian or arab or a number of different nationalities with the right make up. They weren't CIA, John liked to think of themselves as better than the CIA. No government agency was completely fool proof as the government, John surmised was a fool's paradise, each jester more funny than the next. He wondered how to approach Morgan. She was the tpe of person her kept her feelings inside, which was also good, but it made it difficult to gage her responses. So he waited until after class one day before spring recess.

"Morgan, can I talk to you a moment?"

"Sure Professor, what's wrong? I know it isn't my grades, this is the one class I am excelling in."

"I know. What are your plans for the spring recess?"

"No plans really. My father is semi retired so I thought about taking him on a fishing excursion or something to get him out of the house, but I am open to something else."

"How would you like to study with a group of criminologists that work for me?"

"work for you doing what?"

"come to my house Saturday afternoon, here's the address and I will explain it all to you. If you're interested, we can start training immediately, if not, you can go back to your studies, no harm no foul."

"Okay, I'll come, but it sounds so secret."

"Not really secret, just not known. Its better that way. Interested?"

"Intrigued."

"Ah, I knew you would be. See you saturday."

Morgan left for home. She could put off the fishing excursion one day to see what was going on. It did sound interesting and being able to work in her field during the spring recess was more exciting to her than going fishing. She knew her father would enjoy it, but she didn't. She thought that maybe it was about time to get her father a friend to hang out with. He has been sort of reclusive for all these years and Morgan blamed herself for that. There was so much wrong with things back then that they needed the stabilization of a set lifestyle, but that was a long time ago, and her father was getting older. She wasn't planning on spending her whole life with him forfeiting her own. He was planning on her getting married one day and she didn't have marriage on her mind, she wanted to study crimes and solve them.

She arrived at the house and her father was just coming home from a racketball match. He had been playing that a lot lately and she was glad of that.

He was talking a lot about a young new detective that he had taken under his wing. As long as he wasnt' lonely, she didn't mind. Sometimes she worried about him with her at school all the time and she never thought that far into the future back then when everything was going on.

"Hi daddy"

"Hello baby girl? How was your day?"

"fine, school, just like always."

"you need a husband or a friend or something girl. You are much too pretty to be cooped up with an old man all the time."

"Oh, you're not old." she kissed his forehead.

"What did you cook?"

"Wheat germ cakes and brown rice, good for you food."

"Cardboard cakes and shredded cardboard if you ask me. But if it helps."

She picked up a spoonful of the rice and cut a piece of the little cake with it. It didn't taste as bad as it sounded.

"You ready for our fishing trip?"

"Well, baby girl, thats what I need to tell you about, some of the guys at work, a new young detective and I are going fishing this weekend. Going down to the Gulf. Its going to be guy stuff, you know? Maybe you can call some of your girlfriends to come and keep you company, I'm going to be gone this weekend and maybe part of next week. You angry at me?"

"No daddy, thats good. Since when have you decided to hang out with detectives, you said you didn't' trust any of them, wouldn't let me date any."

"Well, I'm getting older and this guy reminds me of me. I want to know what he knows so that I can retire and he replace me, I don't want to be run out and replaced, makes the retirement money smaller."

"You don't need the money anyway."

"Yea baby girl, but I earned it. And I want my full share. The streets are different now and he seems to have a handle on whats going on out there. I need to keep up with my game, just a little while longer."

"Okay daddy, go play with your little friends, I've got some studying to do anyway. But I will call Kathy to see how she is doing."

"This is her third child isn't it? Is she ever going to get married?"

"Apparently she just likes having babies daddy, don't need no husband to keep her happy."

"She should have went to college."

"Yeah, well, she started early with boys, I'm not saying this is how it always ends up but this is how it ended up for her. I'm glad its not me."

"Me too baby girl, me too."

Her father headed for the showers to clean up and Morgan lay on her bed in the room. Her father's suggested cleared the way for her to go to this thing on Saturday. She was excited about it but she was afraid as well. Oh well, nothing ventured, nothing gained.

She listened as her father whistled in the shower, He had not done that since . . . well, she was just glad he was moving around more.

XIII

Steven St John was making a name for himself with the APD. He was tough on crime but also had touch with the neighborhood people who enjoyed talking to him. He was down to earth and fair. The black people didn't mind seeing him come around, treating him like one of the fellows. The white people were comfortable with him too. He was in his element. Doing what he loved to do by day and doing what he needed to do at night.

The detective test had come up and he took it and passed with flying colors. They promoted him and put him under the tutledge of a seasoned detective, a black man. They became friends of a sort. The man didn't say much about his family life except that his wife had passed many years ago and that he had a daughter in college. Steve liked the older man, he reminded him of someone else he loved. He also noticed that the older man had a aura of sadness to him and decided that he would also tutor him in having a life. He taught him how to play racquet ball, and they were going on a fishing trip this weekend. It was like a father he didn't have. He wanted to do all the things he didn't do with his father with this man. Steve didn't pry into the man's background, but when he was comfortable with him, he began to talk to him about his life a little.

Steve knew he was worried that his daughter would not settle down and marry. He said that his daughter was beautiful and bright but she was shying away from men. He felt responsible somewhat for that but would not elaborate on it. Steve didn't want to guess at the issue and hoped that the daughter was not a victim of some sort of sexual crime committed by her father. Those things happened sometimes and in the best families although Steve didn't think this was case. Maybe she was just sheltered too much. Police officers tend to keep their children in the police circle and if that was the case, he wouldn't want his daughter marrying a police officer either. It seemed sort of incestuos.

The fun he was having with this man was taking some of the need for killing away. Miss Eliott was right. Maybe it was the pain of his childhood that made him the way he was. He knew he wasn't cured and wasn't sure that he was even looking for one. He wrestled with his conscience briefly but told himself he was disposing of the trash. He was sorry at how they became trash, but he didn't cause it. He just disposed of it. Their families should have taken better care of them. Sometimes, families do the best they can and other times, like his own, they turn their children into trash to be disposed of by whatever trash collector happens upon their path. Steve did try to be humane about it, not making them suffer too much, and they were getting a little love in the process. He even paid them, although they never got the chance to spend it, they died knowing that they had money for that crack pipe even if the crack man never got it.

Atlanta was one big high time. There were always parties to go to, places to be, people to see. It was as if Atlanta was a little bit of Hollywood in the south. There were beautiful people, black, whit and others all over the place. It was a cornucopia of happenings and although Steve was on the good side of the law, he wanted to be apart of the party side as well. Its been done before. He just had to think of a 'how'. But he was fishing this weekend with his father figure, so that is where he kept his focus.

XIV

Amir had become known as the "gentleman dealer". He listed himself as an art collector for people he needed to know what you did for a living. His parties had become the toast of Altanta and anyone who was anyone was invited. If you didn't get invited to Amir's it was because you were a nobody. That was a fact. He had come a long way from the Bed-Sty hustling days and he thanked God and his mentor who was since passed, everyday for teaching how not to be a street thug and to enjoy the finer things in life. He lived like a king, all he wanted was his queen.

No one knew that Amir held his parties much in the same way that Gatsby did in the book he read. He held the parties and observed, looking for that special someone in the crowd. Amir loved to read and he loved art. He just wanted someone to share it all with. If he could find that special Queen, he would leave the business for good. He had more than enough money and with most of his assets invested in art, he could live the rest of his life without working again. It was how he planned it.

He was having another party this weekend and was in the planning stages right now. Inya was his party planner and was party planner to the stars of Altanta. She could throw you whatever party you wanted. He paid her well to sweat the details. He was flying over to Spain this afternoon to pick up an object he negotiated a buy with and would be back Saturday morning. The party was saturday night, but with Inya in charge, all he had to do was get dressed.

XV

Morgan awoke Saturday morning. The house was quiet. Her father had left last night with his friend. Morgan thought she should have met him but her father was running out the door like a little kid on a camping sleep over. She didn't dare interrupt that good mood. He was happy for the first time in a long time and she didn't feel she had to baby sit for him.

He had left her some of those wheat germ cakes in the microwave and she tossed them out in favor of bacon, eggs and toast. She didn't have to meet with John until later this afternoon so the morning was her own.

She ate quietly, listening to the outdoor sounds, looking around the kitchen. Over the years, the marks that her mother made were all but gone away. She kept her favorite pot holders and towels in a chest in her room. Her pictures of food she had on the walls were stored away. Morgan took them down one by one and replaced them with things so that her father didn't notice the change. It was subtle. After a while, her father even brought home things that he liked to put in places left empty by the quiet disappearance of her mother's memories. She didn't know he if notice that there was somethng missing but he always would comment, 'you know, that space needs something'.

Morgan caught on homework, college was harder than she thought and required a lot more attention than she thought. She had planned to work part time but found that time did not allow for that. Studying was all she could do. She did call her friend Kathy to find out how she was doing.

"Hey girl, how's it going?"

"girl, two of my kids have the flu, the oldest and the baby. I got dirty diaphers everywhere. You should come see."

"I got a few hours to kill. I'll be by there shortly, do you need anything?"

"I always need diaphers and baby food. But I could use a good chardiney."

"I'll be there shortly."

Morgan jumped in the shower and cleaned up. She would leave from kathy's and go to John's. She had mapquested his location and was surprised at how far out in the sticks it was. It was in Marietta but out from the may fray. Mapquest could only get her to the street, she would have to follow the street address to get to John. But it took her past kathy who lived in Marietta near Dave and Buster's.

Traffice on 75/85 north was busy, more than usual or maybe she hadn't driven it during a Saturday in a while, and when she branched off to 75, it slackened some, but it was moving very fast. She liked driving fast on 75. Everyone did it. She got to Kathy's exit and pulled into her apartment complex. It was place that was full of children judging from the small bicycles and toys scattered through the yards in front of many of the townhomes. She walked up to kathy's number and could hear the babies crying before she knocked on the door. She knocked hard so that kathy would hear her and when she did, all the noise stopped. She knocked again softly and Kathy came to the door.

She looked worse than Morgan had ever seen her. Her hair wasn't done, her face wasn't made up. She had put on some weight and her clothing was wrinkled and it didn't seem like she had a shower in a day or two.

"C'mon in Morgan, welcome to my world."

"Kathy, I would ask how things are but I can see."

"Always the little snob."

They laughed.

The children looked at Morgan with interest and the oldest one, who was 4, with a runny nose and old plats in her hair, came and crawled into Morgan's lap. Morgan tried not to appear offended but she didn't relish the idea of getting snot on her clothing. She kissed the child on her forehead and put her onto the floor.

"Oh, don't mind her, she's pretty friendly."

Kathy cleared a spot on her couch and Morgan handed her the wine she asked for.

"I'll save this for when they go to bed. They do sleep soundly, you know? When they are sleep I almost feel normal. Remember when you tried to talk me out of having sex with that guy? I should have listened. Once you get started, its like crack, you can't stop. If I had gotten pregnant every time I laid down, well, this house wouldn't be big enough. I guess I should feel bad about how my life turned out but when I'm with a man, all I think about is right then, not the consequences."

"I wish I could say I know what you mean but . . ."

"You still a virgin girl? Oh my Christ. You couldn't find anyone good enough?"

"It wasn't that. When my mom uh, died, I had to take care of my father."

"Yea, I heard about that. I was so sorry for you. I was going to call you when I thought things had quieted down, but life took over. I'm glad you called me."

"I miss you. You were the only friend I had when I wanted hang out or run around."

"well, those days are mostly over for me now. Mom babysits sometimes but mostly they come by and bring me food and diaphers and leave quickly. I know she's disappointed but I love my babies. All of them. The oldest one's father brings her clothing and gives me money sometimes, the other two never came back. I don't know if they know I have their babies or not. I hadn't heard from them since the night we shared."

Morgan felt sad for her friend but not sorry. This was a choice that she didn't have to make. She chose poorly as her father would say.

They talked a little longer; Morgan left the large bag of diaphers with her friend along with 20.00 dollars (for you—not the kids) and left.

She got off of 75 north onto a winding street that seemed to stretch into nowhere. There were addresses on the street but you could not see the houses. There were long driveways or hidden drives that dotted the street and there weren't that many. John's house happened to be at the end of the long street, where it dead ended. She drove up the driveway, and came to a fence with a guard.

"Miss Morgan, they are expecting you"

The guard opened the gate and she drove through. She was driving a mercedes like her mother, but her father traded for a newer model and a different color and presented it Morgan on her graduation from high school.

At the door, a man servant or someone like that opened the door and ushered her into a huge vestibule. John appeared out of nowhere.

"this is an awfully grand house for a professor, maybe I should be learning to teach instead of learning."

"my salary at the university doesn't pay for this, my sideline business of which I want you to be a part of does."

They walked through the double doors at the end of a long hallway and to an elevator. John pressed the down button and Morgan felt her ears pop.

"Uh, fall out shelter?"

"Privacy."

He looked at Morgan and smiled. She was a beautiful girl. He had a weakness for beautiful, intelligent women. His wife would attest to that. Morgan caught him staring at her but she smiled and didn't feel alarmed.

They exited the elevator and walked into a large common area. There was Brody, who was in her class and two other boys she didn't know. There was an oriental girl in the corner, watching a DVD.

"Gang, this is Morgan." they all approached her and held out there hands.

"Brody, but you remember me don't you. I sat beside you in chemistry."

"I'm Shane but my friends call me Sherlock. You can call me Sherlock, and you can call me anytime."

She laughed.

The tallest boy, who Morgan couldn't tell what his nationality was, he was a mixture of a few things stood above her and looked at her up and down.

"Sherlock would like anyone to call him. I'm Mustafa, but you can call me Musa."

The oriental girl, who was a little guarded held out her hand but there was no feeling in it.

"Pasha"

John herded everyone into a smaller room with seats and a large movie screen. On the table were snacks and booklets and a very beautiful woman, scandinavian Morgan thought, brought water and tea.

"John she is as beautiful as you said. Hello Morgan I am Sasha, John's wife. He has spoken of you often. I hope this won't be the last time we meet."

"I'm sure Morgan will join our little group."

"Yes already and I don't know what it is. It feels exciting though."

John called the meeting to order.

"Musa, I am sending you to Egypt this week. There is a nasty little bugger there who is into child slavery. The dosier contains the details. You are posing as a purchaser."

"I hate those guys. The children are always from some place where money is so important. They make me sick. I'll take care of this."

"I need you to take out the little man in the dozier and infiltrate to the top line, he isn't the top. The man at the time is highly respected business man, You need to get close enough to kill him. We don't even want him in jail."

"got it."

"My china doll, unfortunately you are type cast. You are going to Shangai and take out an opium dealer. He's got a large network of operatives so its going to be you working from the bottom up. I already have you ingratiated into the local trader who thinks you are . . . "

"a drug addicted prostitue?"

" . . . ah, no, an american business woman looking to score for her american boss. No type casting this time."

"thanks, that hooker angle was getting so I was believing her existence."

"Sherlock, I need you to create some information on Morgan, I need passports, driver's licenses, ID's from all fifty states and Holland as well."

"She's going out already?"

"No, but I need her prepared. She won't take long to teach. Brody, I'm sending her with you to Holland."

"the Prince?"

"yes, Morgan is his flavor this year and we need to use that to get to him."

"Sure, but will she be ready."

"She will."

Morgan just looked around.

"ready?"

"yes, you are going to be the bait for us to catch the Prince at his nasty little smuggling game. He smuggles anything of value; guns, women, children, drugs. Two trucks with children and women in them were found in the desert abandoned and the cargo was dead. Death by starvation, heat. He just left them there when the buyer backed out. He has a thing for women of color."

"do you think I'm ready for this?"

"I know you can handle it, do you want to bust some bad guys?"

"sure."

"then there is no time to lose. Your father is one his fishing expedition?"

"yes, he won't be back until next week."

"good, go home, pack a few clothes and be here first thing tomorrow morning. You're going to need I think about a week to get ready—right Brody?"

"At least."

"Can you stay here a week?"

"what will I tell my father?"

"You have taken a job with Milan Modeling agency. Here is all the information. Sherlock, have that passport ready for me in 24 hours okay. Brody, I need another stock of sani-shields and check the computer for news on the Prince. I need to know where to position Morgan."

Morgan was amazed as everyone jumped into action. John escorted her out to her car.

"Don't worry Morgan, you can do this, that is why I chose you. Sorry to throw you into the mix so quickly but I have complete faith in you."

"I'm glad you do. I'm excited but afraid. I've never done . . ."

"don't worry, the training we give you hear will be more than ample and Brody is going to be by your side all the time. You have a great gift for this, now you have to use it."

Morgan smiled at the old man.

"Okay, I'm in."

"I knew you would be. Drive carefully and I will see you tomorrow 8:00 am sharp."

XVI

Steve was rplaying in his mind the events that transpired before the fishing trip he had planned with Morgan's father. Since his promotion he has been privvy to the information on the new drug dealers in town and who was holding all the cards. As they unloaded the gear at Lake Allatoona, Steve, trying to concentrate on his fishing trip, was in a nother world. He felt bad that his mentor would not be a part of the operation, but older detectives look like detectives and the younger guys can make themselves look like the people they are trying to get. They know the language, the street language and its a better fit all around. This fishing trip was supposed to help Steve break the news to him, but he hadn't thought of way to do that yet.

"I haven't been fishing in a long while."

"When you retire, you can fish all the time."

"Yeah, I don't want to retire. This is all I know. I know police work, I know police people, I know police everything. I know nothing about the civilian world. My daughter is part of that world and sometimes I don't know her."

"Morgan's alright, she just needs to find a niche."

"She needs to find a husband. I know that she mistrusts men because of me, and I don't want her to spend her life as a loner."

"Do you have someone in mind? You know daughters hate it when their father's try to fix them up. It usually with someone that their father likes and not what she likes."

"I don't know anyone who she would like, its a whole new generation out there."

Steve was quiet because he could feel where this was going. Morgan wasn't a bad catch. He could be married to her. And having the father's permission would make it that much greater. He would inherit the house, the cars and the daughter. This was something Steve hadn't figure on with the older black gentleman. He listened with a renewed interest.

"Well, you know the young women these days aren't sure what they want because there. is so much for them to get. Its not as simple as it was when you were courting and dating."

"Courting and dating, wow, I hadn't heard that in years. When I met Morgan's mother she was the most beautiful woman to me. Smart, charming, her parents had taught her well. She was everything I wanted."

He looked reflectively out into the surroundings.

"I don't know why I did the things I did to her. She was very devoted and I had women everywhere. Somethng about the uniform of a cop made women want me. I was cocky and stupid. Hell, one day I came home and Morgan could smell the perfume on me. I didn't think about it at the time other than Morgan was just too smart for her own good, it didn't dawn on me that her mother may have been picking up the vibes. She never said. Always tried to be very nice and pleasant. I was so stupid, cocky, blind and stupid. The woman wasn't half as good as my wife."

"you know those things happen man, cops are always getting hit on. You played it the way you knew how."

"which was no way at all. It cost me my wife, my happiness and everthing I planned for the future. I don't want my daughter to grow up alone, a hardened whatever she decides to become."

"Well she does model."

"yea, but she doesn't do it with any type of enthusiasm. People ask her to do it and she does it. I don't think she even knows why they ask her. I don't think she realizes how beautiful she is."

"I never met a woman who didn't know how beautiful she was."

"What about you Steve?"

"I know how beautiful I am."

They laughed.

"No, what are your plans? You want to be married?"

"I never thought about it. I don't think I would ever find the woman I want. She needs to know her own mind, be sophisticated and familiar with a cop's life so that she won't worry about me. I also want her to have her own career so she can be who she is, you know, compliment each other. We can come home at night and talk about our days, what she did, what I did. She has to be beautiful though. Color is not important."

Morgan's father looked at Steve for a long time.

"She sounds familiar."

Steve knew the description sounded familiar. Thats why he said it. Personally, Steve never cared much about marriage, could really give a shit about females except for the obvious. Wives were like his mother and he would make about as good a father as his dad. But opportunity was knocking, in the form of a very kind black man. Steve smiled inside to himself. Why is it that the people who were the nicest to him were the ones he was going to hurt. Miss Elioise was nice to him. His face clouded alittle when he realized that she was the only one who saw who he really was. He wondered about Morgan's father and decided to keep him very close indeed. Fishing, horseback riding, whatever. This opportunity may not come around again and he wasn't going to let it go. It wasn't that he wasn't grateful. He was. You never forget the nice people that are brought into your life, he guess he just wasn't raised enough to really appreciate anything except looking out for himself. It was the way he survived everything he had been through, everything that he does, everything. No one to rely on but himself. Morgan would be a tasty addition to his lifestyle however and he couldn't get over the fact that the old man was actually giving her to him. She just didn't know it.

"Iknow you came from a hard knock life Steve. You know, everyone has a past that they aren't too proud of. Everyone has someone in their family that abandones them, whether in thought or in deed. You are never alone."

"I don't like to talk about my past. You know more than you should already. Who wants to bothered with a hillbilly from the hollows?"

"But you took that adversity and made something of yourself that you like. You are a damn good detective and you have the potential to go far someday. I am proud of you, really. You came to this department fresh from the small town and took on the big city on by storm. You acclamated yourself, you learned, you grew. Now, you are probably in line to take my spot as head detective. I was jealous of you when I first saw you. You were headstrong, brave and a little bit of a hotdog."

"Like you?"

"Just like me. That's what I didn't like. A young gun like myself. Although I must say when I did it, I did it with a little more finesse."

XVII

The caterer had arrived and the party would begin on time. Amir had some representatives from columbia coming to see him. He wasn't supposed to know that but he always gets wind when things like this are coming down. He planned the party for this weekend particular so that they could talk business, people were around, hide in plain sight as it were. He really wasn't interested in dealing with the Columbians, too much politicall bullshit with that. The Feds, the guerrilla fighters. People were thinking that they were using the drug money to fund their own little coup and if they were, it didn't bother Amir. He could give a shit who did what in that little ass country. But to get involved with the drugs could open him up to a whole new set of charges if he was caught. Drug charges were one thing, but conspiracy and wars and bullshit like that was close to treason or something. Uncle Sam would put those shackles back on his feet like they did in the slave days. He would never be free. The thought of doing federal time didn't necessarily bother him. For the drugs they would catch him with he was looking at 5 years max and he was prepared for that. If you are going to do this shit, you have to prepare yourself for that possibility. It happened. Some bull shit cop gets close to you, a girl you wrong drops a dime, people are jeolous and they drop a dime. There are lots of ways to get caught up. He just made sure he didn't. The women didn't know what he did, the general public didn't know what he did. He treated the other dealers in a positive manner so they didn't see him as a rival. The Columbians would be something else. He liked the pre-columbian art that they were bringing. It made it all seem legit. He even went so far as to cook their favorite dishes from home. He was not familiar with the Columbian way of cooking or their culinary delights but he knew a woman who worked at the local market who was columbian he thought. She was and she made a few dishes for him and he paid her well. She enjoyed doing it she said. People don't always like the food. Her family had angloized themselves to the point where if it wasn't from McDonalds they didn't want it. They hated her old ways, wanting her to replace them with the new American way of life they were so integrated into. When the fine black gentleman asked her to cook, she was overjoyed. The money was more than she needed but she heard he was an art dealer so he could probably afford it.

Amir began the process of dressing for the evening. The caterers were gone and everything was set up. All he had to do was get ready and receive his guests. One of his other women in his life, one who was into powder but not so much was the hostess for the evening. He prided himself on having beautiful women to chaperone his events and she was more the able. Blond and almost six feet tall, she had the skin of a california girl and the eyes of an ice blue lake. She was fluent in several languages, working as an investment broker, but her desire for powder and the good life brought her into contact with Amir. She fit the evening.

He showered, wishing that she were here now he could use a little diversion, but he would make sure she was here for after the party. She didn't like having sex with him, but did it because it took the price off her powder. Anything for that. She didn't like his "animalistic" ways. He left bruises on her that lasted for "weeks". Still in all, she didn't refuse his invitation. He had a nice package ready for her when she arrived and another to take with her when she left the next morning. Always out by morning. Amir didn't want anyone to get the impression that he needed someone around forever. Being a bachelor was good for him. He wouldn't change unless he found that special and she had to be REALLY special. So far, that wasn't on the agenda and life was good for the little abused boy from Bed Sty.

XVIII

Morgan drove home a little apprehensive but excited. She wasn't sure what she was getting into but with her father away she wouldn't have to explain anything.

She arrived at the house which was lit up like daylight. Her father had so much security lighting that in some places of the house, it never got dark. She laughed. Just like a cop.

In her closet she looked for her work out clothes and some regular outfits. No one seemed to be dressed anyway but casual. If she was going on an assignment, John would have to have clothing or disguises or whatever around and with all his attention to detail, he probably did.

Funny, there was no apprehension which she felt she should have. She only knew this man from school and not from any other social interaction. The thought of trusting him to keep her safe in some scheme to catch criminals was a bit beyond her comprehension but she packed a bag anyway. It seemed like a real adventure. Her friend Kathy crossed her mind and she shuddered. Having babies and being in her spot was something that she was going to make sure never happened to her. She would remain a virgin until she died if she had to. It wasn't necessarily holding out for some knight in shining armour or some prince, but just someone who was sane, steady, and sure. Her father was under the impression that she disliked men because of him, but it really wasn't the case. She knew that her father had a different type of weakness and her mother did as well. Two weaknesses together never turn out. Someone had to have strength. She didn't necessarily want to be the one in the relationship with strength. Hopefully she would find someone who was a stronger personality than herself. She could wait for that.

Riding back to John's place, for the first time she felt butterflies in her stomach. She never had any thing like that before. Not about any decision she ever made. Confidence was what made everything so easy. She was always taught that she could do anything and she knew it too. It was always a feeling that she had. Now, she was shaken, if not for long.

The training was strenuous. Because they had to amp it up, the repititions were quick, the intensity was enormous. She worked and sweated and paid close attention to everythng that was being said. Her mind opened up like she was a new child and learning for the first time. It was in a realm of world that she liked, crime. What made people do things, which people would be more capable of doing things. She was taught the personality traits and how to read situations. Her intuition was honed to a fine point. She already had good intuition but the games John used to teach were challenging and fun. She was coming into her own.

CPSIA information can be obtained
at www.ICGtesting.com
Printed in the USA
FSHW01n0915130718
50436FS